Praise for

TE KAUHANGA

A Tale of Space(s)

by

ANTONY MILLEN

"How anyone could dream up such characters escapes me. Between them they allow their creator, the author, to weave a story so original, I defy anyone to find one remotely like it. Highly recommended."
Tui Allen, author of *Ripple*

"Complex and captivating … I was hooked from page one! The reader is drawn in as each character, mysterious and fascinating, full of flaws and eccentricities, is delicately unfolded and exposed by the author. Beautifully written … an enthralling tale."
Chad Dick, manuscript assessor & editor, *100% Proof Ltd*

"This book races along. Amazing characters, whacky as hell, brilliantly structured and hugely entertaining."
James Russell, author of *The Dragon Brothers Trilogy*

"*Te Kauhanga* is brilliant. The author reveals an almost supernatural understanding of what makes people 'tick'."
E.M. Wilson

antonymillen.com

TE KAUHANGA

A Tale of Space(s)

ANTONY MILLEN

Te Kauhanga

A Tale of Space(s)

Cover Design: Leanne Reynolds

Ordnance Survey symbols © Crown Copyright

Author photo: Mary Millen

Find more information at:

antonymillen.com

Follow Antony Millen on Facebook and Twitter for updates on
future projects.

ISBN: 978-0-473-38759-4

CONTENTS

To DTH & others like him

PROLOGUE

Near the beginning, after Te Kore—the great void—had been filled, there was Te Pō—the perpetual darkness. Darkness was all that Tāne Mahuta had known. In the darkness, he heard the movements and sighs of Ranginui—his sky father—and Papatūānuku—his earth mother.

He heard others as well—his siblings who murmured in the darkness, whose murmurs turned into cries for the light, cries for space to move and breathe and grow—and he heard whispered rumours of something more beyond their parents' embrace.

Then there was stirring, as the siblings shared their restlessness with one another and with their parents. Papatūānuku felt the pushing and kicking in her belly but only clung tighter to Ranginui, who grumbled reassurance to her, and she received his love once again.

"Tāne Mahuta!" cried the siblings. "Tāne Mahuta!" They didn't need to say more. Tāne Mahuta heard the cries of his siblings and coiled himself, seed-like. Tight within his parents' embrace and surrounded by his restless, pleading siblings, Tāne Mahuta rooted his shoulders deep into his mother's body and strained against his father's heavy canopy.

The light entered slowly at first, but as he pushed his legs against his father, and the invigorating rays brushed his limbs, Tāne Mahuta brought light and space to the world—and as the space increased, the cries of his parents decreased.

Towering above his mother but still rooted in her, stretching just out of reach of his father but still nourished by him, Tāne Mahuta reigns in the space he created.

PART 1D

WINTER

ONE

Some say you could almost see it from space. Were you to descend into this world, moving within the edges of our sphere towards the largest areas of blue, the tree would seem to reach past you to the stars, rising from the northern island of Aotearoa—the land of the long white cloud.

On the first day of winter there was no cloud, but the grey mountains gave way to their white caps, and the blue lake glistened under a winter's sun. To the north of the three ancient maunga, greenery sprawled in two distinct shades: the matte green of farmland and the dense green of native bush.

And there were townships, at night seen from above by lighted houses, street-lamps, cars and reflected starlight from iron roofs. In the day, the towns could be recognised by their own greyness, patches sewn into the land as if intended to mend it.

North of the mountains and to the west of the lake, the tree stood in the town as if pioneers had encompassed it in search of an obelisk. *Ranginui's sun-dial*—it seemed to mark a spot long destined to inspire attachment and growth.

It would be more accurate to say it stood above the town, for the town proper rested along the river at the deepest part of the valley. This was the town of Te Kauhanga, and one arm of the valley pushed a small neighbourhood to the highest point above. This was Taumata.

Taumata was both the raised neighbourhood and the tree which dominated it. The name means *resting place* or *brow of a hill*. It is a word used to describe places Māori ascend for direction and enlightenment. Of course, it was just such a place before it became a neighbourhood. The first European settlers, late arrivals to this region, also recognised a good look-off. And so it was settled. A grid of streets grew, entering in from Hauāuru Street to the west, along Tūāraki street, turning south down Rāwhiti Street and back out to the west along Tonga. But the division of Taumata formed no simple circuit. One final street joined the midpoints of Tūāraki and Tonga—Centre Street—and this meridian was itself split, one lane on either side of the tree, forming a roundabout flanked on the east by the church and on the west by Koro Hohepa's house.

In that centre stood the tree that had no business growing there. It was a karaka tree, or that is what the arborists and Department of Conservation agents claimed it was. It may have been related to the coastal karaka and, if so, this fact only emphasised its bold alienness. Some in this region claimed that it was Kupe who brought the karaka tree to Aotearoa. The locals also called it *Kōwhi* and so, to those who had never seen this specimen, it was thought to be related to the kōwhai tree. Those who knew better recognised its connection with the kōpi tree of the Chatham Islands, a karaka tree so-named by the inhabitants of that lonely and distraught isle.

The tree was enormous, far bigger than any karaka tree and far bigger than any tree known to man; taller than the giant sequoias of the Pacific North West of America and more rotund than its spiritual cousin, Tāne Mahuta—the great kauri to the north in Hokianga. The people of Hokianga had long-since claimed the name of their ancestor for their tree but acknowledged Taumata as the other leg of Tāne Mahuta. It was a debate longstanding.

To stand beneath it was to feel the weight of air below its evergreen branches above. It took eighteen men, joining hands, to circumnavigate its trunk, and no one man could see more than four of his fellow links in the chain. Its bark was soft—soft enough to accept lovers' initials without flaking or breaking. It was always dark under its leafy canopy which grew thick several meters above admirers' heads. Looking up through this darkness and into the leathery leaves, it was impossible to say more about this tree's nature—its true height never measured, its full stretch never scaled.

The tree was tapu—sacred to local Māori and never to be

climbed. While rivers flowed and mountains rose nearby, some local iwi identified themselves with Taumata in their mihimihi: *Ko Taumata te maunga—My mountain is Taumata.* Such was the mana the tree held for them, such was their deference to it, as if to an ancient ancestor. It stood as their maunga and as their kaitiaki—their guardian.

What they did not know was that this winter, Taumata had grown his final ring.

Taumata, the hill, presented the people of Te Kauhanga with their highest view of the valley, but the best view from this hill belonged to the owner of 22 Tūāraki Street. Directly north of the tree, past the church grounds on the left and four more homes on either side, across Tūāraki to the very edge of the hillside and standing three stories high, Montreal Perec's house easily towered above the typical bungalows of Central North Island townships. The house had seen better days and better views when it was built for the town's first civil engineer, Clive Graham, who had established himself and his family on the trusses of two bridges and several railway system marvels.

The top floor consisted of only one room, constructed much like a lighthouse—circular with large picture windows framing circumnavigational views of the township, the lower hills of the opposite side of the valley and the neighbourhood of Taumata itself. Leaving no heir, Graham's extended family from the South Island had entrusted it to the community who used it variously as a convent, a retreat for returning war veterans and, for a short time, a storage unit for a kayaking company. Despite its decline and state of ill-repair, Montreal Perec bought this house when he arrived in Te Kauhanga thirty years prior for one feature: the view. This created an irony, not lost on the townspeople, that the man who wanted to see everything was rarely seen outside his house for almost three decades.

He was an immigrant, which made it all the more confusing for his neighbours. Why move to a new country only to sequester yourself inside a house—a house that may as well be standing anywhere in the world? The interior was the same as any comparable dwelling: walls, furniture, appliances and, later, a computer. The view was essentially the same as when Perec moved in: the hills, the river, the rail, the tree. The township had changed, naturally, but surely not enough to interest a stranger.

But inside that lighthouse window, hidden from the eyes of constables and shopkeepers, Perec gazed over the valley daily, then systematically dipping his eyes back to the work in front of him. Sketching and ruling, Perec mapped the area once again. It was winter, and winter meant mapping the town, the leaves having thinned enough along Donaldson Street. Last year's town map lay at his feet, not as a template but as a fascination for Perec. *How things have changed*, he thought. He made note of the new signage for the café on the corner of Donaldson and Drew, and lamented that the scale of his map did not allow much room in capturing it. He took satisfaction, however, in stencilling a new symbol for the skate park added to the domain last spring, listing it under the category of *Recreational Facilities* in his legend.

He watched the people, too, from his desktop perch, but made no note of them in his map. Years before, he had toyed with the topological idea of including certain individuals in his map, symbolically portraying their positions and perhaps their personalities in an attempt to capture the moment in time in which the map was created. He imagined tracing the lines of their movements and thus, their lives as they navigated their way around the township, crossing and criss-crossing each other's paths, twisting, turning and intersecting, unaware of the patterns they were illustrating. But people were too changeable for Perec, too colourful to isolate. So he maintained his focus on more immutable features. Besides, he was a cartographer, not a painter or a photographer. His art was in description not prescription, in delineation not creation. He portrayed things as they were, not as he would have them otherwise.

Still, he did dream of another reality, another way. Sometimes he would dream of living in his maps—not the place the map represented—but in the map itself amongst the symbols and the contour lines. He imagined scaling himself down to walk along red-lined roads and meandering blue-lined rivers, ascending hills covered in uniform green and stopping to admire the symbols of significant landmarks.

This day, he put away his colouring pencils and his T-square, stood up from his draftsman's table and descended his lighthouse steps, pausing long enough to appreciate the branch from the tree which had continued its annual stretching almost to the point of contact with his roof. This observation could wait for a future map. The sun had dipped below the hills, the hills which limited yet contained his view, so he could see no more of Te Kauhanga except by street lights. At one time, night meant sketching the heavens, imaginatively connecting the dots to create his own pantheon of constellations pinwheeling around our milky way; but this had been replaced by other projects—modern projects—and so he moved to his lounge on the street level floor of his house where he sat at his computer.

The Internet had affected Perec's life in more ways than you might imagine for a cartographer. After so many years inside, so many years sketching his maps with pencils or crude software, the Internet had landed it. Programs with topological images allowed him to add his own features: photographs from space, railway lines, political jurisdictions, names attached to famous sites and even events that occurred there. For a time, it was a paradise for Perec. Long-starved of new vistas, he wiled away his time in sleepless sojourns around the globe, tracking roads he would never travel in the flesh, immersing himself in the land of the map.

But the paradise didn't last. It didn't satisfy his dream, for, as he zoomed in from the map to the realistic images, he lost his perspective, he lost his symbology, and it became the same as it was before his self-imposed hermitage. As much as it was all so different, it was all too much the same. Pyramids were rough and rocky, water fountains were transparent and unshapely, the evidence of human intrusion was everywhere. Why did people ever need to explore so wide and far anyway? Why did they need to move from one place to do the same thing in a new place? Perec was aware, of course, of how he must be perceived of doing just that, but he knew he had made his move and found it wanting.

And so, this night, he returned to his computer, not to explore the scenic splendours you and I crave, but to follow his maps—to enter into the world of lines and symbols and trace his way around and back again.

======::::::

Stanley Kowalczyk loved straight lines. His father always told him:

The shortest distance between any two points is a straight line. It was the only advice Stanley ever accepted from his parents, and he placed it at the very core of his being.

For his walk home from work, Stanley had mapped out the most efficient path for himself. He exited the back of the Aotea Insurance Agency, passing through the front doors at an angle to the sidewalk, altering his course only slightly to aim for the crossing at the intersection to his left. Stanley never walked along the sidewalk to the crossing only to turn right to cross the street. In fact, Stanley hardly ever crossed at crossings at all. Instead, he was the consummate jaywalker and had a series of hand gestures at the ready for oncoming traffic from both sides. His first posture was to stroll into the street without looking in either direction, a way of communicating to drivers that, in fact, *he* had the right-of-way, and it was they who should stop for him regardless of whatever congestion presented itself. To him, it was not an arrogance. To Stanley, it was efficiency— the one driving value in his life.

Cars that did not stop immediately were, of course, given the open palm by Stanley and, only if necessary, a stuttering step to avoid collision. Invariably it was the car that stopped as Stanley knew it would be, and he carried on his line of action, ignoring any verbal or non-verbal protestations behind him. By the time he reached the middle of any street, oncoming traffic from the opposite direction would take notice of this man's intentions and courage and submit to his command, stopping without any need of a signal.

In the event that a car slowed but did not stop, Stanley would simply stop himself and wait for the car to proceed rather than break his line. He would not say anything to the driver but merely wave him by patiently, knowing there was far more pressure on the driver to keep traffic flowing from behind him.

After crossing Drew Street and arriving as close as possible to the next intersection's corner, Stanley would continue in this fashion, not quite travelling *as the crow flies* as was his dream, but as close to the ideal as he could navigate.

Stanley walked home every day, covering a distance of 2.2 kilometres. He had an option of travelling in a co-worker's car which would have delivered him faster, but saving time was not his concern. The inefficiencies of the car's turnings, stoppings, and startings drove him mad. It was far better for him to sacrifice time and maintain his sanity.

One of Stanley's great gratitudes in life was reserved for Te Kauhanga's underground, not an underground transit system (Te Kauhanga was far too small for that), but a subterranean tunnel dipping below street level under the railway tracks and emerging across from the incline leading up to Taumata hill. So grateful was Stanley, that he would often stop and say a little prayer of thanks at the exit beside the last pieces of tagging and graffiti. "Thank you wise civil engineers and council members who so thoughtfully constructed and maintain this underground," he would say and then carry on towards home.

To his right, Stanley would continue, at a loping pace, up and around the curving incline road. At the top, he cut across Tūāraki Street at a dangerous angle, completely out of sight of any traffic that might whip round the turn. But this was the quickest way to his short-cut across the Taumata neighbourhood, a brush-laden path carved through Mr Findlayson's property. For the past five years, Stanley had been the one human being permitted to cut across the Findlayson property, a privilege negotiated after several heated exchanges convinced Mr Findlayson he could not contain this stubborn man.

A Māori family lived behind the Findlayson's backyard. This was the Heke family, a large whanau who always said a friendly, "G'day", to Stanley as he passed. There was always a different child playing in the yard. No-one seemed threatened by the daily intrusion.

Past the Heke's, Stanley continued down the long driveway by the tennis courts, out across Tonga street, and straight through his front gate which led directly south up to his front door. Stanley lived south-west of the tree. His house spent a good deal of the day in the shade, but Stanley enjoyed the sun on his front porch for the last remaining minutes of a winter's evening initiated by the sun's setting.

If she could have smelled him, she would have at least recognised his presence, but it had been too long since he crawled into the mound of rags and worn out shirts. Did he curl up there intending to die? Or was he buried alive while he attempted to rehabilitate himself?

She didn't mean to do it. She didn't mean to do a lot of things. She loved cats, and they surely must have loved her because they kept coming, despite the smell, and perhaps in honour of it.

Those bones that once supported the fur and flesh that she had cuddled and kissed were now swathed in wrapping paper and cardboard. The darkness of his eye sockets was filled with disintegrated plastic from a collection of restaurant toys. His tail, which up until a month ago had been protruding from the mound like a drowning boy's hand, was disintegrating—a skeletal reminder of days spent running through an owner's petting fingers.

Magazines piled on the cat's coverings like a rugby maul, and on top of these, their heavier cousins: books upon books, scattered and opened with pages torn and yellowing. It was the books that started it and, it would seem, it was the books that would have the last word.

Surrounding the pile were stacks of more books, these ones betraying an order that once existed in the house. Hardcovers huddled together on hidden desktops and dressers. Paperbacks leaned haphazardly by the doorframe. The corridor leading out from her sitting room looked no different. There were shelves once, long neglected after braces had broken from the strain of the texts. You could see the shape of them in the angle of the books entering from the front lounge. Turning the corner, the scene remained the same, but for the attractive woman standing next to the wood burner in a wing of this labyrinth of clutter.

No-one in Te Kauhanga knew Sharon Pellerine's secret. This was because Sharon did her best to live the right way. She got up every morning and went to work each day. She dressed immaculately, spoke with a fine, educated Kiwi accent, kept her lawns mowed and watered, and even assisted the local historian in organising his archives. With a grown daughter living out of town, and still just in her mid-forties, Sharon was certainly among the top ten most eligible single women in the area—perhaps the top five.

Her house, with its shuttered windows and tidy front gardens, was stationed to the south-east of the tree. Sharon caught plenty of the sun's early morning rays but endured cool evenings after almost a full afternoon in the shade of those leathery leaves. Sometimes, especially in winter, she wondered what it would be like if there was no tree.

There are many reasons why a man would stay inside a house for thirty years: perhaps fear, or misanthropy; perhaps some sinister scheme or self-loathing; perhaps some malady or addiction.

Montreal Perec was not afraid, at least, not in the conventional sense. He disliked change and never felt fully recovered from his shift from Canada—an abrupt shift, ill-conceived and jarring. But this did not breed fear in him, and he had no traumatic experiences from which to draw his reclusive tendencies.

Nor did he hate people. In fact, he enjoyed the limited social interactions he shared with the posties and supermarket delivery agents who had serviced him in Te Kauhanga across the decades. He had never married, so his resentments were few. His schemes were not sinister, he was conveniently satisfied with his personality, he suffered no physical nor mental illness, and any addiction he did maintain was harmless to others and, at any rate, would still have manifested whether he stayed indoors or not.

Montreal Perec stayed in his home because he chose to stay there. He chose to stay because he saw no reason to leave. Where others sought explorative variety in new places, Perec found infinite variety in the same place. For, in a house, there is so much to explore and investigate, so much to study and extrapolate, particularly for a cartographer of Perec's temperament.

When he was not mapping the town to the north of his lighthouse, he was mapping Taumata, the hill and neighbourhood to the south of his front gate. He enjoyed mapping his house each winter, detailing floor plans and furniture arrangements. A single room provided fodder for a map. Ornaments were represented, and he had created his own symbols for picture frames, lamps, and various receptacles for letters and bric-a-brac. The closer he looked, the more he saw, and the more he saw, the more he mapped. It is important to note again that he did not sketch these items as they were, as in a diagram. Instead, Perec represented them as in a schematic, sometimes to scale and always by legend.

He had been doing such things, in some form, since he was a child. He did not owe this to his parents. They were fantastical creatures, scattered and vague in their jobs and in their child-rearing. His mother owned a bakery, and his father was a school-teacher, but both the sorts you find in a Hans Christian Anderson tale. They were both of the whimsical variety—his mother as flaky as her pastries, his father as scattered as the papers on his desk. Their favourite mantra for their son was: *Don't live your life one-dimensionally! Variety adds volume!* And often it seemed that variety was pursued for variety's sake, at the expense of the minimum of stability a young boy craves.

But there were excursions—walks along seashores and voyages around the bay in the family dory. Mahone Bay, Nova Scotia was a paradise for a small boy with footloose parents, a picturesque area with post-card popular churches and a fine settlement in nearby Chester. The town itself was not much bigger than Te Kauhanga but distinctly New England. Residents and visitors would feel just as comfortable in New Hampshire or Massachusetts.

It was the bay that intrigued, with its sheltered waters and plethora of islands. It was still a favourite pastime of Perec's to close his eyes and create a mental map of the islands and coves. He never sketched this map on paper, content to enter into it by memory and imagination alone.

In his map, Perec would start from the shore, circling out beyond the collection of islands until he reached the Atlantic Ocean, then turn back into the bay, marking islands as he sailed, curving with each pass and drawing closer to his centre—his final destination—the island tucked away behind the others, out of view of any passing ocean-going vessels: Oak Island.

TWO

The builder had struggled with the concept that Stanley Kowalczyk presented to him shortly after he had arrived in Te Kauhanga.

"You want a square house?"

"Yes, but the point is not to have it square, it must be linear," Stanley had said with an emphatic smile.

"Linear," the builder had repeated. "Well, I can't imagine I could build it any other way than linear. Unless you want a roundhouse." He had laughed at this, cocking his arm in a feigned punching motion. Stanley didn't flinch or laugh.

"The walls would be linear, of course," said Stanley, "but it's the passages that need to be linear ... linear and equidistant."

"Right," said the builder. "Yeah, you mentioned that."

Five years on, and Stanley still stopped inside his front door each day to appreciate his creation. It was a square house ... and it needed to be. How else could each room be joined by a passage which ensured a direct route from one room to another, regardless of which room he vacated and which room he entered? The builder had shaped the corners of the rooms in the centre of the house, allowing for criss-crossed passageways running south-west to north-east and south-east to north-west. Similarly, doors opened from the other corners of each room creating pathways around the perimeter of the structure. Stanley inhaled the efficiency when he arrived home. Here, he could fly like a crow.

So, his evening routine began with a turn into his bedroom where he changed out of his work clothes; then, a walk back across the main passage to his kitchen where he prepared his tea, followed by a diagonal trip to his lounge at the back of the house to watch some television with his cat, Stripes. Throughout the evening, the bachelor moved between toilet, lounge, kitchen, and, finally the bedroom where he set himself to sleep, smugly satisfied with the resourcefulness of it all—a predictable, inornate existence—and so efficient.

Sharon had endured a tedious day. It had started well enough before running into Frances whom she had avoided since Monday.

"Hey, I didn't catch-up with you at all yesterday," Frances had said. "I thought we had a really good time on Saturday night."

Saturday night—the frustrating vibrations of the events and personalities still resonated in Sharon's brain.

Sharon had said something like, "It was good to try something new," but only nodded incoherently when Frances suggested they do it again sometime.

"I just think that we five should spend more time together, you know what I mean?" Frances had pressed, following Sharon who had walked towards the front desk of the council offices, hoping to sit at her computer as a way of screening her face from her co-worker while she continued, as she knew she would.

"Do you think I went too far talking about Paora like that in front of Veronica? You know, I was just trying to get her out of her shell a bit, eh?"

Sharon had nodded, thankfully having settled at her desk so she didn't need to reveal more through eye contact. *Still*, she had thought, *better to say something.*

"I don't imagine Veronica would mind. I haven't heard her talk about Paora since she and Georgia told us about their designs last year."

Frances had laughed at this, then leaned in conspiratorially, saying, "Those two were funny—it's obvious that Paora has no interest in either one of them."

Whatever, Sharon had thought. She was growing tired of the gossip and Saturday night had been an intensive session of it, with Frances leading the charge. Surely, on a Queen's Birthday weekend, the last thing you would want to talk about would be work, but Frances was obsessed and ambitious. Sharon was not. Sharon was eight years weary-worn. Yes, she was horny, too, but knew by now that no workmate was going to solve that problem.

Intuitively, Frances had asked, "So, where are you at with Blake? Has he asked you out again? It is just past the first of the month." Frances had reached out to brush Sharon's hair away from her eyes as she spoke, an attempt to extort a look, disguised as affection.

Sharon had not wanted to answer the question. Blake had asked her out and she, once again, had declined. The running joke was not lost on her. Blake was a workmate, aide to the mayor—new, younger, attractive and, for some reason, interested. She was not.

"I'm not interested," she had said to Frances.

Frances had leaned back, studying Sharon's face, reading her. Despite her internal protestations, Sharon finally looked up at Frances and immediately regretted it.

"Hmmm ... I don't know. I think you are." And that was enough. She knew better than to play along with Frances' bullshit, but this comment had meant the end of a productive day for her. She had moiled away the afternoon, monotonously sifting e-mails and moving paperwork from one pile to another, often catching herself ignoring customers waiting at her desk. Sharon, normally an astute, professional, hospitable clerk, had been derailed. Not once had she seen Blake today, but she found herself falling for him. And that could only lead to one thing.

The walls of Perec's home were adorned with maps, some common and some treasured: prints of world maps by Anaximander and Piri Reis, fictional maps from *Treasure Island* and *Lord of the Rings*, painted models illustrating Alfred Wegener's theory of Pangea and continental drift. His shelves supported globes, sextants, and weighty atlases. Drawers and closets concealed further documents. Some of his favourites featured illustrations of dragons and sea monsters, once deemed suitable and even desirable substitutes for uncharted regions. Like Joseph Conrad, however, Perec desired no substitutes, but was excited by lands and seas unknown which offered the life-enhancing possibility of discovery.

The two maps given pride-of-place on his lounge's feature wall had hung side-by-side since he had moved into the lighthouse. He owned other, modern versions, but they lacked the sentimentality he attached to these. Plus, he preferred the classical colours and lines created in the seventies. He had carefully scissored his map of New Zealand from a *National Geographic* magazine in the Mahone Bay library. The article had focused on the geological wonders throughout the country, from the volcanic plateau of the North Island to the fiords in the South. His map of Nova Scotia belonged to a university friend who had visited from Ontario and bought it to guide his way from Halifax to Chester one summer. It was well-creased with a coffee stain leaking into Clark's Harbour and Barrington.

While the New Zealand map was hung as it was designed, with north at the top, the Nova Scotian map was tilted so that north rotated to the north-west. Perec had also drawn a line which looked like it was highlighting the trans-Canada highway from Antigonish to Truro but which was intended to fabricate a separation of the peninsula from the isthmus connecting the province to New Brunswick and the rest of Canada. By doing this, Perec had emphasised a curious comparison for himself: the shape and dimensions of this little province in Atlantic Canada shared a remarkable resemblance to the largest Polynesian nation positioned deep in the South Pacific. Both land masses were dominated by a *mainland*, a larger island to the south, with a smaller island roughly one-third the size to the north.

It was a forced comparison, and Perec had never conjectured about any significance, but he enjoyed the pattern, the symmetry, the connection his two homelands shared in the two-dimensional world.

Sometimes he would place a hand on each map, New Zealand on his left, Nova Scotia on his right, and feel that connection through him. If only it were as easy to do in our three-dimensional world. Montreal Perec had not visited his homeland since his emigration. He had not yet finished his task.

═════:::::::

You might think monotony would plague Stanley Kowalczyk in his routined travel method.

"You know, I've heard of drivers who have deliberately, though unconsciously, put themselves in a ditch after taking the same route home every day without any variation," his co-worker, Raima, said to him one morning over coffee. "I sometimes drive around the back of Keller Road, just to change it up, especially if I want to delay my arrival at work."

"Not at all," Stanley said. "Monotony is a state-of-mind. A bored person is a boring person. It's like any of the *mono* words. You tease me because I don't multi-task like you—such a typical Kiwi woman's joke—but I advocate monotasking. It's far more efficient to do something right the first time and retain focus."

Raima sighed. She was accustomed to his diatribic responses. With Stanley, it was like pushing a button on a cassette player—select the topic and out spouts his entire thought. He had once told her that, "sound-bite conversations were too inefficient," and that it was better to allow a person to develop all their thinking in their response, even if it meant listening to an essay, and then using your opportunity to speak similarly, as if life was a debate meet—three minutes for each side and time for rebuttals after. She suspected he was sincere in his thinking but was also aware that he was the only one who ever spoke like this, meaning everyone else issued sound bites and were then forced to listen to him pontificate.

"I'm just saying, Stanley," Raima replied, "that efficiency isn't the be-all-to-end-all. Efficiency is good for work tasks, maybe, but not to live every second by."

"Well, I disagree entirely of course ...," Stanley said, and Raima switched off early into his exposition.

Still, in many ways he was not a terrible man to work with. His paperwork was immaculate, his customers were happy with his dependability and assured service, and he didn't play mind-games or try to undermine Raima's client-base. He was the same each day, and that sameness had grown on her.

Sharon followed her own routines at home despite any visual evidence to the contrary.

Arriving home, she pushed her door open through the piles of newspapers in the front corridor, and tossed the latest editions into the back corner, unread. She hung her purse neatly on a hook inside the kitchen, above the recipe books stacked high on the low floor-shelving unit. Then she squeezed past the plastic bins crammed into the lounge doorway to climb over another pile, this one a mixture of newspapers, magazines, and plastic file folders. This pile was especially difficult to navigate as it had been steadily growing ceiling-ward over the past months.

In the spring, I'm going to go through this house room-by-room, she would often say to herself, especially in the grey days of winter when she spent that much more time indoors.

Over the pile, up to the ceiling and down again to the further corner where she still managed to sit in her lounge chair, she parked in front of a small television set on an overflowing bookshelf opposite.

Then, each night, Sharon would cry. It always started in the same place and always waited until she had taken her seat and removed her shoes and coat. Maybe it was the uncertainty of where to put her coat that sparked it, for uncertainty had always troubled her, or perhaps it was the certainty that she was shut in now—shut away from the world of customer service, impatient councillors, and the incessant demands of her society for order, or at least the appearance of order.

She cried and it always started in the same place—in her chair and in her throat. The tears seemed to be planted there, rooted deep in her heart and welling up in racking sobs that finally forced the salty water from her eyes. She cried—and she cried for hours. The need for it was greater than for hunger or companionship.

While she cried, various cats might call on her—some for food from the kitchen, some for stroking once they emerged from their hiding places. They brought stink with them—urine and feces and infection. Her tears didn't cure them, and they weren't curing her.

Eventually, she would rise, wipe her face, and feed the cats and herself. Sometimes she managed to scrape and wash dishes, but, more-often-than-not, she would focus her energies on laundry and personal hygiene—whatever it took to prepare for her performance the following day.

I have to go to New Zealand. Twenty-eight year old Montreal Atlas Perec had announced this to his parents at the dawn of the eighties. *I have to see where this leads. I have to chart this out.*

Oak Island had inspired and haunted Perec as it has generations of Nova Scotians and treasure hunters from around the world. You may not know the story—it started in 1795 when teenaged Daniel McGinnis discovered a depression on the island below a tackle block hanging from a tree branch. He and his friends, hoping to find a quick reward, discovered a layer of flagstones followed by intermittent layers of oak logs every three meters. The subsequently named *money pit* yielded nothing but even more dramatic mysteries over the next two centuries: coconut fibres, spruce platforms, symbols inscribed on a stone. Even more confounding, in 1861 a collapse in the bottom of the shaft revealed a series of flood tunnels engineered to punish and prevent any who managed to dig deeper than 30 metres. Six lives have been claimed by the island. In the absence of further evidence, speculations have abounded: Captain Kidd's pirate treasure, the original manuscripts of Shakespeare, Marie Antoinette's jewels and, of course, the Holy Grail. Young Perec grew up ensconced in it all, then enamoured with it. Oak Island was his muse as a cartographer, his Beatrice, the one who calls you in and then sends you forth.

Imagine a mind like Montreal's, seeking stability yet buoyed by his parents' flamboyance and bohemia. To his mind, Oak Island ranged with possibilities, sparking a lifetime of imaginary sojourns. Even President FDR was captivated. But beneath the conjectures and the meandering plotlines stood a bedrock of purpose, of unyielding devotion to a cause, like a topographical map before the additions of man-made lines of road and rail. To know that purpose would be to found a religion for a mind such as his, searching for faith and meaning in his world of representations.

And so it is with all treasures. There is purpose and there is prize; and there is theory and with all theories for the stout-of-heart, there is testing, there is action. Faith without works is dead. By twenty-eight, Perec had completed his degree at Carlton University and returned to Mahone Bay, working for R.C. Becker Surveying and living with his parents. But it wasn't family or work that drew him back. It was Oak Island. There were theories upon theories, but young Montreal had developed his own—a unique theory which was the only type in which he could be interested.

Despite his upbringing, Perec would still have been voted least likely to travel so far from his family and home province. He owned little and travelled light, hopeful that his search in New Zealand would last no more than three years. He still owned little—prepared to return to home and family when the task was complete or exhausted of trails.

THREE

Winter moves slowly through Te Kauhanga. No holidays break up the work weeks and the grey permeates the rain and stillness. Skiers and tourists fill the supermarket and petrol stations, their accents punctuating the soundscape with otherness, but their presence never impresses upon the locals. The foreigners could be a reminder to them that there is more beyond this valley—diverse nations and values—but invariably they threaten and only emphasise the immutability of the place.

In addition to the patterns of sun and shade it created, Stanley enjoyed Tuamata's tree for the same reason he admired all trees: it grew straight and true.

Prior to his move to Te Kauhanga, Stanley had lived as a city boy. He grew up in Dunedin then moved to Hamilton where he had studied and was licensed to sell insurance. He loved the city for the most part—the grids and blocks made sense to him even when they interfered. There were usually plenty of underpasses, alley-ways and discrete passages through private property. In Dunedin, he had enjoyed consistent sloping which always returned one to the Octagon and the harbour.

He moved to Te Kauhanga for work but also for the rural lifestyle. He looked forward to open spaces, less congested with the structures of civilisation which facilitate and impede. He liked to watch the magpies and tuis.

He had not anticipated living near the famous Kōwhi tree of

Taumata. It was magnificent. Its size, to be sure, was overwhelming and awe-inspiring to any visitor or resident. The local iwi held it in great esteem and why not? Yes, there were others who resented it. The shade blocked life-giving rays to sun-worshippers. There were occasional bursts of paranoia about branches falling or fruit. However, according to the locals, this tree had never fruited. It seemed it was the last of its kind, and legends said that no branch had ever fallen from above.

All of this was terrific, but none of it was what magnetised Stanley. *The shortest distance between two points is a straight line*, his father had said, and there was no better illustration of this than the tree of Taumata Hill. It was so straight that sometimes Stanley believed the tree formed a direct line between Te Kauhanga and God.

Every day, Sharon ate lunch in town, away from the council offices. In winter, she preferred the arcade—an indoor strip between the main street and a back parking lot, complete with a diner-style café and some second-hand shops. She ate alone, deflecting hints or even self-invitations from workmates to join her. Of course, Frances was the worst, going so far as to accuse Sharon of elitism or having secret sexual rendezvous.

Sharon didn't mind company over a lunch menu, but she needed time alone for her shopping excursions at the second-hand shops, the pharmacy, the book store, of course, and any number of craft and clothing enterprises which had thrived or failed during her years in Te Kauhanga.

She was not a shop-o-holic. She was a collector and hated to see a precious book or article wile away its existence on a shelf or rack, destined to be ignored and neglected by the second-rate denizens of the town. She was a collector—and a saviour, a rescuer of history. Hadn't she found that saddle belonging to Archibald Mackenzie, pioneer in this area? If it wasn't for her, it would have hung perpetually on a hook purposed for old rugs and shovels. And hadn't she recovered that *Listener* magazine featuring the article about James K Baxter—the one now treasured by the Ngāti Hau people of Jerusalem?

No, it wasn't about her collection, it was about the artefacts. It was about history itself and the people who also held history as taonga—treasured memories locked in sacred objects. It was her vocation—her calling in life.

She'd made a career of it in Wellington—seven years at the Alexander Turnbull Library. A dream job for Sharon, she'd earned it with good fortune, fresh out from finishing her library science degree at Victoria University. Six years of purpose and fulfilment and one of frustration and disgrace. Tom. If it hadn't been for Tom ....

You would think that thirty years of indoor living would produce one bloated cartographer, but Montreal Perec maintained a rigid fitness routine, if not a regime. After all, he did have one unique feature not shared with any other house in Te Kauhanga: two flights of stairs.

Ascending and descending twenty-six times each way, Perec paced himself through an intense ritual, increasing speed for each of the first four climbs, with relaxed intervals between, followed by a corresponding decrease in speed over the next four climbs, and repeated. In winter months, when the heat didn't trap in the house, Perec carried heavy books under his arms for extra resistance. In the summer, he might relax his routine unless he was keen to work out in the morning when the tree's shade shrouded his place.

He had re-upholstered his stairs several times, explicitly aware of when the material became unsightly and dangerous. He was no slob and no savage. While most of us clean our homes or brush our teeth motivated by social interaction and potential exposure, Perec acknowledged genuine purpose in his day-to-day habits of self-care. He kept his hair, curled as it was, brushed, and he kept his large beard uniformly trimmed. Besides, he enjoyed the routine. Performing aspects of his daily schedule was like driving, sailing or hiking over familiar terrain: well scouted, well thought out, well mapped. Maps were useless without someone to follow them. He knew that. He was inevitably pragmatic, desperate to match his behaviour with his philosophy.

Still, once he had performed his rituals, he was free to continue his great hunt. In thirty years of writing new routines and re-routing old ones, he had never forgotten his original purpose and daily used the time remaining to search. Only, after so many years, the time remaining had dwindled, and he often lay his head on his pillow regretting the hours spent. Futility had cast a longer shadow in recent years.

———————::::::

Hanover Findlayson liked Stanley Kowalczyk. He enjoyed sharing the stories of his first encounters with him most Wednesday nights at the Cosmopolitan Club quiz.

"He didn't even pretend ignorance of what he was doing—just walked on through like he owned the place."

His friends had heard the stories before but knew they would have to listen to them through again. It was Graham who had raised the topic of neighbours, one of the many that set Hanover ranting. At least this rant was always told in good humour.

"I never saw him the first time—Melvina Burrows told me about it. She had seen him cut through my yard when I was down here with you guys one night. She said she'd seen him do it two nights before too—thought he was new in town."

"When did you see him first?" Graham Lowry asked, raising his beer glass so it obscured a winking eye directed at Topia Stevens, the group's trivia savant.

"I still remember the first time I saw him for myself," Hanover continued, oblivious. "I stayed home from the Guy Fawkes preparations after Melvina said she'd seen him the night before. I reckoned he might be walking home from work or something.

"Sure enough, he marches on through. I was sure I'd catch him skulking through the yard, maybe ducking down below window level, or at least trying to move along closer to the fence. Nope—he just waltzed on through so comfortable I half-expected him to tip his hat to me—if he'd been wearing a hat."

Hanover laughed, "I didn't say anything to him until he'd almost got right the way through, I was that taken aback. Finally, I says to him out my window, 'Whatdya think you're doing?' but he just kept on walking, past the Heke's place and across the road. He didn't stop—just walked straight across and in through his front door."

Topia, who had left to buy another round of drinks for the group, returned to his stool and said, "Yeah, he's a strange fella all right there, Hanover. Why did you let him cut through? That's not like you." He returned a wink to Graham, who smirked but sighed as well.

"Damn right it's not like me," Hanover said, "and I let him have it the next night when he came traipsing through again. This time, I waited outside along the back fence. I could see him coming. He was dressed in his suit—we all know the one—and he had his briefcase with him. I caught his eye and he didn't look away. Just as he came up to me, he nodded his head and said, 'G'day,' and walked right by me—straight onto my own property like he had just walked into the town square.

"I yelled at him, eh? I said, 'Hey buddy, whatdya think you're doing?' and he kept walking again, just like the night before. Only this time, I marched after him. I followed him past the Heke's and across the road and up his front steps. I banged on his door and he opened it straight away. 'Yes?' he says, like he was opening up to some door-to-door salesman." Hanover paused, awaiting and receiving the raised eyebrows indicating the supposed interest of his mates.

"'Whatdya think you're doing?' I asked him, and get this: he asks me, 'Do you mean, what am I doing right this moment? Or do you mean what am I doing in my life in general?' Imagine that. Imagine bloody that," Hanover said, and Topia and Graham exchanged another look. The table of trivia team-members nearest them also looked over at this latest exclamation but returned to their drinks and their own chatter.

Hanover continued, "I said, 'Don't be smart with me. Whatdya think you're doing walking through my property like that?' He looked behind me and said, 'I was walking straight home. That's all. No harm intended.' That's what he said: 'No harm intended.' No, 'Sorry about that,' or, 'I didn't know that was your property.' He basically said, 'I know what I was doing and it's OK, get over it.'

"I told him not to walk through my property again or I'd ring the police or thump him, whichever suited my mood that particular day."

Topia smirked at Graham. They had been blustered by Hanover before and had never known him to strike anyone. "That should have scared him," he said.

"Too right—at least you'd think so anyway. The next night, I waited at the same spot. This time I stayed home from taking Magdalene to the movies to make sure this guy had learned his lesson. I saw him come over the top of the hill and then walk my way the same as he did the night before! I didn't wait for him to come close. 'Whatdya think you're doing?' I yelled out to him, but he didn't stop or even flinch a little. He came right up to me the same as he did before, and I knew he was going to walk by me again and keep ignoring me. So I stood in front of him and—this was the damnedest thing—he stopped short and gave me the most hateful look I've ever seen a man give, even from my time in the army." Graham and Topia looked away. They knew Hanover had only joined the army for three days before opting out for a medical condition—*Inertia*, he had told them once.

"That look was enough to make me step back but not out of his way, and—here's the thing—he had plenty of room to go around me, but he didn't even try. He just stood there with that look on his face.

"I told him that he wasn't coming through my property, and he said—I'll never forget his words—he said, 'Well, I'm not turning back.' What the hell did that mean? Talk about a full-on challenge—I thought he was going to do a haka on me, Topia!" Topia shook his head.

"I said to him, 'I told you that if you tried to come back through here I'd call the police or sort you myself.' He didn't budge or look away. He said, 'Are you going to move or not?' Imagine that, Graham! It was like I hadn't said anything at all. He was creeping me out, that's for sure. I told him I wasn't, and before I knew it, he was walking straight into me! He just started walking—his face was pressed into my chest, and I had to plant my legs to stop from being bowled over. I pushed him back, just firmly at first, just enough to get him off me. 'Whatdya think you're doing?' I said to him, but he didn't say anything—just started pushing into me again."

"Why didn't you clobber him Hanover?" Graham asked.

"Well, I didn't really want to hurt him, you know?" Hanover said. "Besides, I reckoned I could ring the police later anyway. So that's when I decided to let him go through. He was acting like some kind of mental patient or something. I said, 'All right, all right, you egg. Stop pushing, I'll let you go through this once. Settle down. As soon as I moved out of the way his face returned to normal, and he carried on to the Heke's as if nothing had happened." Hanover sipped his beer, satisfied.

"So, did you phone the police?" Topia asked.

"Nah, I couldn't be bothered," Hanover said, lowering his glass. "I figured he was pretty fucked up—probably wouldn't hurt anybody, just wanted to take a short cut, I guess. And that's all he's ever done as far as I can tell. The Hekes don't worry about him, so why should I? Geez, that's going on five years now."

"Well," said Graham, "that's a heck of a story. Isn't that a heck of a story, Topia?"

Topia nodded. "Yes, bro, that is a heck of a story."

Hanover nodded with him. "It sure is," he said.

✠

Sharon was proud of her collection. She had stuck to her rule: never retain more than one copy of the same item. All her drinking glasses were different, she had no sets of plates or utensils, she wore selections of underwear from different brands. Even her collection of books and magazines contained no duplicates. Of course, this rule didn't apply to different editions of the same book.

She also kept only one picture of Tom. Appropriately, she kept this hidden inside her most treasured memento of her time at the Alexander Turnbull, and she had stolen many treasured mementos. This particular item was not stolen as much as it was appropriated as a gift. It was a *Book of Hours*, one of the finest examples of incunabula from the original collection of Alexander Turnbull himself, and it was her wedding gift from Tom. Not that there had been a wedding. Beautifully illustrated and filled with monastic prayers printed in the 15th century, this was a gift from the ages, a gift designed for a woman from her man, never intended to be stored away for some curator's pleasure alone.

But Tom had not been that kind of curator. He was generous and real. He would have given it to her if he could have—if he hadn't been turned away, turned away by that witch, Felicity. Hadn't he neglected to try and retrieve it from her? Surely if she were not meant to have it, he would have pursued Sharon for it. No, he wanted her to have it even if he couldn't have her, even if he was doomed to choose that woman.

And that's why Tom's picture stayed in *The Book of Hours*. The picture was between pages 72-73, marking the passage about the Holy Family's flight into Egypt. The vellum leaves were beautifully decorated with a central painting of the family on a donkey. The leaves were bound in 18th century dark brown sheep leather with gilt edges. It was wrapped neatly in brown paper and stored in a box. The box was now crushed under the weight of other stolen items less neatly stored. Some of these were torn or falling loose of their bindings. Another cat had made a nest nearby, and one old map in the collection had urine stains. The smell had not reached Sharon's nose through the assortment of clothing and periodicals stacked high atop these once proud items. Beyond the clothing, including winter coats and torn socks, Sharon sat in her chair and cried.

PART 2D

SPRING

FOUR

Spring starts with a date in Te Kauhanga: 1 September. It doesn't matter what the trees say or the birds—if the calendar says it's spring, it's spring. And nobody complains really. If the trees say it is spring and the calendar agrees, everyone is happy to enjoy the resurrection and rejuvenation offered. If the trees disagree with the calendar and withhold their prosperity regardless of the time, the people of Te Kauhanga cheer themselves with the hope and faith the calendar inspires.

Of course, in Taumata, people looked to their tree, their kaitiaki, for signs of spring out of a genetic legacy more than sense, for the tree, other than exponential growth, had not shown evidence of change in a thousand years. Its leaves may have altered colour, but they did not drop until pushed off the stem by their almost fully grown green replacements. The shade was omnipresent through the seasons even as the tree fluctuated its feel, if not its look.

Branches stretched, but never fell, and another ring manifested itself as slowly as a minute hand or a snail trail—larger and larger for over a thousand years

For thirty years, Montreal Perec had aged alongside the tree, growing

31

his own rings, his own lines in his face and in his hands like contour lines charted by eroding time. Like the tree, his search had been fruitless, and losing grip on his heart and mind. He had begun to think of home once again and of death and where that might mean for him.

So it was until the intruder arrived.

Perec's space could allow for a visitor—he had hosted plenty of electricians, plumbers, and builders inside his house over the years. He had suffered neighbours dropping in when he was ill or when they invited him to participate in a Christmas function. One did not receive an invitation readily into 22 Tūāraki Street, but Perec was not opposed to human beings entering the premises.

What he did object to was any intrusion into his work. More and more his work had moved online—freelance survey work, collaborative cybercartography projects, or programming for companies in New Zealand and overseas. In addition, geological enterprises, fact gathering for councils, even some intel for the U.S. government in the late nineties had led him deeper into the social aspect of online cartography, an inevitable blurring of lines between the interactions of professionals, hobbyists, and any common owner of a broadband connection.

Perec's preferred site was WiCharts—a combination of mapping, legend construction, and photographs from the ground. It wasn't as advanced as its competitors, offering no 3D views, but was an easily manipulated site for enthusiasts. Too easily manipulated, as it turned out.

Perec's pride in the site was in his legend constructions, and this was linked to his search amongst maps from Nova Scotia and France and the UK and New Zealand and the islands populating the ocean above it—across centuries of maps from hand-drawn sketches to amply navigated and charted regions. To original, scanned documents written on parchment hundreds of years earlier, Perec had added his own symbols consistent with an elaborate legend incorporating time signatures in addition to the classical elements of purpose and size. With the advancement of the Internet, he had meshed these with hyperlinks and photographs provided by other sites or by individuals within his network.

Occasionally, he had dealt with mild hacking by casual users who added irrelevant or irreverent photographs to his collection, but these were easily removed. This was the down-side of using an open sharing site and one that required Perec to carry out periodic spring cleaning.

However, the intruder in early September had deigned to add his own symbols to Perec's work, symbols that did not correspond with his legend.

To understand the significance of this better, imagine plotting your own family tree across several generations and across multiple branches, then having someone insert their own friends and family— relatives with absolutely no connection to yours other than belonging to the same race or originating from the same homeland.

Perec was furious and panicked. Not actually owning the site, only an account, Perec contacted the administrators, asking them to trace the changes made and identify who was responsible. He quickly received the information along with an advisement that, as an open site, there was little the site administrator could do to stop the addenda unless they were deemed to be pornographic, racist, or otherwise offensive. Perec claimed they were offensive to him. He argued that he had spent over a decade on the site creating a work of art, a researched chart with a specific purpose, but also, "a chart and legend worthy of the Smithsonian—and here it was being denigrated by some rogue."

The site administrator advised him, "As this is an open site, you may raise your issue with your fellow user. Please be aware that there is an expectation that any dialogue between site users should be respectful at all times, even in private messaging."

Subsequently, Perec wrote a private message to the intruder:

Re: The legend of Perec22

Sir:

I have noticed that you have been adding symbols to maps and documents that I have uploaded and been developing here on WiCharts. I understand this is an open site, however, please be advised that these pages are part of a larger project I have been researching and charting for the better part of the last decade. In the spirit of cartography, of which I am sure you share, please remove any symbols I have not located and desist from adding any in future.

Kind regards,

Perec22

To which he received a reply that same evening:

Re: The legend of Perec22

G'day, Perec. 10 years is a long time to be doing this shit—got nothing better to do, aye? Your legend is choice, and I'm really enjoying working out your systems and everything. As for my little contributions, I think I'll keep putting them up. It's fun, and I love the way they look next to yours.

BloodyLegend180

To say the least, Perec was dumbfounded by the cheek of the response. *Fun?* he thought. *Ruining a man's life's work was fun to this miscreant?* He tried to impress the gravity of the matter on the intruder:

Re: The legend of Perec22

BloodyLegend180:

Thank you for your reply and for your kind words about my legend. Since you show such an appreciation for it, you must understand something of the complexity and intended artistry of the work. It has taken me a great deal of time to construct, even prior to my ten years on this site, and only maintains its usefulness and aesthetic qualities when it is left intact and consistent. Please recognise that, by adding your own symbols, you are detracting from both of these qualities. Once again, I implore you to leave my work unhindered and unelaborated. Perhaps start your own legend with your own uploads. I have no copyright on my pages, so I am perfectly agreeable to other users downloading my documents and re-uploading them for their own endeavours.

Thank you in advance,

Montreal Perec
BSc, MGeog

Perec did not receive a response from the intruder for almost a week—a painful six days of noting ever-increasing additions, each one tagged publicly with the moniker, *BloodyLegend180*. Each day of that week, Perec devoted more time to deleting symbols and writing e-mails, copying the body of his originals and again formally repeating his request for understanding and compliance.

Finally, the intruder responded:

Ha-ha—you sure are determined aren't you? Yeah, I can see how much work you've done and it's awesome, it really is! It's so awesome, I've gotta have a go, you know? Besides, I think I can help you ... 'cause I'm a bloody legend!

—————:::::::

While Stanley Kowalczyk did not concern himself with time as he did space, he invariably did tend to follow a routine of time as we all do. He left for work at close to the same hour each morning—8:10am—unless he felt an urge for a stop at the bakery to buy his lunch for the day. He returned home at the same time, stepping out of his offices after 5pm, with no stops along the way unless required to divert ninety meters to the supermarket. These two rhythms, combined with his unique habits, created a very predictable, very vulnerable situation for Stanley. His friends had warned him in Hamilton: *People will catch on with you, Stanley. It's not good for people to know exactly where and when you will be each day.* He understood, and tried to vary his times or pace each morning and night, but it didn't prevent the robbery.

A single man in the city, who drew attention to himself with his unusually purposeful gait and even more unusual habits, was bound to fall victim to the criminally astute members of society. They took everything and, worse, left Stanley feeling that his search for efficiency had cost him more than it was worth. How efficient was it to spend years working and filling a life with items that can be taken away in the smallest fraction of the time? And, while his friends' advice made sense to Stanley, he could do little to change. So, he decided that city-life was the problem and the expendable factor that could be remedied more easily.

He felt safe in Te Kauhanga. Five years with no break-ins, no suspicious characters giving him odd looks except the harmless Findlayson. Instead, his patterns of time and pathway only served to create new, sustainable relationships with others in the town. Each morning he passed the same three people on his way to work: Mrs Taituma, who walked her dog down and up the hillside; the McNamara twins, always waiting outside the town entrance to the underground, deposited there by their parents where they caught the town bus to school; and Benson, the one-armed retired police officer who manned the busiest zebra-crossing in town, ensuring children and others were safe during the first of the town's daily rush "hours" between 8:20-8:30am.

Five years of this routine—Mrs Taituma was on her second dog in this time, the twins had grown taller and uglier into their early teenage years, and Benson had earned a record of five years clear of pedestrian incidents. Five years of routine caused new occasions to stand out.

He first noticed her on the third Tuesday of September. She was running. She was running and ignoring Benson's zebra-crossing, electing instead to charge into traffic in front of the pharmacy and towards the twins and Stanley, who had emerged from the underground. She was following his pathway exactly and only veered to the left slightly to avoid running into him, flashing him a double eyebrow raise. She ran so close that Stanley could feel a breeze brush his briefcase hand and smell her sweat lingering long moments after she'd gone. He stopped and turned, not enough to take him off course, of course, but enough to look back at her disappearing figure—the straightness of her back, the broadness of her small shoulders beneath a dark, long-sleeved top, the roundness of her bottom, the evenness of her footfalls, and, disconcertingly, the weaving of her route as if she were running some imaginary slalom through town.

After watching her vanish, Stanley continued on his way, greeting the twins, avoiding Benson's zebra-crossing, and proceeding towards the insurance company offices, wondering if he would see the strange new figure again.

✠

Perhaps it was the spring in the air or the spring in his step, but Sharon had decided, not only to say yes to Blake the next time he asked her out, but that she would ask him out herself if he failed to meet his first of the month deadline.

He did not fail.

"Hey, Sharon," Blake said, placing his hands on the swivel chair beside her, recently vacated by Frances. It was the end of a long work day. His greeting echoed faintly in the hollow foyer.

Sharon smiled and turned towards him. She wasn't sure how to feel or what expression to show him. She only knew her decision. "Hi Blake," she said. It was too loose, too much like she knew what he was going to ask. It seemed to cause him to shy away, so she added, "Are you staying late too?"

The question enticed him to stay.

"Oh ... no ... not really. I was just waiting for Frances to leave so I could ... you know ...." He raised his eyes hopefully. He did have nice eyes.

Sharon, feeling coy, said, "OK."

This threw him. Was she saying she understood or that she was agreeing? Not a stranger to this, however, Blake asked, "Well, I was wondering ... again, ha-ha ... if you'd like to go out, even just for a drink this afternoon. It's the first of the month—sort of a tradition of mine."

"A tradition to have a drink ... or to ask your co-workers out?"

This scared him. "OK, well, never mind ... maybe another time then, Sharon." He turned to go, but Sharon reached out and took him by the arm.

"I'd like to, Blake. Sure, let's have that drink, eh?"

"Trust me," BloodyLegend180 had written, and Perec, primarily in a spirit of surrender but also in a vein of curiosity, had decided to give him some leeway. For two weeks, he allowed the other to add his own symbols to Perec's maps and documents. He still monitored him closely, especially in the beginning, to ensure he did not tamper with his work in any other manner. The intruder had earned some trust, seemingly leaving Perec's symbols and commentary unmolested—no pictures deleted, no alterations to his legend. Still, he had no idea what he was up to.

The two communicated by instant messaging, though infrequently, as Perec watched the other work. Occasionally, he would ask him a question such as, "Which document are you working on now?" and BloodyLegend180 might respond and point him to it, other times he did not.

Perec spent some time trying to find out about the stranger, searching online for any references to his username, but with no results. He had no hacking skills himself, so he searched for ways to trace a user back through IP addresses, but he found no readily understandable method and was not sure if one even existed.

In between sessions in cyberspace, Perec returned to his hand-drawn maps of the plumbing systems in his house. This was a relatively new annual project for him, the first one completed three years prior, after he had a new water main installed from his toby. Seeing the pipes in the raw inspired him to imagine the connections behind the scrim, and sometimes he poked holes in his walls or lifted floorboards. He felt like Leonardo da Vinci, peeling back skin and flesh to sketch circulatory systems and, again, Perec did not sketch what he found or imagined but constructed another legend and system of symbols to represent joins, elbows, faucets, and valves. So much to study right here in his own house.

Two weeks on, Perec finally received an unprompted message from BloodyLegend180: "Are you starting to see it?"

Intrigued, Perec trolled through his documents. He might have asked the puzzle-maker where he should look specifically, but he was now enjoying this mystery trail.

He studied his maps of New Zealand, noting some symbols clustered around the Hokianga region, but saw nothing special that BloodyLegend might be alluding to. He found some more around various islands in the Pacific—Tahiti, Hawaii, Tonga, the Marquesas, as far west as Taiwan and as far east as Easter Island. One or two more appeared along the west coast of Canada on his maps from the late 18th century, but, even on his large scale maps, he could see that Nova Scotia had been cluster-bombed with symbols, even more than the UK and France.

The symbols appeared, mainly concentrated on his detailed maps of Nova Scotia, both modern and circa 1750-1800. Flipping through them in chronological order, dating back to pre-European times to the era of French Acadian settlement—the time of his ancestors— through the late 1700s, Perec noted the increase in symbols but recognised no pattern. He felt a need to satisfy his challenger and resisted asking for help or admitting defeat.

Finally, he wrote back to him, "If by 'it' you mean the clusters, then yes I see it."

To which BloodyLegend replied, "Keep looking—closely—it's almost finished."

Where some men might find this gamesmanship intolerably manipulative, Perec found it irresistible. Dutifully, he returned to the map with the greatest cluster of symbols: the *Carte de l'Acadie, Isle Royale* of Jacques-Nicolas Bellin, circa 1773. He knew he was in the right place when he observed new symbols appearing in real-time. Somewhere out there, his communicant was pasting and presumably sketching something of significance.

New symbols appeared at Port Royal and Lunenburg, then further north at Tatamagouche and Pictou. As they did, Perec absorbed the new data, collating it with the previous images and reworking these parts, looking for a new whole his brain could understand. Finally the symbols stopped appearing. There was no new message from their creator, but Perec knew he was waiting. He closed his eyes and scanned the globe in his imagination, an image more real to him than the floor beneath his feet or the tree in the centre of Taumata. He scanned the globe as if by scanning he could locate him, see him sitting at his computer, a mirror image of Perec.

He opened his eyes again, quickly, thinking that his mind might subconsciously interpret the message for him before his prefrontal cortex could over-analyse the problem. He sat back in an attempt to gain a wider perspective, peering through the screen as one does with 3D stereograms, but nothing dawned except a realisation that he was going about it the wrong way.

He leaned forward, closer to the screen, moving slowly and allowing his peripheral vision to detect the edges of the map as his nose pressed against the image.

Then he saw them.

Spirals—multiple spirals formed by invisible curving lines connecting symbols in various regions of the provincial map, each one of equal dimensions to the others. One spiral to the south west, near Yarmouth and Kejimkujik; another to the north below the Bay of Fundy, including the Annapolis Valley; further west, a spiral included points in the Milford-Stewiake area; another encompassed a section of Cape Breton and seemed to grow out of Fortress Louisbourg.

But the most striking spiral, the most colourful, the most dynamic, stretched into the Atlantic Ocean and seemed to fairly spotlight its epicentre, a familiar piece of real estate: Oak Island.

The island glowed in Perec's vision and, as he pulled away from the screen, his eyesight failed and he fell into blackness.

⸻

During those same weeks of Montreal Perec's online encounter and subsequent Damascian collapse, Stanley Kowalczyk did not see the strange new figure again. But that did not stop him from thinking about her—or her bottom—and he caught himself looking more to his left and to his right as he walked to and from work.

Sex had eluded Stanley for many years, certainly since his arrival in Te Kauhanga. There had been women in Hamilton—there have always been women in Hamilton—and some shared a bed with Stanley, though none for very long. He had tried to behave normally then, in his new city where he might establish a different reputation from that in Dunedin. Nancy, from High Tower insurance, had slept with him after an ill-fated fall-out with their mutual boss, Mr Sandiston. Stanley knew there was a relationship between the two and that he was part of her revenge for some slight.

It was not a wild event but straight-forward, as you can imagine— missionary position preceded by efficient foreplay. But she had left satisfied and Stanley could feel that, for an evening, he had been a normal bloke, free from hang-ups, an adventurer off the straight and narrow. Morality had little to do with it, or love, or affection. These things were not even third-nature to Stanley.

But he did like a round bottom.

The next time he saw the runner was on his way home from work at the end a fateful first week in October. As he approached the main street and prepared to cut across and into traffic, he saw her running further up from him and the pharmacy. She appeared to be running in much the same direction as before but had stopped for traffic amidst Te Kauhanga's other rush hour between 4:55 and 5:15pm. She wasn't running on the spot, as some joggers do, but was bent with hands on her knees, moving her head from side-to-side with the traffic as if the cars were tennis balls.

Stanley noted her figure again, this time wrapped in t-shirt and slightly baggy shorts which did not betray the lines of her body as before. Uncharacteristically, he stopped at the curb as well. He pretended to watch traffic in similar fashion and let some gaps pass when he saw that she made no move to fill them. In the minute that passed, he admired her long hair tied in a single knot, and the side of her face.

For a moment, he felt an urge to walk towards her, a desire immediately checked by five years of habit and pride. In that moment, she propelled forward, dodging and weaving, avoiding the braking cars. She had not been waiting for traffic to ebb! Stanley felt so akin to her in this, so enraptured by the connection that he wanted to run after her, briefcase pressed against his chest, and suit-tie flung over his shoulder.

Instead, he smiled and watched her disappear into the underground, longing to cross her path again.

Once again Sharon avoided Frances, going so far as to skip her lunch and shopping routine and stay with Manu at the office, knowing that Frances had errands to run around town. Manu was a bore but the safe option after Friday's date with Blake.

"So we're planning a trip in January this year," Manu said, slouching in her staffroom chair. "Last year, we found it so hectic leaving right after Hori finished school. I had all his prizegivings and final assemblies to go to, and then we had to pack at the same time— or I should say, *I* had to pack—Steven wasn't helpful at all. He'd finished work at three, and I still had to do everything when I got home. No, this year we'll relax for a couple of weeks, just see Mum and Dad over Christmas then go to the bach after New Year's. It'll be busier traffic-wise, but Hori will be rested and ready for a trip, and this way you can have annual leave earlier, just like you said after last year."

Sharon nodded. She was thinking about Blake. She had heard all this from Manu before, and it was easy to nod and add comments without much thought.

Yes, she was thinking about Blake but was grateful that Manu hadn't asked about him yet. She knew that her co-workers would find out about Friday night. She and Blake had managed to keep their coffees secret for almost a month, but Frances had seen them at the Korean restaurant. She had given Sharon her shocked look and waved a finger at her like a scolding schoolmarm. All weekend, she dreaded having to answer for it. She had no intention of playing along.

"... too many relatives at the camp ground, and everyone expecting me to feed and entertain them while Hori and Elizabeth missed out on time with me. They had to run around the beach all day without me, collecting shells on their own ...."

Blake was nice, no doubt, and he seemed genuinely interested in her. That was a problem. Perhaps she would feel more positive if he'd only wanted to get in her slacks. It was less crowded in there.

"... constant dishes. This year, I'm throwing every dish away after meals, and I told Steven to tell his parents we're arriving at the site two days later than when we actually are. At least then we can have a couple of days to ourselves ...."

She had stolen glances to see how crowded he was. It was difficult to tell, but he looked to be amply crowded at certain angles. He was nice—and maybe more. He did have cool eyes. They seemed to be hiding something but nothing sinister, probably just opinions—the kind you keep to yourself when you are first dating. Tom had told her he had done that, and she'd admitted the same. Certainly not enough to prevent her seeing Blake again. And she had decided to see him again—this time for a meal on Saturday night, upstairs in Zoebel's restaurant above the Arts centre, out of sight of co-workers.

"... Frances. Did you get everything done that you needed?"

Sharon turned towards the door to meet Frances' knowing look, another affectacious standard.

"Hello, beautiful," Frances said. She only called them beautiful when she was about to dig. Well, this time Sharon wasn't open for prospecting.

"Hello, Frances," she said, impassively. "All good downtown?"

Frances ignored the question. "So ... c'mon now, what happened on Friday? Did you finally say yes?"

Obviously, thought Sharon. "No, he dragged me out. Threatened to date you if I didn't agree to it."

"Ooh, nice one, Sharon. You know I wouldn't date him, don't you? Not since you two are in love now and all." She drew out the word *love* and winked at Manu.

Sharon smiled flatly. Before she could deflect the conversation, Frances asked, "Are you going out with him again? Tell us you're going out with him again. We need some interesting gossip around here. When? Saturday night maybe? You two should so go to Zoebel's. It's not flash, but it's secluded, and you could whisper your sweet-nothings easier up there. I promise I won't listen. I'll just stay at the bar and witness true love develop from infancy to the strip-down-throw-me-down stage." She bit her lip and gyrated her hips, dancing over and behind Manu. "Strip-down, throw-me-down, strip-down, throw-me-down," she chanted, laughing.

Sharon stood to leave. "Very funny, Frances. No, I don't think Zoebel's is for us. Maybe we'll just stick to coffees after work. I'd better get back to the desk."

"Aw, darling, don't leave now. Are you mad?" Frances asked.

"No, I've got nothing to be mad about," Sharon said, too sharply. "It's all good, Frances. Thanks for pushing me to try it. We had a nice enough time."

Sharon walked out of the staffroom and back to her reception area. Why did she give Frances that? It would only encourage her.

Creating shapes out of points is the most natural geometrical process. Geometry—measuring the earth—starts with points and extends into lines, covering one dimension from Point A to Point B. Add two more lines, connected at points, and you have your most basic two-dimensional shape, that basis for the vast field of Trigonometry: the triangle. Three points, three lines, two dimensions. Increase the number of points and lines, even infinitely, along a plane surface, staying earth-bound, and you still only operate in two-dimensional space. Polygons—rectangles (or oblongs), squares (which are simply specialised rectangles), pentagons, hexagons, heptagons, octagons, nonagons, decagons—are all created by points connected by lines. As simple as connecting the dots.

This was the world Montreal Perec lived in, at least in his imagination. It was the world he dreamed to live in. As if he rejected the space created by the legs of Tāne Mahuta, Perec longed for the re-joining of earth and sky. To him, that would be heaven on earth.

Yes, he lived in the realm of points and lines and knew their nuances intimately. But the spirals were disconcerting to him, discombobulating. For, how do you create spirals from points? Once you lay out the points, they are like the stars—joined in any number of ways. How could you arrange them to insist they are connected by one spiralling line? But BloodyLegend180 had done just that.

A true spiral originates from a central point and radiates out, encircling the lines of its past. Each new curvature forms at the same distance from its predecessor just as that line formed from its own predecessor. Unlike concentric circles, a spiral's arcs are joined, one continuous line which, were it made of string, could be unravelled to its full length.

The spiral is iconic in New Zealand, of course. It adorns Māori meeting houses and pouwhenua and even human flesh in the form of moko tattoo. The spiral can represent whirlpools as much as it can represent the sun, and so covers at least two elements. The koru patterns, inspired by the unfurling silver fern frond, emphasise how embedded the shape is in the landscape—spirals birthed from soil and seed.

But a spiral formed on a map? Unheard of. It is believed that a cross is marked on Oak Island, but crosses are difficult to assign absolute assurance of human design. Like constellations in the night sky, ley lines, or faces on Mars, the shape is too often found in nature as a result of human imagination and dot-connecting.

Shortly after his collapse, Montreal Perec recovered himself and surveyed his screen again. The spirals were indiscernible from his angle and distance. The *l'Acadie* map was certainly covered in BloodyLegend's symbols, and Perec now recognised the clusters in the same geographic areas of the province, but, even with imagination, he could not see how the symbols could form a spiral pattern. Perec reflected on his experience. Not only had he felt consumed by the patterns, he had felt a connection with his homeland and ancestry unlike anything since his departure. He considered pressing close once again but did not want to risk his foggy brain so soon.

"Spirals," he typed. One word was enough.

BloodyLegend180 responded, "Good."

"Where are you?" Perec asked.

"Close—and that may prove useful ... or not."

Perec paused over his keyboard, studying the map again. "You marked symbols in other places. Why?"

"Connections," was the only reply.

"Are you from Nova Scotia too?" Perec asked.

"No."

"New Zealand?"

"No ... but I have access there."

Access? Perec thought. He typed, "Is this about Oak Island?"

There was a longer pause across cyberspace, then Perec read, "That's what you want, isn't it?"

Of course it was what he wanted, Perec thought. He'd wanted little else in life. It's why he returned to Nova Scotia, it's why he left Nova Scotia for New Zealand, it's why he came to Te Kauhanga, why he needed to keep looking closely ....

"Yes," he wrote.

"I could tell by your work on here," BloodyLegend180 typed. "I see the connections you have been making. Are you in Pureora?"

Pureora? Pureora was a forest park some hundred kilometres north west of Te Kauhanga.

"No," Perec wrote.

"You should be."

FIVE

This time, Stanley did not need to wait as long before seeing the runner again. It was the next weekend, a Saturday morning, that Stanley went on his weekly walk for exercise. For this excursion, Stanley travelled in the opposite direction of town—south—down the back road where the hill joined a five kilometre loop, wrapping around small subdivisions of Te Kauhanga. You may think that circuits such as these would be anathema to Stanley, but he recognised the circle as a straight line joined at head and tail, like the Midgard serpent, Jormungandr. Ironically, it was much more pleasant and satisfying to Stanley than walking an "out-and-back" in which the inefficiencies of retracing steps, for the purpose of exercise, irritated.

It was a grungy morning. It had rained overnight, and evidence of the rainfall flowed through muddy ditches alongside the footpaths. Unperturbed, Stanley tramped briskly up and over the hilly terrain, quite willing to walk through depressions of stubborn stagnant patches of water where the drains did not flow evenly. He passed the dairy and the wealthier houses on Tōtara Street, around the back of the golf course where the road narrowed and paddocks of sheep looked on, returning, ever clockwise, towards Taumata, and down Half-Mile Hill into a mini gorge when he saw her.

She was stationed on the bridge at the vertex of the gorge, leaning against the rail, staring into the small river flowing swiftly below. She wore her running clothes, this time with the long-sleeved shirt. Traffic had escalated as there was an event of some sort at the golf

46

club, now behind Stanley. So, as he neared, he realised he would need to stop on the bridge with the woman until she either shifted out of his way or until the traffic relented enough for him to exit the footpath, slightly, and walk around her. Even Stanley would not advance into moving traffic barrelling headlong towards him.

Unsure of how to present himself, Stanley slowed awkwardly, walking onto the bridge and stopping a metre from the runner. A large sheep truck rumbled past, followed by a line of cars. She had kept her head lowered until then but, at his approach, raised it to look at him. Stanley was conscious of her lack of awkwardness—the way she looked so directly at him, the way in which she stood straight with her shoulders back and her breasts steady.

"Am I in your way?" she asked. Her voice was exhilarating.

"Yes," Stanley answered, stupidly.

The woman smirked and Stanley lusted after her lips.

"I thought so," she said, then looked over her shoulder at the relentless traffic, unheard of on a Saturday morning in Te Kauhanga. Stanley did not mind at this point. His awkwardness was easing enough to allow for intrigue and infatuation.

She looked down at the bridge rail, upon which she still rested her arm, blocking any space between Stanley and the footpath behind her. "What are you going to do about it?" she asked.

The directness of it! Stanley loved it. He didn't know what to do with it, but he loved it.

"I'll wait," said Stanley.

"Well, what are you waiting for?" she asked.

A smaller truck jangled by, leaving an echo of chains and tools in the empty space behind it. Now was Stanley's chance. What was he waiting for?

The runner looked at him curiously, with a slight glance towards the road, then removed her barrier from the rail. Stanley looked at the space proffered but did not budge.

"I'm waiting for...," he started.

"Never mind, it's all good, Mr Straight-Line Man," she chirped, winking at him. She pushed past him and up the hill, brushing against his arm. He turned to watch her go, his eyes automatically watching her wriggle as she started into her run. She looked back at him and called out, "Caught you!" then slapped herself on her left cheek, exaggerated two swings of her hips, and launched at speed up the hill

47

and out of sight. Despite the returning awkwardness, Stanley enjoyed watching her go.

Zoebel's restaurant had seen better days, or at least the venue for the business had. The owner, Karl Zoebel, had initially established himself with a café on a side street, next to the Opportunity Shop and Bin Inn. Despite the poor location, he had earned favourable reviews from locals for his cabinet selection of quiches and meat pies. Encouraged, he shifted to the main street to the improved location, neighbouring the outdoor pursuits shop and one of Te Kauhanga's three banks. He began to draw group bookings there, prompting him to look further for a space capable of hosting larger functions. The loft above the hair salon and book store was not ideal for foot traffic, and Karl still needed to renovate beyond the kitchen and dining room, but customers enjoyed the airy spaciousness of his restaurant, one of the few places in town offering elevation above the humdrum of small town affairs.

Sharon hoped it would be an ideal place to avoid the eyes, ears and mouth of Frances. She had enough to think about with Blake in her life now.

"It's funny being up here," Blake said, leaning back in his chair having placed his order with the waitress, "after passing under it all my life and wondering what was up here when we were kids."

Blake Mānukau was a Kauhangian—born in the town, raised there until secondary school age, then returning to live and work after leaving high school in Whanganui.

"Haven't you been up here before, then?" Sharon asked.

Blake shook his head. "No, I don't eat in restaurants very often. When we had our initial coffee last month, it was the first time I'd eaten out in years."

Surprised, Sharon asked, "Why is that Blake? Is the council not paying you enough?"

Blake laughed, "Of course they're not paying me enough, but that's not why I don't eat out. Never mind, though, this is cool. I'm looking forward to a kumara salad. Are you sure you're happy sharing, Sharon?"

Sharon smiled. "Yes, that's fine. I haven't had a kumara salad before, so I guess we're both venturing outside our comfort zones tonight."

They sat in silence for a few minutes. The restaurant was not full. Shortly after they arrived, a collection of schoolteachers broke up their session of drinks near the bar. A few remained, speaking quickly, but covertly, with animated gesticulations. A waitress cleaned the tables left behind by the group. Otherwise, they were the sum population of the place.

"So, if you don't eat out much, does that mean you like to cook?" Sharon asked.

"Not really," Blake laughed. "But it does give me more control over things. I like to know where my food comes from and how it's prepared."

"I think your salad comes from the ground and is being prepared in the kitchen," Sharon joked.

"Ha-ha ... fair enough, Sharon," Blake said. "But what about the wheat used for those teachers' beers, or the beans for the coffees we had last week? Some products have travelled a long way from plant to plate. Do you know that when you buy a chocolate bar, that bar has been transported here to Te Kauhanga from Auckland, where it was imported from Australia, where it was imported from France, where it was manufactured from cocoa beans grown God-knows-where? The chocolate bar companies import their cocoa beans from other companies, who source them from different suppliers, who harvest them from all sorts of obscure third-world locations, often with no paper trail. The next chocolate bar you eat will probably have been made from slave-picked cocoa beans and delivered to you by multiple trucks, planes and boats. If it works that way for chocolate, you can bet it works the same for lettuce or blueberries or milk."

Sharon was taken aback, though interested. She had never seen this side of Blake in the staff lunch room or in his shy requests for coffee.

"So, how do you do things differently? Do you read labels at the supermarket, then?"

"I do, yeah, but I do more than that. I buy my fruit and veg from Gary V, you know, the guy who visits town each Friday? He either grows his produce himself or can tell you where he got it—and you can bet it's come from within thirty kilometres of here."

"That's interesting, Blake. Yes, I've seen that man, but I didn't think his prices were that much better than our supermarket, and his vegetables were all good but nothing spectacularly different."

"But, don't you see that's not my point? It's not about price or quality—although I can show you how much cleaner and fresher his stuff is—it's about our use of resources world-wide. We expect fruits out of season, and we expect oranges to be orange. So, we all join together to have this stuff shipped to us from around the world. I mean, our supermarket is currently selling lobsters from Nova Scotia, Canada! Think about what those poor little buggers have been through to make it here. Besides, we have plenty of our own crayfish, why do we need Nova Scotian lobster?"

"Well, they are different, I suppose, but I think they look too creepy to eat," Sharon said.

Blake paused and lowered his voice from the higher register he had been using. "Sorry, I went on a bit of a rant there. This stuff just really makes sense to me, you know? So when I say I haven't been in a restaurant for a while, it's a lifestyle choice. Restaurants are part of the whole system—"

"Well ... we can go if you'd like," Sharon interrupted.

Blake's face fell. "Oh, shit ... sorry, I didn't mean it like that. No, really ... I want to have a good time with you tonight. I'll behave, I promise."

Sharon nodded. "It's all good, Blake. Hey, isn't that man who lives in the lighthouse from Nova Scotia ...?"

Several November days had passed since Perec had heard from BloodyLegend180. However, the puzzle maker had left him with homework. It was not difficult with the technology provided by WiCharts. The points marked by BloodyLegend were specifically set and labelled with GPS co-ordinates so that, if he could not discern directly from the map, Perec could use the Internet to identify the exact place or feature.

He started with Oak Island, of course. From there, he identified various historical landmarks in the Mahone Bay and Chester Basin regions: first church constructions for the early colonists from New England; the site of the *HMS Mars* shipwreck of 1761; and what appeared to be sites significant to the Mi'kmaq, the first nations people of Nova Scotia.

Further north, in the Annapolis Valley region, the spiral emerged from its centre at Grand Pre, famous for the church in which Perec's ancestors, the Acadians, had been herded by the British prior to their expulsion and forced diaspora around the globe. Perec identified more sites of significance for the Mi'kmaq, including Cape Blomidon.

These were areas with which Perec was familiar. He knew their context and some of their stories. He certainly knew of their locations, and he mentally constructed his own symbols that he would use to represent them at a later date. He searched for information about sites marked in the Yarmouth areas and around Milford and north-east to Louisbourg, on Cape Breton Island. However, it was the Milford site that puzzled him most, because he could not identify its centre.

And there was something else.

Having pored over the maps for the better part of eighteen hours, Perec was transitioning from his screen to the comfort of his bed, when a message from BloodyLegend180 materialised.

"So?"

Perec thought about sharing his findings straight away, but he was still wary of this stranger, curious to know more before offering.

"Where have you been?" Perec wrote.

"Overseas," was the reply.

"That doesn't tell me much."

"Does it matter?"

Perec, annoyed, tried a different tack. "How did you find me on here?"

This question seemed to cause a pause.

"Well, I wasn't looking for you, if that's what you're worried about."

Games, thought Perec. *He's playing games with me.* He wrote as much to him.

"No games," the other wrote back. "Serendipity, maybe. Fate. Destiny. Connectivity. Synchronicity."

Perec leaned forward in his chair. The hum of his computer had grown louder, the fan working overtime to cool his machine. It was dark outside and in, the only light from the screen which illuminated his face and his reflection in the mirror on the wall left of him. His correspondent paused as well.

Perec wrote, "I've been doing some research."

"Of course."

"I've been researching the sites marked by your symbols. They're a jumble, a mixture of all sorts of things."

"Yes?"

"What's to say they're more significant than any others you've left out? There are plenty of historic sites in Nova Scotia. Why those ones?" Perec asked.

"Those ones make the spirals."

Perec shook his head. He typed, "Do you mean you've chosen them for just that reason? So there's no significance at all then. They're random until you shape them."

"No," was the only response.

"Yes," Perec wrote back after waiting to see if the other would say more. "That's exactly it."

"No, not random. Look again."

Perec rubbed his eyes. He really was tired. The adrenaline that had propelled him so hard through the week subsided at the thought that this intruder had led him astray. But he looked again. This time, he looked closer, with the captioned information revealed next to each of the symbols. He leaned in and saw the words blur as the symbols tried to recreate the spirals in their clusters of colour. But the words in between interfered. Perec leaned back, intending to hide the words and try again, when he saw another pattern.

"All the sites are pre-1770."

"Try 1768," BloodyLegend wrote back.

Perec considered his findings again. "OK," he wrote. He scratched his head. Then he typed, "I don't see how that makes any difference."

"Then you have more homework to do. Think about other sites I've omitted, pre and post 1768, and try plotting them on the spirals."

I will, Perec thought, but then wrote, "I take it they won't fit?"

There was a pause, then, "There's something else. Look closer."

Frustrated, Perec surveyed the map in front of him. At first, he didn't lean in, as he had done before, but considered that maybe it would be better to look from afar. But then, the appeal of all those flat, coloured lines, those symbols for towns and provincial parks and historic landmarks drew him in. He had barely moved, however, when he saw it—a large spiral encompassing the entire province, not including all the points of the others, but connecting first with those on the outskirts: the shipwrecks and islands and ports, then swirling inland. Perec felt like he was descending into the heart of a tornado, surrounded by debris from ancient scouting posts and homestead foundations until he saw the very core, a point of uttermost importance but that included no man-made construct or natural feature.

Once again, overwhelmed but still conscious, Perec shook himself and leaned back, breathing heavily. Re-composed, he wrote, "Another one—a big one—joining all the others."

"One spiral to rule them all," BloodyLegend replied.

"Yes," wrote Perec. "Ruled by the spiral around Milford."

<hr>

Those who have lived in a small town know the *Law of Multiple Encounters*. The Law of Multiple Encounters states that, for every acquaintance you have in the town, you will experience a long period of non-contact followed by multiple encounters within a very short space of time. This could be two-to-three times within a week, or even several times within one day. Stanley Kowalczyk endured over two weeks without re-crossing the runner's path since their meeting on the bridge. And it was an endurance, because Stanley was by then longing to encounter her. He longed for a chance encounter and, in his dreams, he longed for a sexual encounter. If it were up to him, and if he were brave enough, he would encounter her several times a day, and he would encounter her good.

He was terrified of her, of course, and this only fed his longing. It would be difficult to explain to Stanley. He really was a simple man. But during his period of abstinence, and the frustration that complemented it, Stanley had forgotten about the Law of Multiple Encounters.

Behind the Aotea Insurance Company's offices splayed an outdoor patio, a space set aside for staff to eat lunch or hold more informal meetings with clients. Stanley often ate lunch at the modest picnic table, under the shade of the umbrella. This day of multiple encounters, Stanley sat with his back to the offices and the sliding glass doors, looking at and through the fence surrounding the patio, enjoying the spaces between the palings with the sunlight causing an anti-shadow on the asphalt beyond.

As he ate his carrot and cucumber sandwich, he saw the runner disturb the panorama as she appeared suddenly from the right and quickly disappeared to the left.

He wanted to leap to his feet, scramble from the picnic table, push through the umbrella like a turnstile and race to the fencing to see what he could see of her. But he knew the noise would be too obvious, so he moved fast enough to reach the palings and see her lovely figure pace past a car parked at the corner and veer left towards the main street. His lungs stirred at her absence, filling until he sighed. He did not know that the Law of Multiple Encounters had been invoked.

Of course, in a small town, the places and spaces that people meet are limited and the probability is that you will see a person in one of the more common venues. Despite his tendencies, Stanley did need to shop for food on his way home some nights, and that meant visiting the one supermarket in town. Selling wares was not the only service the establishment offered the people of Te Kauhanga. Most afternoons, shoppers filed into its narrow aisles as if they were taking a seat in a town hall. The conversations ranged from the state of the local high school to which new business owner had recently imported a bride. Everyone could be found at the supermarket at least once during the week.

And so it was that Stanley encountered his runner again that same day. The aisles were full, especially Confectionery Lane, and, as you can imagine, Stanley was tracing his usual efficient route through the store—starting at the start and finishing at the finish with no backtracks, diversions or deviations. He sometimes bypassed an aisle if he did not need anything in it but would only do so if there was a second aisle to circumvent in order to even out his northbound aisles with his southbound. If only one aisle was unnecessary, Stanley would still pass through, otherwise he would end up stuck at the back of the store with nothing but the distasteful option of retracing his steps.

Hence, Stanley was selecting items for his cat Stripes in the pet food aisle when he came face to face with the runner.

"Hi there," she said to him, as if he was a friend who had pre-arranged an appointment. She balanced a can of dog food in her hand. "Do you like dogs?" she asked.

Stanley looked at the can. "Dogs are OK, I guess," he said, "but I don't have one. I haven't since I was a kid."

"You were a kid once? Geez, I wonder what that must have been like," she said. "All rulers and no compasses, I bet."

Stanley was puzzled. She had formed an impression of him somehow. "You called me the straight-line guy."

"Sorry?" For the first time, she seemed puzzled.

"On the bridge. You called me Mr Straight-Line Guy. Why did you call me that?"

The woman nodded, and her eyes smirked. "I see you when I'm out running. You always walk in straight lines—through parks, across the streets, even in here I bet. I've watched you do it. You've got yourself a pretty weird thing happening there."

Stanley felt embarrassed and aroused at the same time. She'd been watching him.

"It's not weird, it's efficient. The shortest distance between two points is a straight line."

She laughed. "You sound like a Maths text book." Stanley shifted his feet on his spot. "I watched you the other day," she continued. "You were walking into the underground and you dropped something. Do you remember? You dropped it and I watched you stop a few metres away, turn around to look at it, and then you just kept going! You just left it there! So I ran up to see what it was." She reached into the back pocket of her jeans and presented an envelope. "It was your new bloody bank card! You left your new bank card out on the footpath for anyone else to come along and take it? Why would you do that?"

Stanley, of course, had fielded questions about his quirks before but had never been confronted in this way—so publicly by a stranger, by a beautiful stranger, for this was the first time he had seen her dressed out of her running clothes. She was made up with her hair down over her shoulders. Her top was much the same as her long-sleeved numbers but more formal. While she was talking, he was captivated by her living eyes and her graceful mouth, but he also stole several glances at her chest which was breathing in time with her oratory. *Oratory*, thought Stanley.

"I cancelled it when I got home," he said.

This left her open-mouthed for a moment and then she laughed, "Well, did you order a new one too? I bet you ordered a new one—to replace the one you wouldn't just pick up off the ground."

"That's right," said Stanley.

"You're worse than I thought," she said. "So, here we are again, like we were on the bridge. I'm in your way aren't I? What do you do when this happens?"

"I usually wait. Or I might say, 'Excuse me'."

She looked hard at him. "Well, go on then," she said.

Stanley looked away. Her eyes were vibrant and he was getting lost in their intensity. "What do you mean?"

"Well, you said you either wait or say, 'Excuse me'. So go ahead and do one of those things." She hadn't budged during the conversation but had stood steadfast in the centre of the aisle, at times with her arms folded to allow customers to pass the pair, at times with her arms stretched to either side of the aisle as if holding items on the shelf in an earthquake.

Stanley spoke, sounding like a child, "Excuse me."

"No," she said.

"No?"

"No, I won't excuse you," she said.

"What do you mean?"

"You said 'Excuse me', which really means, 'Get out of my way,' and I'm saying, 'No'."

"You mean, you won't move out of my way?"

"That's right," she said.

"Even when I say, 'Excuse me'?" said Stanley.

"Even then," she said. "So ... what next?"

Stanley looked over her shoulder at the space behind her. "I'll wait," he said.

"Well, I don't want to wait here with you."

With that, the runner removed both hands from the shelves and rammed them into Stanley's chest, forcing him backwards down the aisle in the direction he'd come. He was too stunned to protest but only tried to regain his feet, which had instinctively stumbled back and under him in an effort to stay upright. As soon as he recaptured his balance, another blow would force him back until, sure enough, she had shoved him to the beginning of the aisle where, with one final assault, she pushed him so hard that he did fall over, landing on his backside between the paper-towels and the cat toys.

She didn't stop to help him up, she didn't apologise to him or explain herself, she didn't say anything. Stanley watched her walk off from his floor seat, thinking, despite his cognitive dissonance, *She's been watching me.*

Sharon Pellerine was also shopping in the supermarket the night Stanley Kowalczyk took ten steps back in the pet food aisle. She was collecting materials for her home dinner date with Blake. This would be their first date at home, to be held at his house, of course. They had agreed that Blake would source the vegetables and venison from a friend while she looked after drinks and desert, preferably a New Zealand wine and a pavlova made from local free-range eggs.

Over the weeks, they had continued their conversations about such matters, and Blake's reasoning and approach was impressing Sharon. So, she returned to her house to prepare the pav, feeling very good indeed about the night ahead. There was, in fact, another item on the agenda for the night.

Dating Blake had given Sharon some incentive to think about her living quarters. Movement in her kitchen was easier as she had shifted some piles of magazines, freeing the doorway, and, for tonight at least, she had a clear bench and a safe space between her oven and her periodicals. Yes, it would be a good night, a spring night, a night of new starts and fresh discoveries. Who knew where it might lead?

"Where do you live?" Blake had asked at work a day earlier, after they had arranged plans for dinner at his house.

"Taumata," she had said.

"Oh, well, I live up there too," Blake had said. "Which house are you in?"

"Oh, I don't live in a house," she'd lied. "I live in a flat above someone else's house."

"Really? I didn't know there was anything like that in Taumata. I thought the only multi-story place was the lighthouse."

"Oh, no," Sharon had said, "there's another one. I should know. I live in it."

After deflecting him onto another topic, Sharon had been happy—happy enough to enjoy their planning and their night for what it was: pure, conventional pleasure.

She arrived at Blake's house at eight o'clock. He lived in a modest yellow bungalow on Tūāraki Street, north-east of the tree. He lived in the same block as Sharon but between her place and town, a situation that enabled her to know more about where he lived than he did about her as he would have less cause to travel in her direction. His house had no driveway of its own, instead set on a hill on a small section in front of a larger property behind. Sharon ascended the steps from the footpath with the setting sun brightening her right side to compensate for the long shadow of the tree. It was a beautiful pre-summer evening. The air was still.

Blake met her at the door, having spied her through the front picture window. He was dressed casually, not in his usual work ensemble, wearing long khaki shorts with a polo shirt and jandals. He held tongs in his hand which he wielded wide from their bodies as he welcomed Sharon with a hug.

"Come in. Welcome to *Chez Mānukau*," he said.

Sharon smiled and followed him inside. The first thing she noted was the space available to her. She knew, naturally, that he would not live as cluttered a life as hers, even as a man, but she did not anticipate the sparseness of his house. The front foyer had one pair of dress shoes inside the door under a small table balancing a single ring of keys. The walls were devoid of ornamentation—no pictures or artwork. As he led her through and into his kitchen in the back, he placed the tongs on a plate on the bench. He had been preparing their salad. The cupboard doors were opened, revealing the barest minimum of whiteware—two plates, four juice glasses, two mugs, two wine glasses. In the centre of the kitchen, completely exposed except for the filled salad bowl, stood a simple table with two chairs on either side.

"I thought we'd eat outside," Blake said. "I've just finished with the barbecue." He sounded confident in these surroundings, like a man who knows the end of a story that intends to surprise.

The next few hours passed as you might expect. Sharon asked Blake about his house, and he told her about the renovations he had completed and the plans he had for development. Blake asked Sharon how she ended up in Te Kauhanga, and she obscured her story about why she left Wellington for the more placid lifestyle of a rural town. The neighbours started playing a stereo which threatened to disturb their meal and conversation, but this only lasted half an hour or so which was a good thing for Blake as he tended to overreact when under pressure to alter surroundings out of his control.

As the night cooled and jerseys no longer sufficed, the pair moved inside, sitting on Blake's best sofa, one on either end but close enough to touch. Until this moment, the two had always sat across café and restaurant tables. It was cosy and promising.

"Tell me more about your job at the library. What was the most interesting item you had contact with there?" Blake asked. He held his wine glass with both hands, one leg folded under the other, his knee barely brushing against hers as she sat in similar posture.

Sharon thought of *The Book of Hours*, somewhere in her house. "Oh, I loved the Milton stuff. It all came from Turnbull's original collection, considered one of the finest in the world. It's not so much that I'm a fan of Milton, or even poetry, but I do love contact with the antiquity created by objects like those. You know, maps and things too."

"Really? What sorts of maps? I only think of books in places like that."

Sharon shifted in her seat, moving her knee away from his, instantly regretting it, but unsure how to casually reconnect. "We had some maps from early European navigators. Some were copies, especially the ones made by Cook. The originals were all kept by the Royal Society in England. We did have some hand-drawn ones too. Most were unidentified. We had Tuki's map, of course."

"Whose map?" Blake asked. He shifted his own position, relieving his right hand of the wine glass and stretching it across the back of the sofa, close enough for his fingers to rest against her shoulder and the ends of her hair. *Contact re-established*, Sharon thought.

"Tuki—he was a Māori tohunga. He and another Māori, a warrior named Huru, were taken captive by Philip Gidley King so they could teach colonists how to treat the flax on Norfolk Island. We're talking 1792 or something. They were only young guys, twenty-four or so—not weavers, but skilled navigators. Anyway, Tuki drew a map of New Zealand for King, copied on parchment. It's pretty special." She laughed, "Some legends say that Tuki was able to draw the map because he had entered a trance and levitated over the country, but if that was the case, he didn't fly very high. Anything south of Hokianga is largely unaccounted for, and the South Island is a lumpy mass without much detail." Sharon paused. "Are you sure this is interesting to you?"

Blake smiled and nodded. "Sure. I like old stuff—not that it's much use to us now, but it's interesting enough."

Sharon motioned with her head around the bare walls of the room. "I notice you don't have very many belongings in your house, Blake. You don't even have a book shelf in here. Are you expecting to move house or something?"

"Nope, this is a lifestyle choice, Sharon. I live with as few belongings as I can. No books for me. I do read, but I have an e-reader. I have an electronic library with over a thousand books and they all fit on one wee device. No paper wasted, no trees harvested, no space taken up in my house. Do you have an e-reader?"

Sharon flushed. "Oh, yes, sure," she lied again, "but I still prefer books."

"But see, we really do need to change what we're doing, Sharon. I mean, places like the Turnbull Library are important for holding onto things from the past but not the past we're living in. Our present is electronic storage, there's no need for double-up. The publishing industry has had its time of ripping down forests. It's all part of what I've been saying. We've been so consumeristic that we maintain our hunger for the planet's natural resources even while we've created solutions that are already in our shops and homes. I'm not saying books are the main source of deforestation, but the attitudes of bibliophiles who snub e-reading for the smell and touch of a paper copy are indicative of the selfishness in our society. We don't just inherit the earth from our ancestors, we borrow it from our children. Besides, imagine if you and I were in a novel right now and people are reading our words. Do you think the person with a paperback would be enjoying the story more than the person with an e-reader?"

Sharon's stomach spiralled. Without meaning to, she had moved her shoulders inward, ashamed of herself as she listened to Blake's words. She had read about the pros of e-books and had debated topically with others in the council offices about them, but she had never heard these points made nor felt them made so forcefully, and she felt all the more wounded hearing them from Blake for whom she had been genuinely falling.

Blake sensed the disconnection. He reached out more deliberately, firmly placing his hand on her shoulder, then took her under the chin to lift her head and look directly into her eyes. "Are you OK?" he asked.

Sharon asked, "Do you really feel that way?"

"Well, yeah, I do, absolutely, but ... I get excited when I rant like that, and I sound judgmental ... it's not a hill I'm prepared to die on—at least not tonight."

Sharon sighed and tried to smile. Blake identified vulnerability in this and stroked her chin and cheek. He felt her shaking. He swept her hair from her face and neck, resting his hand on her opposite shoulder. Then he kissed her.

Sharon, still nauseous, kept her lips tight out of survival instinct more than resistance. Blake drew back to check on her, but she looked at him to tell him it was all right, and this encouraged him enough to have another go. So he did, and they did.

Measuring the centre of a circle is easy. By definition, any point on the edge of a circle is the same distance from its centre. Ellipses are trickier. Examining an ellipse, whether in two-dimensional form or in an egg-like object, we would always say that there is indeed a centre. Yet, how is this measured? One way is to draw two lines, like cross-hairs, joining the points where the arcs of the ellipse reach their vertices. In other words, much as you might do with a rectangle.

But what about irregular shapes? What about random blobs of putty, or ponds, or spilled milk, or a crumpled shirt on the floor? What about islands or peninsulas? What about provinces?

There are methods for measuring these, although there are also debates about these methods among geographers, surveyors, mathematicians and cartographers. But like most things scientific or mathematical, once you spend enough time drawing conclusions from data and formulas, you begin to see the conclusion first and provide the proof after. Call it an educated guess, call it intuition, but Montreal Perec knew what he had discovered or what he had been shown.

"The geographic centre," he wrote to BloodyLegend180.

"Yes."

"Near Milford," he wrote.

"Yes."

"And you're saying that all these spirals emanate from there,"

Perec wrote.

"Yes."

Perec wiped his forehead. It was late but still humid after a number of hot spring days in his house on the hill. "What does all this mean?" he asked.

"I was hoping you could tell me," was the response. "You're from there ... and you're living in the land of spirals."

Of course, Perec had thought of that after his first revelation from the map. He was, however, scientific enough not to assume there was a necessary causality involved. He also realised that, if there was a connection, he was not intuitive enough to see more than he had. Serendipity, he felt, was an enemy to both the scientific and the intuitive mind, spinning strands that were most often found untethered.

BloodyLegend wrote, "Why did you move to New Zealand?"

It was an old question, one that is asked of any immigrant and one that he had endured from residents for the first few years of his life in Te Kauhanga. More mystifying to those residents was the fact that, other than a brief stay in Wellington, Perec had settled in their isolated piece of real estate having travelled straight from Nova Scotia. Perec had always answered, "Came here for work," or, "Always wanted to see this end of the world." It satisfied people, especially if said in flattering terms and tones, but also because it made sense that someone with such an interest in geography would settle in this part of the Central North Island.

But this is not what he said to BloodyLegend180, the puzzle-maker, the intruder.

"I'm following Cook," Perec typed, and then waited several minutes for a response.

"I thought so," the other replied. Was it possible to sound smug in an instant message? "Cook charted New Zealand but learned to do it in Nova Scotia?"

"That's right," Perec said. He hesitated, and BloodyLegend seemed to sense he needed time, as he did not type anything for several minutes. Perec used this time to flick through maps, maps sketched by various French cartographers, charts plotting voyage routes across the Atlantic and the Pacific, even around the world. Perec scanned through them quickly, not searching for anything, but surveying his life's work. Was this the time to share? Was it the time to share with this fellow who might be an interloper or a potential aide?

Thirty years living in New Zealand. Thirty years tucked away inside the lighthouse of Te Kauhanga. Thirty years under the shadow of the great Taumata tree. Thirty years of searching, following leads that dried or, worse, created whole series of endlessly propagating leads. Wasn't it the time? Wasn't it the place, here in cyberspace?

Perec typed. He typed like a man expunging a lifetime of sins. He told BloodyLegend180 that he had left Nova Scotia on the wave of a theory, a theory he had devised partly from research, partly from stories from his parents, and partly from intuition. Oak Island had contained a treasure. Of that, there could be no doubt. Someone, some group with great engineering aptitude, and with a plethora of either resources or time, had constructed the series of shafts from the ocean, causing seawater to flood the *money pit*. Someone had buried something deep below the periodic platforms of oak, leaving clues of coconut fibres and cryptic messages behind.

Some said it was Captain Kidd—not enough engineering. Others said the Mi'kmaq—plenty of time, but no access to coconut or the tools needed to construct the shafts. Some said the treasure must be a hoard of money, others said it must be a sacred item, worthy of the pharaohs of Egypt who, likewise, poured so much into their pyramids.

Perec believed none of the theories. His hunt was much more personal, he told BloodyLegend180. The treasure, he said, belonged to his ancestors, the Acadians. His people had lived in Nova Scotia, descended from the earliest French settlers in the land, friends to the Mi'kmaq people, and destined to separate themselves from the incessant wars between their homeland and England. As the war raged inland, in New France and at Louisbourg, the Acadians tilled land and grew their own distinct culture. They also protected a valuable treasure.

Perec did not know what that treasure was, nor did his parents, though they did know the legends amongst their fellow descendants. Whatever it was, the Acadians had buried it. Perec was sure they had the help of French engineers. There were plenty about in the 1700s. Boatloads of engineers, labourers, and money regularly visited those shores during the construction of Fortress Louisbourg. And the Acadians, despite their years of separation from the motherland, still spoke the mother tongue and maintained good relations with the French, providing food and supplies to Louisbourg.

Sometime between the British conquest of Acadia in 1710 and the expulsion of the Acadians in the 1750s, his ancestors had buried their treasure in Oak Island. His own ancestors had been expelled from Grand Pre in 1755, only returning after 1764. The stories told by the poets and historians said the British cast the Acadians out because they refused to swear allegiance to their King and because they feared their loyalty to France. This was true, Perec typed, but the British didn't hold them in the church at Grand Pre for five weeks simply to wait for transports to arrive. An interrogation had taken place. Whether someone broke during that period or after was unknown, but the British found the treasure.

"You mean it's no longer on Oak Island?" BloodyLegend interrupted.

"That's right. Hundreds of years of searching for a treasure that is long gone."

"And you think it's in New Zealand?"

"That's right," wrote Perec.

"And you think Cook took it there?"

"Yes."

"Then why are you in Te Kauhanga?"

Perec removed his hands from the keyboard. He lifted his head to look at the stars through his window. Then he wrote, "I don't know anymore."

Stanley Kowalczyk never received visitors. While not a recluse, his life in Te Kauhanga existed between his house and the insurance offices, two points that satisfied most of his needs but did not open the way for many friendships or multiple encounters. He did go out—he had dinners with Raima to celebrate spiking sales figures; he had visited her house for family barbecues; he enjoyed attending plays and musicals at the little theatre in town. But he did not entertain company often, and he certainly did not have visitors come knocking at five minutes to midnight.

The sound of the knocking woke him from a sound sleep. He wondered how many times the knocker had tried to elicit his attention, as it seemed familiar to him when he did finally ascertain what the noise was. Dressed in shorts and t-shirt, the only preparation he needed before opening the door was to pull a beanie over his unruly hair.

He opened his solid wooden door, stretching its chain lock to full capacity.

It was the runner.

She stood on his stoop in her track pants and a hoodie in which she tucked both hands. She wore her own beanie, but her hair hung loose to her shoulders.

"Yeah, so anyway," she said, "I came by to check on you. Are you all good?"

Stanley unlocked the chain and opened the door wider. His heart was pounding at the excitement of this vision, but he was confused. "I'm OK," he said, more meekly than he wanted.

"All right then," she said. "Look, I wanted to say sorry for pushing you over in the supermarket today—just wanted to make sure you were OK."

"I'm OK," he said.

She nodded her head once and bit her lip. "Well, OK then." She raised her eyebrows and said, "Goodnight," and turned back down his steps.

"Wait," Stanley said, unsure of what his next words would be. "Do you know this is the third time we've seen each other today?"

She turned back slightly, not seeming eager to leave. "No, it's only the second isn't it?"

"No, it's the third. I saw you run by my offices today, down behind Aotea Insurance."

She smiled and took two steps towards him. "Do you watch me?"

Stanley stumbled for words. "Well, I've seen you, of course. Usually when I'm walking to and from work—just like you said."

She nodded again, looking at her feet and then back up slyly. "But when you see me, do you watch me?" she asked.

Stanley leaned against his door-frame and put his hand on his chin to cover his mouth, taking care with his next response. He wanted her to know, but—

She filled the space for him.

"Do you like what you see when you watch me? Or do I annoy you?"

"I like what I see," he said.

She stepped backwards down the stairs until she reached the ground, looking at him the entire way. She put her hands on her hips and said, "OK, well, come see me tomorrow then."

Stanley wanted to walk after her now, to reduce the distance to what it had been on the bridge and in the supermarket, but he held his ground trying to play the game properly. "Where should I meet you?"

She looked over her shoulder, past the street lights at the blotch in the sky where the stars were shut out. "Under the tree," she said. "Eight o'clock."

"Why there? What will we do?"

"Leave that with me. I think you could do with some mystery." She held his eyes for a few last moments before walking to the gate, and jogging out to the right down Tonga Street.

SIX

"You look different today, Sharon," prodded Frances within the first five minutes of work on Monday morning. "You look ... uncluttered."

Sharon had expected this and had avoided the staffroom, but Frances had found her sorting her diary at the front counter. Manu followed closely which affirmed they'd been talking about her. Sharon offered a short smile over her shoulder and a murmured mumble of acknowledgment. It wouldn't work.

"So," Frances' voice was closer and Sharon felt a hand on her shoulder, "how was Friday night?"

Sharon put her pen down. "It was ... private."

"Oh-ho-ho," Frances laughed. "Nice one, Sharon. C'mon tell us about your evening. We're your friends. Blake looked pretty satisfied with himself this morning. Did you unpop his cork? Did you blow the lid off his rubbish bin? Huh, Sharon? C'mon, love, tell us how things went." Manu laughed behind her.

Sharon had never been good at this banter—the post-date, potentially post-coital pestering from friends. They weren't her friends though—but was that her fault?

"Hey guys," Sharon said, turning on her stool, "you should know by now that I don't kiss and tell—"

"So, there was kissing!" Frances said, her eyes alight and winking at Manu.

Sharon caught herself smiling. She had waded into that one. Maybe it was time to open up, time to consider letting these people into more of her life. "OK," she said, "so there was kissing."

Frances, recognising the moment, put her arm around their co-worker. "Look, Manu," she said, "our little Sharon is growing up so fast. I wonder what she'll do next, eh?" To Sharon she said, "Blake looks far too satisfied for just kissing, though, Sharon."

But that was all Sharon gave them. She managed to navigate the remainder of the day with distraction, diversion and some shopping in town.

When she arrived home, and had positioned herself in front of the television with a bowl of ice-cream after eating take-aways, she didn't cry. But she did think about friendships and opening up—and she thought about Blake. She hadn't opened up to him fully on Friday night. He was good about it. "It's still too early," she told him. "I need to take things slower than my last relationship." But she had lied about that too. She had taken things slow with Tom. That was part of the problem. She fell for him all right. Her heart hadn't moved slowly then. She threw herself into their relationship like a born-again woman.

Blake said he understood, and they watched a movie together, cuddling on the couch. It was a beautiful evening, they both had agreed.

But sitting amongst her collections, cloistered in her piles and stacks, she saw a pattern. She was too closed in many ways. An impassioned idea was born and she deposited her bowl under her chair. She stood and removed one magazine from the mountain on her right. She flipped through it until she found the article advertised on the cover. She tore one page out, then another, until the article was wholly removed. She maneuvered through her maze into the den where she found her stapler buried at the bottom of an overflowing drawer. She stapled the article together and placed it on top of everything else on her desk.

She looked around her. This was going to take a while.

Captain James Cook is most famous for his charting of the New Zealand coastline during his first circumnavigation of the earth in the late eighteenth century and for his subsequent voyages around the

Pacific, including a journey to the western coast of Canada. However, these accomplishments were on the end of a life-time of seamanship and service to the mighty British Royal Navy. In those years of service, he spent ten years along the north-eastern coast of North America, spending most of his time in the newly established harbour city of Halifax, but also under the tutelage of the Dutch engineer Samuel Holland, charting the Gulf of St Lawrence and the St Lawrence River in preparation for a siege on Quebec. He also created several maps of what is now known as the province of Newfoundland.

He did not set out to chart the coast of New Zealand, a land discovered to Europeans over a century earlier by the Dutch explorer, Abel Tasman. No, his mission was three-fold: to travel to recently contacted Tahiti and befriend the inhabitants there; to observe the transit of Venus across the face of the sun on 3 June 1769; and to complete a secret mission known only to himself and his closest officers. The intelligentsia in London were convinced of a large, fertile, mineral-rich landmass in the south—a counterbalance to the weight of Europe, Asia and Russia. Aristotle himself had proposed this as the fabled *Terra Australis Incognita*. Upon reaching 40 degrees latitude, Cook was destined instead to turn and find the less glamorous east coast of New Zealand.

So, what did this have to do with Oak Island and the treasure-hunting Acadian descendant Montreal Perec? Despite his claim to BloodyLegend180 that he didn't know why he was in Te Kauhanga, there had, of course, been reasons at his time of moving there. But his reasons at that point were intuitive. He tried explaining this to his new online companion.

"There is a story around Oak Island of strange lights and men in red coats seen there in the years before Daniel McGinnis found the tackle block in the tree and people started digging in what we call the money pit. People use this story as proof that the British were responsible for the traps and the treasure. But, although they had the money and the engineers, they had nothing to bury. All their treasures were safe in those days—there are no stories of missing British treasure or any need for valuables to be stored anywhere but in the heart of the burgeoning British empire.

"The red coats were there to uncover the treasure, and they did so with knowledge provided to them by the beleaguered Acadians. The traps are all a distraction. There was always another way in, but everyone naturally thinks the traps guard the entrance."

"How do you know all this?" wrote BloodyLegend.

"Research, stories, logic, intuition—I just know."

"Not very convincing," was the response.

"That's why I've gone it alone. I wouldn't expect anyone else to believe me—I wouldn't ask them to."

"And you think James Cook found this treasure?"

"Not necessarily, in fact, probably not. Cook worked for the royal navy—the treasure easily passed hands and ships. It would have been taken back to Britain and then sent with Cook to New Zealand under the guise of other missions. I mean, really, a search for a lost continent that balances the earth? The Royal Society was filled with the pre-eminent scientists of the day. Foolishness."

There was no response from the other, and Perec recognised that he must be considering the foolishness of this conversation.

Then he read, "So, Cook took a treasure to New Zealand. For what purpose?"

"To bury it."

"In Te Kauhanga?"

"I believe so."

"But why Te Kauhanga? You said there was no need for the British to hide treasure outside of their isle."

"Unless it was something so valuable or so dangerous they wanted it far from their own people as well."

BloodyLegend did not respond for several minutes. Perec re-read his own messages, believing in their legitimacy, but wondering how he could connect the dots for his companion.

Finally, the other wrote, "There's no record of Cook travelling inland. And how would he have got there?"

Perec replied, "There's no record, but he had plenty of time. There are stories in this area, legends of white men who visited up the river, aided by the river tribes in their canoes ... and guided by a priest from Hawaiiki."

Perec was enjoying himself. He had never shared his theories with anyone. Prior to leaving Nova Scotia, he had, of course, tried to explain it to his parents, but his father had grown tired of theories, tired of hearing the fanciful stories about Oak Island or of other treasures buried by his Acadian ancestors. He had moved on, happy to enjoy beaches and harbours without any regard to history. Sometimes treasures were meant to be buried, he would say, sometimes life passes by those who have their hands on a shovel and their head in the clouds. Better to stay in this air, this place between pits and pantheons.

"You must have more than that."

"What evidence do you look for when you're following clues? There are other signs—at the same time as Cook, Jules Dumont d'Urville led a French fleet through here, narrowly missing an encounter with Cook's *Endeavour*. The French and English were fighting all around the globe at that time—in Europe, in North America—but there were no altercations on a grand scale in the Pacific. Yet, their presence was here. You can see it in my maps where it looks like trails have been left from a great car chase or space pursuit—French and English vessels zig-zagging all over the place—and for what? A mythical continent meant to balance the earth? More tiny islands with more species of flax trees? It was a game of cat-and-mouse."

"A game that centres on Te Kauhanga?"

"Perhaps, yes."

"And how long have you been there?"

Perec hesitated to say, but he had gone this far. He told him.

"You must be right, then."

Perec laughed at the response. He had expected critique. He wrote, "Let me ask you something."

"Sure," wrote BloodyLegend.

"When you first found me on here, you said I should be in Pureora. Why?"

"It's the geographic centre of the North Island of New Zealand. Didn't you know that?"

He had known that—a long time ago—but it had ceased to be important or interesting to him until now. He wrote, "Do you think there is a link between that and Milford?"

"Of course!" wrote BloodyLegend. "It's pretty cool what we see on that map of Nova Scotia. You have to admit it's more than coincidence."

"Yes," typed Perec, troubled. "Can you do me a favour?"

"Well, I don't know if we're at that stage in our relationship yet, but what is it?"

"Can you try charting New Zealand like you did Nova Scotia? Can you see if there are more spirals?"

"Sure, but it will take time. Do you reckon I should stick to the same time cap?"

"Yes. No—extend it to 1779."

"Give me a week."

———————:::::::

The rains fall heavily in Te Kauhanga twice each year: in the winter months and in October. The spring rains make for fat lawns but ease towards Christmas. A November rain is received by inhabitants with mixed feelings. Tired of the damp, they are wary but appreciative of the relief from growing summer heat.

In Taumata, the rain only reaches the houses beyond the circumference of the tree's canopy. Some houses are protected from the rain and the harsh sun. They save money on paint but miss the sleep-inducing sounds of a downfall on a corrugated iron roof. Others, across that shadowy line, live a more typical Kiwi lifestyle, happy to be in the sun even if it means a good drenching in between.

Stanley's house was situated outside the tree's influence, but his front yard remained dry. His lawns grew slowly. On this Saturday morning, Stanley awoke to the punching rain on his roof, climbed out of bed, showered, and considered what he should wear. How was he supposed to know what to wear since the runner hadn't told him what they were doing? Regardless, something rainproof was in order. He donned his typical Saturday clothes, threw on his most protective jacket shell and stepped out his front door, through a metre of rain and straight under the shelter of the tree.

Cutting across the church grounds, he looked for his date near the trunk. She had ten minutes to spare, so he didn't worry when he didn't see her. Would he look too eager by arriving first? He didn't want to miss her.

As he emerged from the church grounds and onto Centre Street, he saw her appear outside a drive about seven houses down Tonga to the east. She lived on the same street as him, then, south-east of the tree. He kept walking, however, pretending he hadn't seen her. He would meet her at the tree as planned.

Thirty seconds hadn't passed before she rounded the corner,

running, and slowed down upon reaching the sheltered area several metres away. She smiled when she saw him, as if surprised, and then escalated her pace again until she joined him next to the trunk.

"This is pretty cool, eh?" she said, looking back at the rain that was thundering out of reach. She stretched up to touch the bark of the tree, tracing the outline of some initials carved above Stanley's shoulder. "Isn't this amazing?" she asked. "It's so big, so straight, so thick. Did you know these initials used to be lower? Down here." She indicated a portion of the trunk half a metre beneath the markings.

Stanley didn't say a word but looked at her dumbly.

She laughed, "Don't you get it? Trees don't grow that way." She shook her head. "It's because of Kupe ... never mind. Are you ready to go dressed like that?"

"Go where? It's pouring out," Stanley said.

"It's only water," she said, taking him by the hand. "Come on, follow me. It'll be fun."

Stanley held his ground, resisting her tug. "Where are we going?" he asked. "I need to know before we start."

She relaxed her grip, noting the tension in his jaw, the trepidation in his eyes. "It's not the rain you're worried about, is it?"

Stanley shook his head. She was beautiful. Her hair was tied back, wet. Her dark eyes, so intelligent and free, pierced him, drawing desire out of him. She bit her lip. She was always biting her lip.

"Hey ... hey!" she said, tilting her head to shake him out of his trance. "Let's go for a run together. I'll go at whatever pace you're up for."

"What's your name?" he asked.

"Kiri. My name's Kiri."

Stanley squeezed her hand and pushed himself away from the tree. He and Kiri walked together to the edge of the shade, pausing out of the rain's range. Wisps of water brushed their faces. Then they released hands, and Kiri led them out into the rain and down to Tūāraki Street across from Montreal Perec's lighthouse. At the corner, she turned left, and he ran alongside her, enjoying the occasional touch of his arm against her shoulder. To the end of Tūāraki and turning right, down the incline, across Taylor Road, through the underground and into town—essentially following Stanley's route to work. Kiri eventually led him to his offices before she stopped under the agency's awning. Stanley was panting. He was not used to running, although he was not suffering after years of walking and hiking.

"So this is where you work?" Kiri asked.

"Yes, five years now."

"So five years of walking up and down that hill?"

Stanley nodded.

"Don't you have a car?"

"Yes," he said, "it's parked in my garage."

"Do you ever drive it?"

"Yes, when I go out of town," he said, still breathing heavily.

She laughed and said, "C'mon," taking him by the hand again and running along the back street. It was quiet today. Most of Te Kauhanga's businesses were on the main street, Donaldson, or on the back street which ran parallel but contained agencies and outlets closed on Saturday mornings. It was a good place to run for the weekend warrior.

Shoulder to shoulder they ran, as if Kiri wanted to keep him close, safe from running away from her and out into the passing traffic. She took him off the road, down the long ramp into the town's domain, across the grass and under and around trees towards the river. The rain had not relented during their run and ensured they were alone.

Kiri only stopped when they reached the riverside. They had run through the domain, over a stop bank, climbed a fence and then pushed their way through light brush until they stood with their toes in the water where it met the sandy bank. The rain danced on the flowing surface, but its power had receded enough for them to talk comfortably.

"Do you ever come down here?" Kiri asked.

"No, I don't like rivers," said Stanley.

Kiri stooped to let the water squeeze between her fingers. "What's not to like?" she asked. "It's beautiful—it's always changing, but it's always here. It's cool how the same water I'm touching now will be in the ocean tomorrow, maybe tonight. It's a connection between two points. I thought you'd like that." She stood again, searching his face, looking for signs of the stress she'd seen under the tree.

But Stanley was surprisingly relaxed, captivated by the attention of this sensuous woman who liked to touch the world around her. How could he explain himself without sounding like a complete nutter?

"You're right," he said. "I hadn't thought about rivers like that. It's

74

just that they are ... they twist too much in getting there. Why can't they move straight downhill?" He laughed at himself. He sounded so stupid, like a child.

Kiri looked at him in wonder. "You really are far gone aren't you? How did you get like this?"

Stanley stumbled on his words. He wanted to respond but wasn't sure what was going to come out. Thankfully, she moved on.

"Never mind. It's not important—and we're missing things. C'mon!" She took him by the hand yet again and, to his horror, wrenched him into the river.

He protested as his feet were submerged to his ankles, but as he pulled away from it and her, he caused her to slip, and she fell on her bottom, the river covering her above the waist. Shocked, Stanley stammered multiple apologies and clambered out to help her to her feet.

She was laughing. "It's OK, man, it's OK. I deserved that, I guess. Thanks," she said, shaking water out of her shorts, "I'm fine, really. We're already wet anyway—but we'd better get back and dry off, eh?"

Stanley nodded gratefully. He so wanted to go home. "OK," he said, "but let me lead the way."

And so, Stanley took Kiri by the hand and led her back to Taumata on a straight path.

Almost a week had passed since BloodyLegend180 began his search for spirals in New Zealand, since Kiri tried to lead Stanley from his straight-and-narrow path, and since Sharon Pellerine had torn out and stapled that first article from her magazine. Blake Mānukau determined he would find out why she hadn't been to work in four days. She had phoned in sick of course. On Tuesday morning, according to Frances, she had rung to say she'd developed a migraine. On Wednesday, she'd rung again with the same complaint. On Thursday, she'd said she'd deteriorated further and needed the rest of the week off.

Her friends, whom Blake regarded as overly cheeky and gossipy, had started to rag on her. "It must be some migraine," he'd heard Frances say to Manu and Candice. "I think we should take her story with a migraine of salt." By the end of the week, the comments had turned vitriolic.

"We've been doing her job all week—on top of ours, thank you very much," the ladies started telling customers on the phone. It was true that the council did not hire temps—the town was too small to cater for that—and it was the norm to cover your co-worker's shift for short periods of time.

"If she's not here on Monday, I think we need to speak to Douglas about a replacement," Frances told Manu.

"This is getting ridiculous," Manu agreed.

"She could have at least offered to type something for me at home. She knows I have a monthly report due next week. You'd think since we are helping her in here, she could help us out from there."

And so on. It was enough to concern Blake. He suggested that maybe someone should check on her, but both ladies claimed excuses of out-of-town visitors. So much for friendship. Besides, they said, shouldn't that be the boyfriend's job?

Blake had, in fact, walked around Taumata on Thursday night, looking for the other two-story dwelling besides the lighthouse, but, of course, could not find it. Friday morning, he asked Frances where Sharon lived.

"I have no idea, actually. Somewhere on that hill, near the tree maybe?"

Manu didn't know either, but she did allow him to use her administrative password to find Sharon's address. He didn't recognise the house from the street number, but he did when parked outside it. It certainly was not a two-story building but was easily recognisable, as its front yard was immaculate. *This must be it*, he thought. *The yard just says, "Sharon". Still—why lie?*

After receiving no response to his knock on the door, Blake stepped back to look into the house casements. All were shuttered, the interior completely locked away from view. Undaunted, he walked down the driveway and up to the garage doors. He was able to pull the thin metal door away at the side, enough to see in. Sharon's car was parked inside. He continued, passing around the back of the property in search of a rear door. The backyard was almost non-existent—a very small patch of grass inside a fenced area, decorated with several rosebushes which had grown to the top of the fence but that had been neatly trimmed.

The back door, too, was locked fast and offered no glimpses of the inside. He knocked again. Perhaps she was in a bedroom near the rear of the house. He listened for any movement from inside, but could only hear his breathing and a fantail which had come to investigate him. From under the house, he heard a cat meow but saw no visual evidence of the animal. He looked over the fence into the neighbour's yard but saw no-one. It was quiet in Taumata this afternoon. He had left work early, ahead of the modest traffic and his working neighbours.

"Sharon!" he called out, close to the door so she could hear him better than anyone listening. He didn't think she would appreciate her neighbours being disturbed, but he really was beginning to worry.

He called again. Was that a footstep? He waited and listened. Another sound—this time a shuffling, growing nearer until he could hear someone turn a latch from inside.

The door opened, and Sharon peered at him through the small space she had created. "Blake," she said, squinting her eyes from the sun.

"I'm sorry to wake you. Are you all right?" Blake asked.

Sharon's lips quivered, and she shook her head causing tears to shake loose from her eyes and fall to her chin and to the floor. "No," she said, "I'm not."

"Can I come in, Sharon?" he asked.

She raised her eyes to meet his. It had to come to this—and she had been so hopeful, but maybe this time ...?

She opened the door wider and Blake stepped in. He hugged her and she cried into his shoulder. He pulled her in close, pressing his cheek against her. Then he saw it.

There was a smell to match but unlike any he had ever encountered. It smelled like a used book store built in a barn; it smelled of paper mill and manure; it smelled of tree bark and sewerage.

Paper was everywhere: countless books, many with covers ripped off; endless mountains of magazines scattered and opened—some looked intact while many looked as if they had been chewed through, loose papers scattered amongst them. This room was so entombed by the mess that he could not tell what sort of room it was. It might have been a kitchen stove hidden against the wall or it might have been a toilet.

Sharon, oblivious to Blake's stunned silence, continually repeated, "I tried, I tried, I tried ...."

During that final week of November—the final week of spring, the week in which Stanley Kowalczyk's world was shaken up by the sleek Kiri, the week in which Sharon Pellerine attempted to spring clean—Montreal Perec had been biding his time, waiting for BloodyLegend180 to complete his task. But biding time for Perec was about looking closer.

Excited by their conversations, and with a renewed passion for his field and hunt, Perec deviated from his annual mapping routine to create a new kind of map. He even abandoned his half-completed chart of the electrical wiring in his house. Instead, Perec moved himself and his cartographical materials into his study on the second floor, the room in the centre of his lighthouse. Between meals and sleeping, Perec spent his entire week in that room, mapping. He could not see any stars, or hills, or streets. He mapped only what he could see.

He started with a birds-eye view of the room, not dissimilar to a nine-year-old's Mathematics homework assignment. He sketched symbols for the desk, the bookshelves, the various maps on the walls, the computer on his desk, his chair. He even sketched a symbol for himself sitting amongst it all. He loved it. He loved his own symbol, a simple cursive-style letter P like the one he had been taught to write as a child, shaded in and with a longer, curving tail. To anyone else, it might resemble a lock's key which, of course, suited Perec just fine.

But his week didn't end there. In fact, he was able to complete the study room map in less than twenty-four hours. No, when he finished, he wanted to look even closer. He sketched a map of his desktop, creating symbols for the cartography tools themselves and designing a system accounting for scratches, which looked like rivers etched into the earth's surface.

After the desk, Perec sketched a wall including book shelves, framed photographs, paint chips—all accounted for, measured and drawn to scale or represented by a Perecian symbol. Bliss.

His reverie was marred only by the disappointment of not hearing from BloodyLegend180 sooner than he had requested. With each break for food or toileting, Perec checked his computer in hopes that the other had found something more significant.

Finally, he read the message, "Are you there?" on his screen. It had been posted almost an hour earlier. Perec's wait was over.

"Yes," he wrote back, hoping that his companion was still online.

Perec held his breath. A minute passed before a message flashed, "No spirals."

Perec deflated. He typed, "No? It was a hunch, but are you sure?"

"I'm sure. There are some strange patterns around Puketapu, near Maunganui Bluff, and at Waitapu. The Atiamuri stones feature curiously, and I see some other shapes, but no spirals."

"What other shapes?" asked Perec.

"Crosses mainly. These are potentially related to pre-Māori times. Sketchy."

"What about Pureora?" Perec wrote, "Anything emerging there?"

"No." Came the instant reply.

"So, you don't think there's any connection between here and Nova Scotia?"

"Not saying that. But no spirals."

Perec thought about something BloodyLegend had said before—that New Zealand was the land of spirals. He reminded him of it.

"That's true," was all he received.

He wrote, "So, don't you think there must be some connection to do with spirals?"

"Probably," was the reply. "That's why I contacted you."

Perec flicked through his maps of New Zealand online. He felt something. He started with Antonio Zatta's *Map of the South Pacific*, a beautiful specimen created in 1799 from information fed by Cook's travels. He zoomed in on the North Island of New Zealand, found Pureora forest and punched in the GPS co-ordinates for the geometric centre. He leaned in and looked closer, holding his gaze for several minutes. BloodyLegend either knew he needed time for this, or he had abandoned Perec entirely, or at least for the night.

Perec likewise conceded, seeing nothing at the central point. Instead, he flicked through other maps, official ones from both the British and the French, and unofficial ones from missionaries and whalers. He repeated the process, zooming in, locating the co-ordinates and leaning in for a closer view. Nothing was there and nothing happened.

He persisted, travelling back in time with his maps until he reached the Cook era. He quickly did the same with all the maps he had posted, either created by Cook or based on his work. Nothing.

His last chart was Tuki's map, the most unusual one of all. This was a scan of the precious historical document held at the Alexander Turnbull Library. Māori did not make maps, Perec had discovered in his time in New Zealand. Instead, they ingrained their knowledge of the land in their place-names—their toponymy—each place-name infused with allusions to significant landmarks or events at that site. Cursed with no written recording methods or blessed with terrific memories and ingenious mnemonic devices, Māori moved through this land as characters do through a story, for their land was marked with stories in the same way a map is marked with story-inherent symbols. Likewise, they carved their stories into pouwhenua—totems to their ancestors, family members enshrined in the wood, not places.

Tuki's map reflected this approach—it included references to physical features, but it also contained his *imaginary highway* tracing the pathway of the dead north to Cape Reinga where their souls would complete their final journey across the sea to Hawaiiki, that legendary homeland of Māori ancestors whose pathway has been lost to the living.

Perec zoomed in on Tuki's map. He rotated it too, for Tuki had drawn it east-west, not north-south. He zoomed in but knew that GPS co-ordinates would be useless, as Tuki's map was out of proportion, with most of the map consisting of the land between Cape Reinga and Hokianga, the land Tuki knew well, being closer to his home territory around Doubtless Bay. But he looked closer anyhow and, in so doing, saw something. After so many hours studying this map over thirty years, he saw something—a mark he had never seen before.

Leaning back, he typed, "I have another theory—and another task."

══════ :: :: ::

Kiri had been keen to return to Stanley's place.

Without her own change of clothes, she had asked Stanley if she could shower and wear something of his. He readily agreed.

Sitting in his kitchen, her head wrapped in a towel, her torso garnered in one of his few hooded sweatshirts and that wonderful bottom sporting his smallest pair of boxers, Kiri held her cup of tea close to her lips, breathing in steam before sipping noisily.

Normally, Stanley was annoyed by such sounds—he had a slight case of dysphonia—but he was too excited to care.

"Why don't you like rivers—really?" Kiri asked.

Stanley laughed. He was growing accustomed to her direct questioning about his oddities. "I told you, they bend too much. I like train tracks though."

"Train tracks," she repeated and sipped her tea. "They bend too you know."

"I know, but they don't generally wrap around themselves and start heading in opposite directions for seemingly no reason."

"Unless you're on the Raurimu Spiral."

Stanley exaggerated a shiver. "Don't get me started about spirals. I can't think of a worse shape. They give me nightmares."

Kiri laughed aloud, spitting some of her tea. "That's funny," she said. "I guess I can see why they would bother you but, then again, they are just a straight line in disguise."

"A straight line wrapped around and going nowhere in particular. Point A starts in the centre and Point B is practically right next to it, but does the spiral go straight to it? No. It goes round and round eighteen times to get there. It would drive anyone mad. What use are they anyway? No-one walks in a spiral, no-one builds roads in a spiral. Spirals are for whirlpools, dragging everything in and drowning them."

"You picked the wrong place to live if you don't like spirals. They're on all our Māori carvings—on the marae, on our poupou, on the cross at the church up here."

"Yes, they represent the river." Stanley smiled, "Maybe that's another reason I don't like rivers."

"Well, I think they're wonderful. They add variety and they're not so mathematical, or if they are, they are mathematically, mysteriously wonderful. Think about our Milky Way galaxy. Don't we live in a spiral?"

Stanley scoffed. "Who knows what the Milky Way looks like really? And there's plenty of variety in the world without things like that. Take our tree for instance. Now, that's one of the reasons I love living here. Trees grow straight, they don't muck around. They start at Point A and reach up to Point B. They grow branches for you variety-loving types, which also grow pretty straight by the way."

"What about fantails? I suppose you have a problem with fantails?"

"Absolutely. You know what my dream is? To be able to fly as the crow flies. Fantails, hummingbirds, bumblebees—they're all too distracted. But you know what? Even the crow doesn't fly straight enough. If I were to come back as an animal in the next life, it would be as a godwit or an albatross or something like that—designed for pan-oceanic voyages, straight as an arrow." Stanley sighed, as if lost in his fantasy of it. Then he said, "Maybe I'll buy myself a microlight."

"I can help you," Blake said.

He was sitting at Sharon's kitchen table. He had made enough room to uncover a chair and wipe the table clean. He had refused Sharon's offer of a cup of tea.

"No-one can help me," Sharon said. She sat opposite him, with the open window at her back. Blake had insisted they let some air and sunlight into the house. The back door was open as well, and a cross-breeze was blowing through, stirring up new smells but escorting them out to wider spaces.

"How long have you been living like this, Sharon?"

Sharon heard the condescension in his voice. In her weakened state, and because she felt strangely good about hosting him in her home, she had allowed for the window and the door, but she wasn't prepared to be patronised. This had happened too often with Tom, and she knew that once the relationship lost its balance, once reciprocation was lost and one person felt raised above the other's failings, the future lived in either shame or defiance.

"I'm due for some spring cleaning, that's all," she said, no longer wiping tears from her eyes, recomposing herself.

Blake was stunned and looked around the place again without stating the obvious. *Spring's almost over*, he thought. He tried laughing to normalise the conversation.

"Thanks for coming around," Sharon added. "I suppose the girls have been asking about me?"

"Yes," said Blake. "Well, they are missing you, that's for sure. They said you had a migraine."

"Yes, I had a migraine—and I really needed to organise a bit." Sharon fought back more tears. "Do you want to see what I've done?"

"Um ... OK," Blake said, unsure of how he would travel with her or what he might find elsewhere in the house. Sharon walked to the kitchen door between stacks of papers and crawled over a pile blocking the corridor entrance. Blake followed, crawling as well. When was the last time he had crawled over anything? Caving, perhaps?

Over the top of the pile, Sharon led Blake through a narrow passage, turning left into the lounge. She actually had made a dent in the piles, as there was a space of two square metres now available for a table and chair in the centre of the room.

"I've been sorting this room all week," Sharon said.

That's pride in her voice, thought Blake.

"I've taken all these magazines," she said, indicating the stack on her right, "and I've cut out all the articles and catalogued them here," she said, motioning to her left.

Catalogued them? thought Blake. *It's just a hill of papers.*

"I realise it's hard to tell, but I know where each of the articles are. Remember, I used to work at one of the biggest libraries in the country."

Blake had once heard a teacher say that she met her students at a particular point in their learning and tried to lead them as far along as she could to the next point while she had them. He needed to meet Sharon at the point she was at and help her to keep moving. She obviously felt she had accomplished something.

"Wow, Sharon, that's a lot of work. What happens next? Do you want a hand taking the empty magazines to the rubbish tip?"

Sharon's eyes flashed a micro-expression of anger, and she stepped to her right, partially blocking Blake's access to the magazines. "Oh, no," she said, "I'm keeping those. I just need to sort through the advertisements and make sure I have all the bibliographic information."

"OK," Blake said. "Well, is there anything you'd like me to take out of here for you? You must have some trash from all this ... reorganising. I know when I have a clean-out, I fill a few bags' worth."

Sharon nodded, "Yes, I have some trash—in the corner there." She pointed towards a small plastic supermarket bag, half-filled with torn magazine pages.

Blake couldn't contain himself. "Sharon, are you serious? That's it? Out of all these magazines, you're throwing out a couple of pages? There's not even one magazine's worth in there." He regretted his words, seeing Sharon flinch.

"I know," she said, "but I tried. I tried for you—and look at all this work I've done." She stood and pushed him on the arm. "I think you should go now. I'll ... I'll see you Monday. I'll come back to work on Monday."

"No, Sharon, don't send me away. I'm sorry ... I want to help. Look, maybe I can come by tomorrow and give you a hand ... help you sort through some more things. I'm pretty good at being ruthless about this stuff. Let me help you, eh?"

"No, that's not what I need, I ... I don't know ... maybe .... Blake, I'll see you Monday. Let me have another go over the weekend, and I'll see you Monday."

She directed Blake back to the corridor and into the kitchen where he had entered the house. He complied but stopped on the back step. He wanted to say something clever, something re-assuring, something that would allow him re-entry, but everything inside him was so relieved to be outside that he wasn't certain he could proceed honestly.

"All right, Sharon," he said, "I'll see you Monday," and he walked around the corner. Sharon closed the door, climbed her way to the front sitting room window and watched him drive away. Only then, did she allow herself to cry.

SEVEN

Montreal Perec was comfortable with the disproportional perspective of Tuki's map. As a cartographer, he had been trained for exactitude—everything measured, drawn to scale, a specific and consistent ratio between reality and representation. However, the best maps contained more than information. The best maps contained interpretation.

Tuki's map was wonderful because it contained, not only his individual perspective of his land and surroundings, but also his culture's understanding of the land and his people's connection to it. Tuki's land was more than the physical landmarks, it incorporated the spiritual landscape and pointed to something of the past and to something of the future. As the Māori poupou traced genealogy, carved in the figures of ancestors, his map pointed his contemporaries back to their origins, back to Hawaiiki, that supposedly mythical homeland of the Māori people prior to their migration to New Zealand.

Perec loved this aspect of Tuki's map and all other maps like it. He loved the legendary story of Tuki levitating—using his priestly powers as a tohunga to float above Aotearoa, enabling him to later sketch a map for Lieutenant King. It was another legend, and Perec loved legends. They represented reality, and this legend, like his cartographical legends, was all the more real to him.

There were, of course, many legends along the river and regarding the tree. Sometimes these were connected, and sometimes they were not. The legend that drew Perec to Te Kauhanga was the one that he briefly mentioned to BloodyLegend180. When he arrived in New Zealand those decades ago, Perec did not know where to look, where to settle, where to dig. His first priority was to research the maps of this land and that took him to Wellington—to the Alexander Turnbull Library. How he had loved poring through the records of voyages, records of histories, records of first contacts. He read diaries of Cook and his crew: Joseph Banks, the botanist, William Wales, the astronomer, Daniel Solander, the doctor. He skimmed and scanned as he went, looking for any clues to indicate they had a mission of the kind he theorised.

It was through his searching that he learned of the remarkable figure of Tupaia.

Tupaia—the legendary navigator from Tahiti, who had travelled with Cook as he circumnavigated New Zealand on his first voyage; Tupaia—the great avenger who joined Cook in the hopes of soliciting military support from the British Empire against the Boraborans who had decimated his island community in Raiatea; Tupaia—the tohunga-prophet who amazed Māori coastal villages with tales of his homeland, a homeland the Māori believed to be their Hawaiiki.

And, although it interested him little, Perec learned of Hawaiiki, the homeland of Māori, lost to obscurity after a thousand years of living in New Zealand following the initial contact by the navigator, Kupe. The great Kupe inspired waves of migration by ocean-going Polynesians who settled in this land and did not return. Over the centuries, their knowledge of the return journey to their homeland had been lost—until Tupaia arrived. But Tupaia did not show them the way back, so bent was he on revenge. His loyalties lay with his people and his destiny lay with the Europeans.

But the Māori remembered him—and not just the coastal iwi. Perec studied Cook's journals, his dates, his ports of rest, searching for any indication that he may have taken time to complete an alternative mission—a mission to bury the treasure of the Acadians. Months of living in Wellington, alone in the archives of the Turnbull, left Perec bereft of actual human contacts. He spoke with no experts, he spoke with no locals, but chose, in his delight of the search, to read and chart and measure until he found the space he was looking for.

Perec found a gap—a time period of weeks in which no records were made by any of the diarists, and this led him to the west coast of the North Island, south of Hokianga and the region best known to Tuki; south to the Taranaki bight and to the mouth of a great river. It was here that the records stopped until they picked up again at Port Nicholson, known today as Wellington, along what is now called Cook Straight.

Intuition led him to the river. He could have stayed with the archives, he could have measured and read more, but Perec believed in his hunch.

At the mouth of the river, he found more archives, more museums, more records, and he found writers in these records who were more open to recording the oral traditions of the Māori people. These stories told of Tupaia, much as the eastern coast Māori tribes did—a Tupaia from Hawaiiki who had come leading a great expedition of *goblins*. And the stories told of an excursion up the river, an excursion ending at Te Kauhanga.

There was no mention of the purpose of the excursion, although it was said the goblins were amazed at the tree, even at its height over two hundred years before Perec arrived and bought his house due north of its trunk and beyond its ever encroaching shade. In Te Kauhanga, Perec settled and, with fewer written records, spoke with locals who confirmed the stories—the stories of a landing party of their river whanau, escorting goblins who were assisted by the great tohunga, navigator and translator.

And so, Perec was comfortable with legends. He trusted them as much as written record, as much as measured and recorded data. They had led him to his lighthouse in Te Kauhanga and, despite his thirty years of stagnation, he knew that new stories would emerge.

═══════::::::

"I used to be like you, you know."

It was a perfect evening in Te Kauhanga—perfect for a run with a vibrant young woman, and Stanley was happy.

"How so?" Stanley asked, stepping over a bamboo stalk, fallen from the hillside round the corner of the 5K Tautaungara circuit.

"I used to measure everything when I was running. I measured all the kilometres I ran. I used to drive around, making notes of the quarter and half kilometre marks, so I would know how far I had run. That meant I had to run the same routes all the time. It worked pretty well too—I was able to scientifically develop my stamina and speed and run my first marathon."

"That was a good thing then, wasn't it?"

Kiri laughed. "Oh sure, if you want to spend your whole time staring at your watch! I kept track of everything—and this was before you had apps to do it for you on a device. I had one of those too, cranking the tunes while I checked my pace every quarter kilometre. Four years I did that, all round the North Shore bays. Ask me what the scenery was like."

"What was the scenery like?"

"I have no idea! Ask me who else was around."

"Who else was around?"

"Beats me! Ask me what the best moments were."

"What were the best moments?"

"Logging my times online and seeing how they changed my graphs. Aarrggghhh!"

They veered off from the Tautaungara circuit to run, side-by-side, diagonally towards the hill leading back to Taumata. This was their third run together since the rainy Saturday morning. Kiri had suggested an evening run after Stanley finished work. She said she would run her "hard-core" track in the mornings and run her casual pace with him at night. He had agreed as long as they would run his circuit.

"Now," she said, "ask me what the scenery is like around here."

Stanley was puffing. The Taumata climb was not easy for him. "What's the scenery like around here?"

"In the morning, when the fog is light and the trees are still wet from the night's dew, you can see the sunlight reflected from the leaves and even the bark. The hills are silent but rich in sheep, and the fences invite you to climb over and run alongside them. The houses are still dark inside, and you feel like you own the road and the air, which is so fresh it's like everyone in the world stopped breathing overnight and left it all there for the first riser."

Stanley slowed to a walk as he listened to her, studying her eyes, which stared straight ahead, and her mouth which seemed to be echoing the words rather than pronouncing them. She slowed too, to match his pace, and she said, "Ask me who else is around."

"Who else is around?" he asked.

"There's a man, a real old man with a hat and a cane who walks up towards the nursing home on Tautika Avenue, but he doesn't live there. Every day, he sees me coming and lifts his head, preparing to say hello, which he does in a big clear tone, and I'm sure everyone in the houses along there knows his voice. On Tuesdays and Thursdays, there's this really good-looking guy who cycles to the pool. Most days he wears just his togs with a towel over his shoulder—no helmet— and I wonder if he does the same in winter. At the end of the work day, there's this weird dude who dresses pretty well for a salesman, but who walks in straight lines all the time. I think half the town want to drive over him when he cuts into traffic, but he seems to have become part of the woodwork."

Stanley laughed and then, without being prompted, asked, "What are the best moments?"

Kiri stopped and turned towards him, and he stopped with her. She reached out, taking him by both hands and pulled him close so that her breath fell on his neck as she spoke.

"Listening to the birds just after I got here. By the bridge, as you're heading west out of town, there's that stand of clianthus trees—dozens of them—and for a week or so, they were filled with tuis—hundreds of tuis—more than I've ever seen in one place in my life, filling those trees and warbling to one another, single birds coming and going, fluffing their wings like they do. Then, as the sun went down, they made a mass exodus, like you'd expect a group of starlings or sparrows to do, but these guys were all so huge, that the sound of their wings sounded like an orchestra, and the sight of them looked like a thunder cloud rolling away above the hills and away from our town and valley."

She spoke in a whisper, and Stanley, once he knew she had finished, kissed her, and they stayed in that moment until the sun dropped behind the hills.

Alone, Sharon could cope, but she couldn't change.

She kept her promise to Blake and tried again over the weekend. On Saturday, she disembowelled more magazines. She sorted them and ordered them and stacked them, leaving no doubt that she was an organised person with the experiences and skills of a true archivist. So enraptured and adrenalised was she by her process, she contemplated articulating her system in print so that others could benefit from her profound grasp of curatorial methods.

Sunday morning, as her neighbours and fellow parishioners filed past on the footpath outside her bedroom window on their way to her church, Sharon slept in, consciously, dreading the moment she would witness her living condition. Perhaps it was the spiritual energy of the day stirring deeper in her soul, but Sharon had her predictable epiphany: she wasn't accomplishing anything but moving shit around.

By Sunday night, she had not even accomplished that and did not have the will to clean up around the unfinished jobs she had started. Instead, she relegated herself to her old life, preparing her clothes for the next day, and crying herself to sleep in her chair.

Of course, Frances was waiting at work on Monday morning. She watched Sharon from a distance for the first hour or so. She was sensitive to her control of the social atmosphere at the council and liked people to follow routines. Sharon's absence the week prior required a re-integration into the structures Frances monitored, and she needed to observe her and the dynamics around her return. In short, her return from being ill meant she would be garnering attention, and Frances would have to let that situation run its course before she could redirect people's attentions back to herself in a socially acceptable fashion.

During morning tea, Frances was holding court in the staffroom. Sharon forced herself to be present, despite her apprehensions.

"In Whakatāne, we didn't have these problems. Everyone there was much more civilised than here. No offense, Manu, I'm not being racist, like, I don't mean Māori or anything, I just mean the way people behave, regardless of their culture. In Whakatāne, you wouldn't get people calling you up and raging at you about their rates like it's your fault, and you wouldn't have people walking out swearing at you over their shoulder—and we certainly wouldn't see people schlepping into our offices wearing gumboots. I mean, like, c'mon, man."

Why don't you go back to Whakatāne? thought Sharon. She tried to communicate the thought to Manu or Candice but was wary after being away so long. She wasn't sure how far the others were willing to go in order to stay in Frances' good books. It didn't used to be this way ....

But at least Frances was leaving her alone. And so the day passed, and Sharon was able to cope ... until she finally spoke with Blake.

While Sharon had promised to see Blake again on Monday morning, he had been out of office all day, supporting the mayor in one of the smaller outlying towns in the district. Sharon was grateful for the reprieve, but she missed him and was glad to see him return with the mayor as she was walking out.

"G'day, Sharon," said Mayor Nelson Tumai, ever the congenial leader.

"Hello, Nelson," Sharon said. "Hello, Blake."

"Hello, Sharon." Blake looked warm and open. "Have you had a good day back at the office?"

"Yes, thanks," she said. "How did you two get on down in Akauroa?"

"It was a bit sticky at times, Sharon," Mayor Nelson said. "It was good to have the man with the facts with me." He put a playful arm around Blake's shoulders.

"A man of many talents then, eh?" said Sharon.

Mayor Nelson, recognising a flicker between the two, said, "Well, why don't you two kick off? Don't worry about any debrief this afternoon, Blake. We had a good chat in the car."

Blake nodded and shook the mayor's hand. "Sounds good," he said. "Goodnight, boss." He opened the door behind them and proffered the space for Sharon to walk through.

"Do you want to catch-up?" he asked Sharon, once they were alone in the car park.

"Not tonight, Blake," she said, "but I do want to thank you for coming round on Friday. I'm so embarrassed. I think ... if I can have some more time before your next visit, I'll get there."

"I really would like to help you, Sharon."

To her credit, Sharon did take a moment to consider his offer. She looked in his eyes long enough to see there was care there. She examined his mouth—the mouth she would have loved to kiss in that car park. His words seemed to come out in true blue. She looked at his hands and imagined them touching her ... magazines.

Alone, Sharon could cope. She could get to work and prepare meals; she could pretend everything was normal with her workmates and the people of Te Kauhanga; she could even date—and if she could date, what else could she do? Because, alone she could cope, but she couldn't change. Could Blake help her change?

"I ... I could use just a little help," she said and felt terrified watching the words leave her lips, quivering.

"OK ... because I have some ideas. When can I share them with you?"

"How about Friday night again? I really just need to get through the week normally," said Sharon.

"Friday night is good. We'll make it a date, and we'll talk."

"OK," said Sharon, "we'll talk."

Montreal Perec had lived as such a loner, as such a recluse for so long, that it felt good to collaborate with BloodyLegend180. He had collaborated before—cartography was not always the work of solitary figures. As a student, he had learned the crafts of surveying, which often required teamwork, and he studied those ancient mapmakers of the sea like Cook, like Drake, like Polo, who relied on the deep understandings of their constellation interpreters and, as in the case of a Tupaia, the knowledge of locals.

After so long alone, Perec found it difficult to let go, but for some reason he trusted his new friend. And so, he not only collaborated with him, he delegated the task of examining and reconstructing Tuki's map for their cause.

Yes, instead of completing the work himself or pestering BloodyLegend180 by monitoring his progress, Perec found himself pursuing treasure pleasure of a different sort. After mapping his desk, he continued to construct his two-dimensional representation of the study, completing legends and scale sketches of his chair, bookcase (without the books), and the hardwood floor, even removing all furniture to encompass the entire floor space, drawing symbols for significant wood knots, shaved nail heads, and uneven joins. It was during this last exercise, through a widened gap between boards, that Perec discovered a line of pipes he had not accounted for in his previous charts of the house's plumbing. He theorised that these new pipes were obsolete and no longer functioning in his system. He wrote a note to himself to revisit his previous charts to not only add the defunct pipes, but to possibly appraise, with the help of a plumber, the age of the pipes and their former purpose.

He may have proceeded with this plan straight away if not for the tell-tale trill of an incoming instant message from his collaborator.

"Are you there?" read the simple greeting.

"I am. How did you get on?"

"You may have something with this. I reconstructed the map, point-for-point, matching significant sites to Tuki with their GPS co-ordinates. That was the easy part."

Perec did not type anything to interrupt. The two were used to speaking in instant messaging "soundbites". It was intriguing to read BloodyLegend's prose summary of his work.

"When I tried to do the same with the lower half of the North Island—south of Hokianga—the map remained skewed. But then I interpreted the map the way you told me—imagining the coastline accurately as Tuki would have known his way around the island, but allowing that he had no idea of the depth of the landmass between the southern coast and his region. By doing this, and then matching the significant points, Tuki's map stretched out to look a lot more like the map we know today."

Perec held his breath and felt that confidence of a hunch about to be redeemed. "Have you uploaded your image yet?" he asked.

"Almost done."

He waited, flicking through his collection of maps in the folder, looking for an indication that a new one had been added by another user.

"Done," wrote BloodyLegend180.

Beyond the last map he had added himself, Perec found, what first appeared to be, an ordinary map of the North Island of New Zealand with only sparse markings, mainly concentrated on the northern coastlines. From a rough-hewn sketch on ancient parchment to a digital representation on Perec's screen, this was Tuki's map, upgraded to a form readily accessible to a modern cartographer's sensibilities.

Perec was so captivated by this wonder that he momentarily forgot his hunch and simply breathed, "Oh my God." Then he typed as much to show his appreciation.

"And ...," was all that was typed in response, prompting Perec to focus on the purpose. He looked closer.

There in that open space created by BloodyLegend180, was the mark—the same mark he had seen on Tuki's paper map for the first time several nights ago.

"Is it accurate?" Perec wrote to BloodyLegend. "GPS?"

"Yes," wrote BloodyLegend. "What do you think?"

"Pureora."

═══════ : : : : : :

Before you judge Stanley Kowalczyk harshly, ask yourself, what is the most outrageous thing you have ever done? We all live in comfort zones, bubbles, lifestyles, and, perhaps, these equate to our destinies, the plans that are laid out for our lives, embedded in personalities and unfolded in sequence and purpose. Before we judge Stanley harshly, consider his ill-conceived notions, the core values that drove him from flow and trapped him in his tracks. Yes, ponder the factors that led Stanley to this point in his life and that will direct him, very directly, to the next point—and then judge him ... harshly.

Kiri pushed him, you'll see. She had to, and we wanted her to. Remember that—we all did.

On the last night of November, on summer's eve, Kiri arranged to meet Stanley at a new location for their run. She claimed she was already going to be visiting a friend's house on the other side of the golf course, about 2.6 kilometres anti-clockwise from their usual starting place on the 5km loop at the bottom of the back of Taumata Hill. In addition, she told him she needed to drop into another friend's house near the end of their run in order to pick up a book she had loaned her. In doing so, Kiri placed a choice before Stanley: which way should he go round the loop to meet her?

By now, as you know Stanley Kowalczyk, you can imagine the calculations he was completing. It would seem obvious to us that he should travel clockwise, thereby running 2.4 kilometres to meet Kiri faster and more efficiently. However, Kiri had deliberately omitted some vital information that would impact Stanley's decision. What direction did she plan on travelling back? Did she plan on completing the circuit, regardless of the direction he chose, or did she already know which way she needed to go in order to pick up the book? If the latter was the case, he could end up doubling back on the route he chose. And what if her friend lived on the 2.6km stretch of the loop? He could end up running 5.2 kilometres and, though he didn't mind the overall distance for a run, the inefficiencies would ... irritate him. In the end, it was an impossible choice really, and Kiri had more in store for him anyway so, regardless of his choice, he was set up for what happened next.

Stanley chose to run the 2.4 kilometre leg. It was a pleasant evening with none of the traditional omens associated with the dramas that Stanley's life story required. The sun was lowering but not too quickly, and the hills behind Taumata soaked up rays as if they wouldn't see their provider again for many days. The birds and wind had stilled together. Other, slower runners met Stanley as he ran, showing no foreshadowing whatsoever.

Round the bamboo curve and into the isolated dip leading up to the golf course, Stanley felt good. His footfalls, one following the other—first behind then ahead, then behind, then ahead—measured the track in shape and angle if not in distance. His breathing was steady and he felt in the best shape he had in years.

Up out of the dip, alongside the golf course and within sight of houses again, Stanley looked for house number 192 or for Kiri waiting for him alongside the road.

Kiri was not waiting for him—and this created the next challenge for Stanley. He could reverse, backtracking his route, or he could carry on round the loop and complete it as he always had. Both these choices would be a poor showing for a boyfriend, however, who would be expected to hunt out his mate. He could, then, approach the house at 192 and inquire about his love's whereabouts.

And so, Stanley Kowalczyk, for the first time in five years of circling the Tautaungara loop, left the roadside during his run.

The character and demeanour of the house at 192 was not important in Stanley's story. Nor was the personage of the woman who opened the door to him at his knocking. What matters most were her words: "Kiri left five minutes ago."

You can imagine the spinning and whirling in Stanley's brain.

"Which way did she go?" Stanley managed to ask. He already knew the answer.

"I don't know," Kiri's friend said.

Stanley strategised. "Did she say if she was dropping a book at a friend's on the way back? Do you know where her friend lives?"

"She didn't mention that," was the response. Her voice was

conspiratorial.

Stanley thanked her routinely and turned to face the steps back to the roadside. He scanned the area, searching for signs of Kiri, feeling like a lost child. The valley was still. The trees didn't rustle. The birds did not sing. No neighbourhood children cycled along the footpath. There was no sound or sight of vehicles passing. She had got him.

Then he heard her voice. The stillness masked its location, offering no echo, no wind-born aide pointing him back to the source. Not shy, for Stanley's eccentricity was not the same as bashfulness, he called back, unmindful of the occupants of 192 or their neighbours. But Kiri did not respond. She was waiting.

So Stanley moved. He descended the steps and made a beeline back to the spot from which he had left the circuit. From there, he called again. Was this what she wanted?

Yes. She called again. *That bitch*, thought Stanley, for the voice did not come from the left or right, nor from the way he'd come or the way he hoped to go, but from straight in front of him, over the fence, behind trees, from the golf course itself.

Well, he wasn't playing that game. He had complied with her requests as a dutiful boyfriend in hopes, really, that this relationship would lead to sex in the near future. But now that he knew where she was and what she was up to, he felt no obligation to continue with the charade. He turned to his right to complete the remaining 2.6 kilometres of his anti-clockwise circuit.

He was not far round the next corner, when he saw Kiri running towards and then parallel with him, gliding splendidly over hills and through the shallow dales of the manicured golf course.

"There you are!" she yelled. "Where are you going?"

Stanley resisted the urge to ignore her. He replied, "I'm going home. Are you going to run with me?" He didn't look at her.

"Sure, that's why I arranged to meet you over here," she said, breathfully. "Why don't you run in here with me? The grass is wonderful—great for your knees—and there's no-one else out here tonight. It's too dark. We'll have the whole place to ourselves."

"No, you come out here. We can be sure to finish the 5Ks that way. I don't think you're allowed to run on the golf course."

"I do it all the time," Kiri said, edging closer to the fence. "No-one cares—honestly. C'mon, Stanley, it'll be fun. It's so cool in here."

Stanley did not respond. He had said what he had said. She knew his reasons, and he was not going to articulate them and be made a fool of. He rounded the next corner of the shortest end of the circuit and started the last leg towards the back of Taumata hill and home.

Kiri mirrored him on the inside of the fence, manoeuvring lithely around trees, deliberately meandering towards the putting greens, enjoying the unusual surface beneath her feet. She wore no shoes.

"Stanley," she called, trying not to sound teasing, but still trying to create levity, "why don't you come over now? It's all a homestretch from here—nice and straight. You can rejoin the road down the hill there, where the course ends." She moved closer to him, running just on the other side of the fence. They looked the familiar pair then— Kiri on the left, Stanley on the right, with a simple fence-line between them, stitching the course perimeter together but dividing their worlds.

Stanley ran. He wanted it to end. He didn't appreciate what she was doing, despite the taunting pleasure of her presence at his side— the sideways glimpses of her face and body. He ran faster but could never outmatch her speed and stamina.

They counted down metres to the end of the course and the end of Kiri's great endeavour. Unrelenting, Kiri reached across the fence and grabbed his nearest arm, holding tight and pulling him towards the fence. "Stanley, I'm bored when you're straight. C'mon—"

She didn't see the other arm. She didn't feel the blow—or the several that followed.

✠

On Saturday morning, Blake Mānukau arrived at Sharon Pellerine's house with all the gear you would expect from a seasoned clutter-buster. His ute was loaded with plastic containers, file-folders, staplers, rubber gloves, cleaning agents, and rubbish bags—lots of rubbish bags.

He had devised a plan with Sharon over dinner the night before. She had agreed to trust him. His rationale was that he had devoted time to a sparse life-style, that he too had at one time lived with too many things and that, as a convert to this radical new way, he could support and enlighten. Uncomfortable as she was with the topic of conversation, she was comfortable with the man, and the pair were able to enjoy their meal together as they had been doing until that point. Blake joked that this would be the last supper for Hoarder Sharon and that Born Again Sharon would rise after the weekend.

"The place to start is from the outside in," Blake explained, after Sharon greeted him with a tentative hug. "The more we remove from the kitchen out back, the more room we'll have to haul out other things from the interior. Besides," he said with a wink, "then we'll be able to have a cup of tea."

"Well, we'll sort as well, won't we?" Sharon asked. "I mean ... before we remove anything?"

"Trust me," Blake said, putting his hands on both her shoulders. "We can do both at the same time."

"What about all the work I did last week? Why don't we start with that?"

"Trust me, Sharon," he repeated. "Come on."

They unloaded the truck together, placing bins outside the kitchen door. Blake donned a pair of gloves and flicked open one rubbish bag, handing it to Sharon who eyed it suspiciously. Then he flicked open another for himself. He walked up to the back door as if preparing to apprehend a criminal inside.

"Wait!" Sharon called out, louder and more strained than she intended. Blake turned.

"Don't just start throwing things out. Let's do this together."

Blake looked irritated, but nodded. "OK, Sharon."

The two entered the house and surveyed the kitchen. While it did not look any worse than the last time Blake saw it, it had not improved. Magazines still littered the floor and table. Pots and wooden spoons may have been caked, but it was difficult to tell through the tea towels draped over the them. A jug cord could be seen emerging from heaps of empty cat food packets on the corner of the bench. Most of the cupboards were open. One door hung on a single hinge.

Blake's breathing accelerated like a horse behind a starting gate or a dog who has smelled a passing meal. He could not wait.

Spying the rattiest magazine in range, one with half a cover torn from one corner exposing yellow pages within, he shook his rubbish bag like a matador and deftly scooped the offending item in.

"Wait, which one was that?" Sharon asked, taking hold of Blake's bag and looking to its bottom.

"Sharon, believe me, it's past its use-by date."

"I need to see which one it was," she said firmly. "Let me see."

Blake relinquished his hold, and Sharon extracted her property.

"You see?" he said, "It's just rubbish now, Sharon. Look at those stains."

"It's not all rubbish," Sharon said, flipping the pages. "See? This article is about our tree here in Taumata. It shows a picture of it thirty years ago. I have to keep this."

"Why, Sharon?"

"It's a record of a significant landmark in our region, Blake. We can see how the tree has changed in the last thirty years. In ten years time, we'll have forty years to compare."

"It's a *New Zealand Geographic* magazine, Sharon. There are plenty of them around the place. You don't need to keep this one, do you?"

"Look, Blake, if I'm going to do this, I can't throw out stuff that still has a purpose, can I?" Thinking faster, Sharon said, "Let's set up a system, OK? I saw this one on *New Zealand Living*. It was called, *Bin it, bag it or bury it*. We'll go through this stuff, and you can ask me if I want to bin it, which means keep it in a bin for easy access; or if I want to bag it, which means store it away for a rainy day or for sentimental reasons; or if I want to bury it, which means putting it in the rubbish bags to be taken to the dump."

Blake breathed, differently this time. This was going to be a long day. But her system at least sounded reasonable. "OK, Sharon," he said. "I can work with that, but we'd better get stuck in."

And so, they went through the kitchen one item at a time, Blake showing Sharon a magazine and Sharon arguing its case. Some went in a bin, some went in a bag. After the first hour, not one was destined to be buried, and they had sorted a total of thirty-five magazines, each one sifted for historical significance, cultural relevance, and potential necessity.

The two notes of mood juxtaposed in the room could not have been more off-key.

Sharon, while still very much on edge, was delighted with herself and her company. Between decisions, as an item was placed in a bin or a bag, she would sprinkle affirming comments like, "I'm so glad you're here to help me do this," and, "It feels so good to get these things sorted," or, "You're so right how important space is in our lives. I can breathe better in here already."

Blake was untethered. With each magazine passing between their hands and over the empty rubbish bags, he became more judgmental, more hardened by the sickness he saw in her. While she thought she was emitting light and colour, all he saw was an ooze of putrid, defiant filth. With so many precedents set, he waited for his chance to make his point.

The opportunity arose in the form of a *Pacific Jewel* magazine. Sharon had explained to Blake, over dinner the night preceding, that she was an archivist—he would have to accept that—but that she drew a line at holding two copies of the same item in her care. Blake had seen the same issue of this *Pacific Jewel* magazine about twenty-nine periodicals earlier. He recognised the feature article on cave drawings in the South Island. It had gone in the bin.

"Now—this one, Sharon—you already have a copy of this, so we can toss this one, eh?" Blake said, holding it up so Sharon could see the cover clearly.

Sharon squinted her eyes, reading the titles of the articles contained within.

"Remember, Sharon?" Blake prompted. "This is the one about the caves."

"No ... that can't be right," said Sharon. "I don't have two of anything in my collection."

"I know that's what you said, Sharon ... I know that's your policy ... but this is the same issue. Believe me."

Sharon studied the cover again, and Blake watched as recognition illuminated her face. "No, that's right ... this is the same issue, but it's a different edition. Oh, this one's special," she said, excited. "This was the only time that *Pacific Jewel* had to reprint an issue. You know what happened? In the first edition—the one you're holding—they credited the cave drawings to the Moriori people from the Chatham Islands, saying they had lived there prior to any Māori. But then the editors were challenged by Spencer Lampin, professor of Māori Studies at Victoria University—do you remember him?—he told them off because the Moriori people were actually Māori people in the first place, and even so, the Māori who became the Moriori had never lived in that area. There was a big stink about it and some political pressure put on *Pacific Jewel*, so they re-printed the issue. That's a classic."

Blake's sensibilities could sustain little more.

"You know, Sharon, you're impossible, and I'll tell you why. You say you're an archivist, but it's all bullshit." He continued, despite Sharon's dropping face, "An archivist genuinely cares enough about artefacts to store them properly, and a genuine archivist doesn't hoard things away from the world for their own pleasure. That's what you're doing here, Sharon—hoarding stuff for your own pleasure. You're not a curator for the New Zealand public. If this is such a classic, why did I dig it out from underneath a jam-covered tea-towel on top of a pair of underpants? This place is disgusting, Sharon. There must be dead things under all this shit, I can smell them. How long have you been living like this? Five years? Eight years? Before you came to Te Kauhanga? How many critters do you think have crawled in here looking for warmth and food? This place is a bloody health hazard."

"I ... I think you should leave," said Sharon. She felt beaten by his words. She wasn't about to feel that way again. "You need to go," she said, her voice higher, more pitched. "Now."

Blake wasn't finished. He hadn't made his main point yet. "It's not all your fault, Sharon. I'm not blaming you—you're a victim. You're a victim of our society. How many advertisements have we grown up with, all pushing us to want more and more and more? How many messages from our friends and family at Christmas and birthdays telling us that it's a good thing to get things? It's consumerism, Sharon, and it's all over you. It's consumerism, and it's materialism. You're filling your life with stuff and missing what really matters."

"Get out!" Sharon screamed. "Get out of my fucking house right now! I never want to see you again, you useless prick! Get out!" She was standing now, her eyes wide at the tops and bottoms but narrowed from the sides. She pointed at him, not the door, with her arm tucked tight against her side in an effort to keep control while striking with words. "Get out!" she screamed again. "Get out! Get out! Get out!"

Blake, stunned, wanted to argue some more, make his case heard. She was better than all this but didn't know it. He saw it in her. He knew if he could just help her see it ....

But he left. What else could he do? He tried to tell her that he would leave the bins and the bags, but she slammed the door behind him as soon as he walked outside. He could still hear her screaming from inside as he drove away.

If a treasure hunt is preceded by a deliberate act of concealment, there should be a certain logic to uncovering the treasure. There should be an unravelling of clues working from what is known to the unknown via a connected sequence. What should not happen is the solving of one clue to find more mystery than there was before. One clue solved should illuminate, not obfuscate.

Oak Island, over the centuries of digging, had become a pit of obfuscation. As men reached resource-obvious oak platforms, they discovered the outrageous schema of flood tunnels. The further they dug, the more they surfaced obscure and alien artefacts. They found coconut fibres, most likely originating from the Caribbean, and clay tablets with indecipherable hieroglyphs.

So it was with Tuki's map. Tuki, like the navigator Tupaia before him, did not chart the land and sea as the Europeans did. Tupaia, in order to assist Cook, constructed a highly detailed chart of the Polynesian island nations of their Pacific Ocean continent. To the European mind, there were no compass directions indicated, at least using the cardinal points. There were no lines of latitude or longitude. To the European mind, his positioning and distances made no sense in comparison to their later measurements. To the Tahitian mind, these things did not matter. To the Tahitian navigator's mind, what mattered were hundreds of star paths and specific ocean swells and currents, the movement of the boat beneath him indicating these swells even in the darkest nights. The Tahitian navigator noted drift patterns of seaweed, migration patterns of birds and fish, colour changes from coral below. What mattered was time to reach a place, measured by how far a pahī could travel in a day, not in units of distance in space. To all the Polynesian navigators, none of these things were devoid of a reliance on magic and the assistance of Tangaroa, god of navigation and ocean voyages. In drawing a chart for Cook, Tupaia created more mystery for the European mind.

Tuki's map made sense in the same way. As a sketch of the land Tuki knew, it is remarkable how he was able to interpret the European mind's needs and provide for them in map form. For, surely, the map was not the way in which Tuki saw his land. It was too limiting, too two-dimensional when what he clearly understood went beyond even the three-dimensional.

So, what a mystery he created, and what a mystery Perec and his accomplice uncovered when they determined that Tuki had, indeed, marked the geometric centre of the North Island on his map. This discovery eliminated all other endeavours for Perec and BloodyLegend180, even Perec's mapping of his study. It was all they talked about.

"How could he have known where it was?" Perec wrote.

"Levitation?" BloodyLegend replied.

"Even so, for what purpose? He didn't live anywhere near the area. It would have no significance for him."

"Spirals?"

"What do you mean?" asked Perec.

"Should we check for spirals now that we have a centre?"

"On Tuki's map? There are only a few sites marked—and they're all on the coast. Don't waste your time. There are no spirals there."

BloodyLegend did not respond immediately but seemed deep in thought, or so Perec surmised.

"We should check it out," he finally wrote.

"What do you mean?" Perec asked again.

"You and me—let's go to Pureora."

PART 3D

SUMMER

EIGHT

Summer means many things in New Zealand, most of which apply to a small town like Te Kauhanga. Summer means high humidity and the slow death of lawns. Summer means the end of a child's school year once the final reports are written and prizegiving ceremonies are completed. Summer means Christmas beach gatherings, and many citizens of Te Kauhanga have a favourite bach or campground to which they make an annual pilgrimage. The farms are quiet with little lambing or docking.

But specific to Te Kauhanga, summer means the continued growth spurt of the tree, an annual stretching and widening.

And, while this past spring everyone saw the grass growing, and everyone paid witness to their rituals and traditional processes, no-one saw what was no longer happening. For, to be fair, it is harder to see when something is not happening just as it is harder to see nothing than it is to see something. So, no-one saw the rings not growing, and no-one saw that the tree wasn't stretching, wasn't widening as it had for over a thousand years.

No-one saw, but that is not to say that no-one noticed.

Among the ancient taonga found in Te Kauhanga, there was one, besides the tree, most known to the community. His name was Koro Hohepa. Koro Hohepa lived in Taumata and had done for time immemorial. He lived closest to the tree, across from the church grounds, in a very small house, a house once occupied by more than a dozen people, but now only home to this old man—this very old, this very blind man.

Montreal Perec, in his thirty years living in the lighthouse of Taumata, had experienced only a few dealings with Koro Hohepa. When he had moved into his house, he was approached by a group of local Māori who insisted he allow the old man to bless his home. "It is not about getting rid of bad spirits," they had said, "it is about introducing the old to the new. We want you to be welcomed by all who live here in your special house."

So he had relented, and Koro Hohepa had walked through his house, room by room, chanting in Māori, reciting karakia for the benefit, he had supposed, of all its occupants. It may well have worked—Perec had lived free of any bad vibes in the house, and he had certainly spent enough time inside it to know.

Perec looked out his front kitchen window at the old man who had caught his eye an hour earlier, hobbling across the road to sit under the tree and leaning against its trunk. He had just stood to his feet and was walking around the tree, his hand never leaving the bark. He appeared to be talking to it. Perec reflected that Koro Hohepa looked exactly as he had thirty years ago. He was one of those figures that had always been old. Every town has one. Ask a mother or an aunty or a grandfather, and they will tell you of that one who has always been old. They remember them as a child, always old.

He watched the old man stop to look up into the canopy, his blank eyes shrouded in tinted glasses. His lips stopped moving as he did so, and he stood in place for a long time.

Perec's mind drifted from the scene, as curious as he was, and he thought about BloodyLegend's proposition. Perec had declined, of course. There was no way he was going to Pureora. He knew he was destined to look closer, not to start wandering around the place again. But BloodyLegend had insisted that Tuki's mark needed to be investigated, and if that meant him going alone, then so be it. While his mysterious alter-ego did tell Perec that he would be out of contact for several days, he did not say how far he was travelling. For all

Perec knew, he could be crossing the Cook Strait, or he could be crossing the Pacific Ocean.

Further down the street, a younger Māori man walked towards the tree and Koro Hohepa. Perec watched him near, calculated his personality and intention from his clothing and posture, and surmised that he was no threat to the vulnerable old man. As the younger man approached, Koro Hohepa turned towards him, presumably hearing the sound of footfalls or a voice. The younger man took the other by the elbow but released him when Koro Hohepa turned to touch the tree, speaking. The newcomer was nodding, listening, and then he too touched the tree, and Perec watched both speak in unison.

He opened a window slightly, enough to feel the humid early summer air brush his face. It was warmer outside than it was in. However, a chill accompanied the wind, a chill in Perec's spine when he heard the two voices calling together—chanting together in Māori—towards the tree. Their voices filled the soundscape of Taumata and perturbed Perec's spirit.

———————

We use words like *spirit* to describe something that fills the deeper spaces of ourselves. *Spirit-filled, spiritual, inspired* all name something *God-breathed* in us, something we find difficult to define, but that we know defines us. We call someone *spirited* when we recognise this breath in them—this breath which is life-giving and wild, not constrained by the parameters we place on ourselves and others. Kiri was spirited, and she had inspired Stanley. But, as tightly as Stanley held on to his structure, his delineation, she needed to protect her own fire, lest he blow it out.

In other words, she stayed away from him.

Stanley expected nothing less. In fact, if he had expected anything more, it should have been police involvement. She was hurt from the attack, of course—bruised in her sides and in need of physiotherapy for her knee. She was unable to run.

That's what hurt most. Her separation from Stanley was more significant to him than to her. To her, he was a curiosity, an object of flirtation, not a prospective lover. Yes, she had toyed with him, but she enjoyed his company in that context. Perhaps that was why she didn't report the incident—she held herself responsible to a point.

Stanley's days continued as they had before Kiri ran into his life in the early spring. He walked to work along his same route each day. Raima did not notice any change in Stanley while he had been associating with Kiri, so she did not notice any change after their break-up. He showed no evidence of distraction. He maintained his numbers, and client satisfaction remained steady. He still ate the occasional lunch with her, and she still watched him cut into traffic as he walked home in his strange, efficient way. There were no deviations from his norm; no spontaneous tangents in town or, for that matter, in his conversation; no variations of his paths around the office. It was like he had never met his exquisite companion.

But there was one change. Stanley was not a robot or Vulcan after all. He may have been one-dimensional, narrow in his habits, and singular minded, but he was human and, being human, he could not encounter a force like Kiri and walk away unscathed, unchanged.

So, outside of his business life, away from Raima and still within his routine, Stanley ran where he once walked. He ran his circuit daily, following the same path he enjoyed before Kiri and the same path he enjoyed with Kiri. After the incident, he ran as he had run with her, leaving from his house, down the back of Taumata and onto the Tautaungara circuit. He ran past her friend's house, across from Kiri's hiding place. He ran past the site of the attack near the entrance to the golf course with only a flinch of remorse, although he did think of her each time he passed. He was a selfish man, really, so Stanley thought more about what he missed in her than he did her. He missed her shoulder brushing against his. He missed her bottom.

Stanley did consider taking some early vacation time, to return to Hamilton for a week, to reconnect with family and friends, though he hadn't maintained contact with many. But running away was not his modus operandi. He would press on. Raima, who heard about the incident from a cousin living across from the golf course, raised the idea with him as well.

"You know I don't often pry, Stanley, but I wonder if it might be good for your reputation if you left town for a while."

"What reputation is that?" he asked.

"Well … it's just that people in town are talking, and I would think it might be good to leave until the gossip mongers have had their turn and moved onto something else."

"Do you think I'm a bad person, Raima?" he asked.

Raima, who was chagrined when she heard what had happened, had never felt disgusted, despite her expectation that she should. Perhaps it was knowing Stanley that kept her from vilifying him, or perhaps it was because we tend to have compassion for those we know, regardless of their parts in such events.

"No, I don't think you're a bad person, Stanley," she said.

"Then my reputation should be fine."

He saw Kiri once in December. It was near the tree. She was sitting under its shade, on the edge of the concrete curbing separating the trunk from the road. It was a Saturday night, and Stanley had gone to Mass—a ritualistic activity he had not engaged in for some time. Leaving the church building that night, he walked across the grounds in line with his house. As he passed the tree, at a distance of several metres, he saw her there, her legs stretched out onto the road.

She saw him too, but gave no acknowledgment, no indication that he existed. She simply stared past him. He did not wave out nor did he say anything. He held her eyes for several moments—those beautiful eyes now lacking lustre—and continued on his way.

Prior to the first of December, Te Kauhanga had never been inhabited by a homeless person. On the first of December, the first homeless man of Te Kauhanga appeared, seemingly from nowhere. One day he was nowhere, the next he was sitting on one of the benches in front of the train station. The next day, he was still sitting, but with an accumulation of belongings behind the bench: water bottle, blanket, hat. The next day, he was an established fixture.

No-one did or even said anything at first. One of the clerks from the station asked him if he was all right but received little more than a grunt in response. She went home to cook tea for her three children. A well-meaning young man, one of the two male bank-tellers in town, sat on the bench next to him during a lunch break, talked to him about sandwiches for half an hour, and was permitted to give him half an egg salad. Then he went back to work to sell credit cards. Two days later, a woman from the church in Taumata parked in front of the station with the express intent of finding out what his story was, but he told her to get lost. Then she went to Mass that night and told the priest about him.

This is how momentum builds in a small town—a first sighting begets a second sighting, which begets a verbal observation, which begets a comparison of notes, which begets a humble opinion, which begets a shared evaluation, which usually begets inaction, but, given the right confluence of timing and personage, can beget action.

Father Sennheiser was a busy man. Between daily Masses, funerals, weddings, the incessant complaints of pedantic parishioners, and trying to motivate a reluctant parish directorate, he didn't have much time for golf or homeless people. However, he did have experience with vagrants after years of working with city missions in Christchurch and Tauranga, and was intrigued by the tales of the man on the station bench. This sort of story, if you knew Father Sennheiser, was at the heart of his original motivations to join the priesthood. Yes, he thought, he would ignore the saints and their paperwork, and investigate this calling from God.

Others were moved by the tales as well. Sharon first heard of the homeless man of Te Kauhanga at the council office. It was she who took the phone call from the local paper, *The Bulletin*, asking to speak to the mayor about this most recent addition to his constituency.

It had been a lonely two weeks for Sharon since she cast Blake out of her house and out of her life. It's important to understand that she did not blame him for what happened. She knew it was her issue to sort. But she also knew there was no place for him in her life at that moment. And while she did not have an answer for herself, she knew there was no place for his method.

Frances and Manu had been good friends since she told them of her break-up with Blake. That's what she called it in her story—a break-up. They had been gentle with her at work, not alluding to Blake in any way, taking her out to lunches, and generally keeping things low-key. Blake had moved on. He spoke with Sharon as he had before they went out and went about his business of assisting the mayor.

It was Blake who spoke with *The Bulletin*, and it did not go as planned.

That week, *The Bulletin* printed a front page story about the homeless man of Te Kauhanga, including a picture of the figure asleep on his bench. The story told of the reporter's attempts to interview the man, only to be sent away with profanities and threats.

It told similar stories as related by other citizens. It told of the response of the district council via Mayoral aide, Blake Mānukau:

In the absence of the mayor, The Bulletin interviewed Mr Mānukau about the situation: "Te Kauhanga has never had a homeless person before, so it is difficult for me to comment. Without a precedent, we simple have no by-laws to address the issue and so have no action plan in place." When asked if he or the mayor had spoken with the man, Mānukau added, "I think that is for the police to do, not the mayor or his staff. But again, unless he is breaking any laws such as pestering pedestrians or damaging council or private property, then we really can't do very much."

The article was not well received by those who read it.

Sharon and the council staff read the article. In Frances' words, they were, "embarrassed to work for an agency with such a pathetic response to a problem that was obviously in its jurisdiction to solve." But she did not belabour her point.

Stanley Kowalczyk read the article. Once he ascertained that the man was not positioned on his route, he lost interest.

Montreal Perec read the article. He made a note on one of his maps to indicate the man's position in front of the station.

Kiri Rata read the article. At one time, she would have run by to investigate.

Koro Hohepa did not read the article nor did anyone consider reading it to him.

In fact, none of these people paid much attention to it, nor did any of the district's residents. For, on the front page of *The Bulletin,* above the article about Te Kauhanga's first homeless man, was another article announcing the council's proposal to cut down the tree of Taumata.

In Pureora forest, at the geographic centre of the North Island of New Zealand, there is a plinth—a column standing a metre and a half, capped with a four-sided pyramid. On the face of the plinth, there is a plaque which reads:

How This Point Was Located: A large map of the North Island, approximately 1 metre in length, was mounted onto rigid cardboard. The cardboard was then bent to represent the curvature of the earth, and suspended using a pin and thin nylon, until a perfect balance was obtained. This point, the centre of gravity, indicated the North Island's geographic centre.

Montreal Perec, from the information provided by the plaque, could only assume that the picture he was looking at, posted by BloodyLegend180, was indeed taken at that spot. He could also only assume that his correspondent had visited there and taken the picture himself. Assuming these things, BloodyLegend180 was in New Zealand and only an hour's drive from Te Kauhanga.

"When did you take this?" he asked BloodyLegend, who had only then messaged Perec through the WiCharts site.

"Two hours ago. But I've left there."

"Where are you now?"

"Not important. More photos uploading now."

Perec did not protest. He had grown used to his friend's propensity for blunt obfuscation. While he waited for the pictures to upload, he walked to his front door and looked out at the tree.

The council had made a brief statement about cutting down the tree of Taumata, and *The Bulletin* had made a valiant attempt to create a front page story out of it: *"It is with the greatest regret that the mayor, along with several elected members of the council, has conceded the necessity of cutting down the tree of Taumata Hill,"* the mayor's spokesperson, Blake Mānukau, was quoted as saying. *"We do want the people of Te Kauhanga to know that several arborists, both local and from out of district, have been consulted, along with our local kaumātua, Koro Hohepa, who first brought the matter to our attention."*

However, the editor did not quote any definition given for *the matter*, but instead filled the rest of the article with conjecture about tree diseases and promised a follow-up story complete with reactions from locals in the following week's edition.

Perec had read the article curiously and thoroughly. He was not happy. He thought little of the reasons why and more about the drastic changes in his surrounding landscape. In one sense, it was exciting for Perec, an opportunity to create a new map of Taumata, free of the tree. But what would this entail really? The map of

Taumata would essentially remain unchanged—one symbol less. For, in his maps there were no canopy-cast shadows, no sheltered curbs seated round a trunk, no lines demarcating residents within and without the tree's protection. Perec's maps did not account for these things. His two-dimensional world would not miss the tree symbol, so he wondered: why was he unhappy?

He studied the tree from his front door, looking south the same distance he had looked for almost three decades. In that time, the tree's branches had grown nearer to him, almost touching his lighthouse roof when a wind would blow strong and downward. He had watched each year as the shadow of the tree increasingly encroached on his property. Yet the trunk remained at the same distance—the core, the centre, the pivotal point of contact. When that core was gouged, when those branches were downed and with them the shade and the shadows, what would it mean to him? He had no answer, yet he was saddened.

A note from his computer drew him back to BloodyLegend's newly uploaded photographs from Pureora.

"All done. Tell me what you see," Perec read on the screen.

Perec acknowledged the message then scrolled through the pictures. The first shots showed the forest on either side of a metal road, like a causeway leading to the plinth in the distance as in a classic perspective painting. All the trees, the stones, the sky seemed to point to and emanate from the plinth. Each successive photo drew nearer to the plinth, maintaining this perspective. *BloodyLegend,* thought Perec, *he's the real deal if this is the way he sees the world.* As he clicked through the images, Perec felt like he was watching a video, or walking inside BloodyLegend's body, seeing with his eyes. He could almost hear the gravel beneath his feet.

Closer to the plinth, Perec recognised the inscription he had read earlier. As interesting as this was, he did not see anything more significant, and, once he returned to the first close up shot, the final in the sequence, he told the other what he saw: a lovely walk along a country road.

"Is that all?" BloodyLegend wrote back.

"Is there something else you wanted me to see?"

"Yes, of course."

"Why not tell me what it is?" Perec asked.

"Because I don't know what it is."

Perec wasn't sure what to make of their impasse. He didn't respond, but waited for some revelation to fill the space.

"Do what you do," BloodyLegend typed. "Look closer."

Perec looked again at the last and first photograph—the plinth prominent in the centre, with dense native trees surrounding the clearing, some small and fern-like, others large and bulky. The background was a swirl of browns and greens. He used his mouse to zoom in on the images until they became so pixelated it was difficult to distinguish plinth from plaque, tree from track. He zoomed out and stared hard at the plinth, willing it to reveal something beyond words and stolid concrete. Then, rubbing his eyes, he moved his face closer to the screen as he had done with the map of Nova Scotia in the spring.

Closer and closer, until his nose touched the screen, Perec moved slowly, expecting something. He saw nothing. Frustrated, he wrote to BloodyLegend, "There's nothing. Not this time."

"There has to be. Try again," was the only response.

Perec scratched his head and thought about the image. *It's two dimensional*, he reminded himself. *I can't go into it three-dimensionally.*

Again, Perec moved his face towards the screen, his eyes open and taking in the entire image this time. The plinth faded away as he did so, and all that remained were the older trees, standing as they must have done before any human contact—dense and commanding, not standing back for a little plinth or plaque, but owning the space, filling the clearing. Perec saw the trees as they were, and then he saw what was on them: markings up and down trunks, not engraved but embossed, as if written on the trees like ancient cave paintings, swirls with no regular pattern, none joined, but floating on their bark canvases.

Perec saw the spirals.

═══════:::::::

There are many reasons why people run: exercise and weight loss, of course, but those can be satisfied through other activities; fresh air and connection with nature, but those don't require the pounding of feet and the shocking of knees; socialising, but why run when you could have a beer at the RSA? Before Kiri, Stanley had been content with walking. He had run at various times in his life, but drew no more pleasure from it than his daily stroll to and from work. He ran because Kiri ran. It was an opportunity to spend time with a beautiful woman.

After Kiri, Stanley continued to run for reasons he could not articulate if he was questioned on the matter, but the more Stanley ran, the more he wanted to run. The more he ran, the faster and fitter he became.

Most runners of Stanley's burgeoning calibre set goals for themselves: run faster, run further, run a marathon. Stanley found himself running faster around his loop which meant his time spent running was shorter. So, he began running the loop twice.

But, even for a personality like Stanley's, running the same loop twice each day became monotonous. To keep his mind occupied and his will engaged, he measured markers around the loop. He ran intervals during some runs, completing certain sections faster than others, deliberately increasing his stamina and power.

He ran like this through Christmas, through New Year's and through two weeks of annual leave (in which he ran his circuit both morning and night), running himself into the middle of a very hot and humid January. Running in circles, Stanley began to ponder the point of it all, to question his quest, if he had a quest at all. He had no ultimate goal. A marathon did not interest him. Fitness was easily achievable for a young man like Stanley. He had never known what it was to be unfit, so he did not seek fitness. He had never been fat, so he had no need to lose weight.

One mid-January Saturday morning, he sat on his front step—his running shoes laced and tied, his stopwatch reset for his weekend long-run. *Pointless,* he thought. How could a man like Stanley live without a point to aim for? *The shortest distance between two points is a straight line,* he recited to himself, but from what point was he leaving and to what point was he headed? The more he thought about it, the more his mind began to swirl and swim, and he felt like he had that day Kiri had provoked him.

She had tried to make a point and, he had realised in the weeks following, she had only wanted to get him off line, not prevent him from arriving at his destination. It's not as if he would have been lost if he had followed her that day. The road would have eventually led back home, so what was it? This was not the first time Stanley had asked himself why he was the way he was. But this was the first time in years he allowed himself to dwell on the matter.

His mind swirled and filled with the chattering mantra: *the shortest distance between two lines is a straight line.* He closed his eyes and imagined himself leaving that roadside, jumping the fence and joining his Kiri on the golf course. He felt the panic walk through him, but he did not feel overwhelmed. Instead, he watched himself running alongside Kiri the short few metres to the golf course entrance and back onto the roadside of the circuit. His breathing eased, his pulse slowed, and he opened his eyes.

Stanley descended his steps and walked to his front gate. He did not map out a route in his mind. He did start his stopwatch, though he wasn't sure how he would use it. He didn't turn left towards the back of Taumata and the circuit but turned right. He turned right and ran along Tonga Street, past Centre Street and the doomed tree. He ran past Kiri's house and rounded onto Rāwhiti Street, a short jaunt before turning left again onto Tūāraki Street. He ran past the lighthouse owned by the strange Canadian and past the entrance to his shortcut on the Findlayson property until he came to the incline down which he ran until he circled the base of Taumata hill.

Nothing happened—no panic attack, no swirling thoughts, just a general unease, a discomfort like you or I feel when we take a wrong turn in a strange city. To Stanley, they all felt like wrong turns, even when he eventually did join the circuit and complete his loop. For good measure, and acknowledging that he had pushed himself enough for one day, Stanley returned to his house via the southern climb to Taumata Hill.

NINE

In small towns, messengers are rarely shot—it is the receptionists who take the unfriendly fire. Sharon was on the front lines between the council and the district's residents.

"Yes, I have noted your concern and will be sure to pass your message on to the mayor."

It had been six weeks since *The Bulletin* ran its article on the proposed felling of the Taumata tree.

"No, Mr Rangi, I have not lived here as long as you, nor have my ancestors, but I don't think the council sees that as relevant to the issue."

For six weeks, excluding Christmas and New Year's day, Sharon had been fielding calls.

"Yes, I can understand that. I am saddened by the proposal as well."

Sometimes Manu would relieve her, but she was often preoccupied, responding to e-mails or ducking for cover when a resident or a contingency of residents appeared at the front desk.

"We want to see the mayor about Kōwhi."

"I'm sorry, but the mayor is not available at this time. Would you like to make an appointment?"

"He's hiding isn't he? He knows someone's gonna rip him a new one."

"I wouldn't like to comment on that, but I can assure you the mayor is very busy these days."

"How about that other fella then? That fella that was in the paper?"

"I'm afraid he is not in at the moment. Would you like to make an appointment?"

And so forth.

Frances loved the drama. "I'll take over for a while, Sharon," she would offer, and sometimes Sharon would accept. However, she knew Frances took too much pleasure in being at the centre of all the gossip and controversy.

"You'll never guess who that was," she said one afternoon after, what sounded to Sharon, a particularly abusive exchange in which Frances, to her credit, had handled herself diplomatically.

Sharon hated guessing games. "Who was it?" she asked, hoping to take some wind out of *HMS Frances'* sails.

"You'll never guess," she said. "Could you hear her over the phone? She was going off! Someone who's quiet as a mouse all the time, but boy was she wound up about that goddamned tree. C'mon, I'll give you three guesses."

"Was it Sister Jovita?" chimed Manu.

Oh for fuck's sake, Manu, thought Sharon.

Frances shook her head.

"Was it Mrs Bonke, the high school principal?" asked Manu.

Frances shook her head and looked at Sharon, willing her to have a go. Sharon wasn't about to give in.

"Was it Norm Fister's wife?" asked Manu. "She's a lovely little lady."

Frances shook her head and Sharon said, "Well, c'mon then, Frances, tell us now."

Grinning, Frances said, "It was Maria Sanchez, the Mexican librarian."

"She's not Mexican, she's Chilean," Sharon said.

"Well, whatever ... the point is, she's only lived here for five minutes. I don't know why she's so upset. She was really having a go at us." Frances always referred to the council as, *us*.

"She was ranting on about how Kiwis hate shade—that we're sun worshippers and that we're always cutting down trees for no reason. She was flipping out all right."

The conversation was interrupted by the automatic opening of the front doors. All three women turned to see the homeless man walking across the foyer towards their front desk.

Since the publication of the article about him, and its subsequent overshadowing by the tree's story, nothing more had been done to address the first homeless man of Te Kauhanga. He had continued to live on and around the bench in front of the train station. Little else had changed. He had not accumulated more belongings on the site, nor had he broken any laws by vandalising property or harassing passers-by. He did receive assistance in the form of food from Father Sennheiser and some other benevolent citizens, but he had not gone out of his way to ask for assistance from the community. Apparently, he was no beggar.

Frances shouldered past Sharon to the front of the bench. "I'll take this one," she muttered, not low enough for the man not to hear. She looked him up and down as he approached, from his gum boots to the rope wound round his waist, from his swazi top to his unshaven face and holey beanie. "Hello, sir," she said. "What can we do for you today?"

The man spoke with a voice that belied his look. He spoke with an indistinguishable foreign accent, as if he had been born in another country but raised in New Zealand. "I thought it best I come here," he said, "to sort out some ordinances for myself."

Frances smiled. *Poor soul*, she thought, *he's trying to sound intelligent in here.* "I'm sorry, sir, I'm not sure what you mean," she said.

"Some ordinances—you know, by-laws and such. I need to see what laws you have for people like me."

"People like you?" She was playing with him. "What do you mean by that, sir?"

The man looked hard at her, a look she interpreted as frustration with his own inability to communicate. He held his look for several moments, not saying anything. Frances tried to stand her ground, and was about to disrupt the moment by repeating her question, when the man released her, looking over her shoulder as he said, "Let me talk to her."

Frances stopped her own words and looked back at Sharon. She smiled at her, rolled her eyes and shrugged. "Of course, sir," she said, and stepped aside, gesturing for Sharon to step forward as if she was escorting a guest of honour to her seat in a restaurant.

Sharon, nervous, filled the space vacated by the larger woman and asked the man, "Sir, do you mean you want to know what the laws are for sleeping on the train station bench?"

"Thank you very much," the man said, not bothering to look at Frances who was smirking in the background. "That is exactly what I am looking for—the council ordinances regarding homeless people in Te Kauhanga."

"Very good, sir," Sharon said, "but it may take me some time to look into this matter for you. I will need to speak with our archivist or one of our elected representatives. It might take a bit of time."

"We could post it to you," Frances interrupted. Both Sharon and the man ignored her.

"I'll come back in an hour. Is that enough time for you?"

"Yes, sir, that should be fine. I'll see you back here in one hour."

The man nodded and walked back outside.

"You're naughty," Sharon said to Frances.

"You're not," said Frances.

Manu looked at both of them, puzzled.

There are cave paintings in New Zealand—very different from the ones you find in Altamira or Lascaux. There are no pictures of large animals—no bison, deer, horses—nor should there be in a land devoid of anything larger than a kiwi-bird, excepting the giant moa and Haast's Eagle, before the importation of species by Europeans. Instead, in caves scattered around the shores of the South island and in even more scattered sites around the North Island, such as Whakamoenga Cave near Lake Taupo and along the Kaupokonui River in Taranaki, evidence of early New Zealand Māori life is etched in walls more abstractly. In other words, we have no idea what they were on about.

What is known is that the style of art in the caves closely resembles that of the dendroglyphs on the Chatham Islands. These curvilinear tree carvings were sketched by the Moriori people, descendants from Māori in New Zealand, as ways of illustrating their life in the islands—their people, their food, their customs.

There are no spirals in any of these dendroglyphs.

Instead, spirals appear in the much more elaborate carvings of modern Māori art—in kōwhaiwhai panels, on poupou, on wharenui, and also in tau moko, Māori tattooing. It is said that Tuki, the mapmaker himself, had massive spirals tattooed on his upper thighs.

Perec explored this information and more over the early summer months and shared it with BloodyLegend180. His friend made no appearance in Te Kauhanga, nor did he give any further indication that he was even in New Zealand. At one point prior to Christmas, he disappeared from WiCharts as he had done before sending his photos from Pureora forest.

This information was the full extent of anything relevant and useful the two found together or separately. The dendroglyphs connection, though interesting, shed no light on Cook, Oak Island, Tupaia, or Tuki's map. The question that hovered over them remained: was there any connection between Tuki's supposed marking of the geographic centre of the North Island and the spirals carved on the trees there?

There was one other thing Perec pondered which he did not discuss with BloodyLegend, a withholding of information based on a hunch more than on any particular purpose. The spirals on the trees at Pureora were no ordinary spirals. The best way Perec could describe them would be to say they were spirals with tails. Whereas ordinary spirals resembled a circle from a distance, these spirals resembled comets—oblong in shape, somewhere between the sun-representative spirals of Māori carvings and the twisting oval of a paper clip.

It was the same hunch that prompted Perec to dismiss BloodyLegend's repeated propositions that he should visit Pureora himself to investigate. Instead, in those same weeks, Perec alternated time between his computer, his study (in which he mapped the ceiling and the wall facing the corridor), his renewed project of mapping the electrical wiring of his house, and his annual map of Taumata, the last one he would ever draw that included the tree.

For this map, this capturing of a significant time in the history of Te Kauhanga, Perec meditated on creating an especially descriptive symbol for the tree. This slowed him down, but he knew it would be worth it. Inspired by Tuki's map, Perec pursued a symbol that would represent far more than the physical features of the tree—he wanted to capture something of its spiritual importance. This was uncharted territory for Perec, and one that would require a closer look, not only at the tree itself, but at his own soul which, as in Tuki's case, would be the initial interpreter of the symbol.

And so, Perec meditated for long periods each day leading into the middle of January. He would sit with a chair inside his front door, looking out at the tree, looking at its trunk and canopy and also looking at the effect it had on the people of Taumata. He watched children play under the tree's shade and pretend they were climbing its branches so far above their little heads. He watched cars drive round the tree, bending to its will as they paid their respects, often before or after a church service. He watched more strangers than usual visit the tree: tourists, photographers a TVNZ van, and others he assumed had been drawn to the centre of the hill by the newspaper article. Perec reflected that, in all his watching, he did not remember seeing any arborists visit following Koro Hohepa's revelation. But he had been preoccupied at times.

As he meditated one day in mid-January, a particularly hot day, Koro Hohepa reappeared, cane in hand, and walked out of his drive and up to the tree as he had the month before. Perec watched him circle the trunk, lay his hands on it, and chant in Māori. His voice was soothing, not as dramatic as when he was with the younger man. There were no accompanying gesticulations, no rising and falling tones, but a monotone chant—conversational, not oratorical.

Perec looked closer. There was a sense that this moment might provide him with inspiration and, as he stood and walked to his front door, Koro Hohepa's voice faded as the old man turned his head towards the lighthouse.

Perec stood still, staring at this man who could not stare back. The air in the house stopped and the tree, whose branch tips had been bending gently in a warm northerly, settled again and was still. A lawnmower could be heard in the distance, and further behind Koro Hohepa, two children rode their bicycles down Tonga Street.

The old man walked towards Montreal Perec who felt rooted to the spot, unable to retreat to the interior. For a blind man, Koro Hohepa stepped lithely over the curbing, tapping his cane in front of him until he was in Perec's yard and approaching his front steps.

As you know, Perec was not averse to receiving visitors—but he was not used to them.

"Kia ora, Koro," he said through the door which he opened for his unusual guest. His voice was hoarse from disuse.

"Kia ora," the old man said. His voice was a hill's—steep and aloof.

Perec stood dumb for an awkward moment. Compelled by a distant obligation, he said, "Would you like to come in?"

Koro Hohepa tilted his head back in the motion of one surveying the house, casting his dull eyes, unmasked by any shaded glasses, over the door frames and casements, then resting on Perec's face. "No, thank you. I will stay here. You have enough company at the moment."

Perec shook his head, remembering the oddity of this man who had once prayed through his house. Behind him, he heard the familiar tones of a message arriving on his computer. Could that be what he meant?

"Have you heard about our tree?" the old man asked.

"Yes, I have. They say you told the council about it."

Koro Hohepa grunted. "Just because an eel swims upriver doesn't make it a taniwha. No, I didn't tell the council. But I was the first to know and the first to make it known."

"They say arborists were consulted too."

"Yes, our arborists. We know these things."

"You mean, there's been no scientific study? How do you know the tree is sick?"

Again, the old man grunted but with humour this time. "Who said it was sick? No, it's not sick—but its time has come. And that is why I have come to speak with you."

Perec was confused, but he listened.

"How long have you lived in this house?"

"Thirty years now, Koro."

"Thirty years—yes, that sounds about right." He sniffed, then coughed into his sleeve. He lifted his head again. "Before you arrived, my people believed that, one day, the lighthouse keeper would share a great taonga with us. When you arrived, we were sure you were our man—a traveller from afar like our ancestors, like Kupe—the same Kupe who blessed our tree with his karakia—his incantation. But here we are, thirty years after you arrived. We've left you alone and waited. Some who waited have passed on. Some of us are still here, waiting. But now, our tree is leaving us, and that surely means something."

"I'm not following you, Koro," said Perec.

"I've come to ask you: do you have something to share with us?"

Perec took his time in answering, careful not to offend. "Koro, I didn't come here to share something with you. I came to find something for my own people."

Without blinking, the old man turned towards the tree and said, "Then look closer."

━━━━━:::::::

She's so slow, thought Stanley as he ran past the homeless man in front of the train station. He looked at his watch and then past the woman with the red hat, targeting the lamp-post in front of the library. As soon as he passed the end of the station building, he veered into the open parking lot, around the woman without any sign of greeting, and double-timed it up the main street.

Invigorated by his breakaway onto new paths, Stanley had begun charting his running progress with gusto. One night after work, he had thrown a notebook and pencil in his car and driven out his driveway, down Tonga Street and to the bottom of the incline, turning left until his odometer read two hundred and fifty metres. He wrote in his book, *1/4km—give way sign, near bottom of incline*. He then drove another two hundred and fifty metres and wrote, "driveway after panel beaters". He continued driving and recording quarter kilometres until he had measured a unique route for himself, leading back to home in a new loop. In this way, he could also run the opposite direction, counting quarter kilometres.

This new variety so excited him that he had driven out again, this time marking another new route through town, down to the river, across Anzac Bridge and back again via the main roads.

Having so diligently metred his routes, Stanley had spent the next two weeks testing them. As he ran past quarter markers, including the lamp post, he checked his watch and calculated his pace per kilometre. He noticed patterns and challenged himself to break personal bests each time he re-ran a section. He read running magazines and absorbed tips and advice about training methods and diet which would impact on his speed and endurance. In the morning, he measured his pulse before getting out of bed in order to determine his lowest possible resting heart rate. His book lay on his bed-side shelf and, after his watch, was the first thing he reached for in the morning. While he ran, he counted and compared and predicted and planned. At night, after climbing into bed, he selected his next morning's route and pre-wrote the markers and his estimated times for each.

His obsession with times and distances crept into his daily walks to and from work. Stanley began thinking differently about his efficient use of space. He began to think in terms of time and wondered which was more important: the shortest distance between points, or the shortest time between points? He examined hills and their effect on his journey. He considered how time was impacted by his insistence on walking in straight lines. He did not walk any faster necessarily, for he was already hurrying around the place with his morning and evening runs, but he did, for the first instance in many years, reflect on his use of space *and* time.

In his house, Stanley would sit in the centre of his hallway and sketch new designs, wondering if it were possible to reconstruct walls and corridors so that time was not wasted, regardless of how much space might be misused or untrimmed. He thought of the homeless man in town, whom he now passed on one of his running routes, and what he might think of Stanley's house and his pedantic lifestyle.

He also thought of the woman with the red hat. It was remarkable to him, that the same woman would impede his training whenever he ran the town circuit. It didn't matter if Stanley left earlier or later—somewhere, and it always seemed to be in some narrow passage, the woman with the red hat would be there waiting for him, like a stop sign, never looking out for him, but always walking her own path, always in the way, and so slow.

As Blake Mānukau had stated to the editor of *The Bulletin*, there were no ordinances regarding homeless people in Te Kauhanga, nor were there any by-laws, protocols, rules, procedures, policies, or statutes.

Without any of these things, the council, the police, the community had no jurisdiction, legal precedent, authority or a leg to stand on in dealing with the issue. Instead, there was a great deal of hand-wringing, unreturned phone calls, letters to the editor, and verbal abuse of the homeless man himself.

But the man had his mandate. In response to any detractors who criticised him as they walked by his bench in front of the train station, he informed them firmly that he was not breaking the law and that, as there was no law, there was a tacit sanction for what he was doing and he would not move. He liked it there, he would tell them.

Sharon Pellerine had delivered this news to the man one hour after he had approached the council receptionists and endured their smirking and condescension. He was used to it—and he was used to walking away smugly.

It was the end of a long week for Sharon. The council had conducted an open meeting the night before, and the proposed cutting of the Taumata tree had drawn a large crowd. Sharon had acted as stenographer for the meeting—and she felt very much the court reporter as the mayor and her Blake came under fire. A lynch mob would have been welcome.

After some settling of the crowd and a vague statement from the mayor, the floor was opened to the public of Te Kauhanga.

"There is nothing wrong with that tree, Mayor Nelson," Hanover Findlayson said. "Why won't you tell us the real reasons for cutting it down?"

"As I've said," replied Mayor Nelson Tumai, "the council has consulted several arborists in this matter, and we have been advised to cut it down."

Findlayson again: "Which arborists? What was their reasoning?"

"They have requested, and we have agreed, that their identities remain secret. Please understand Hanover, they knew what sort of upset this would cause, not just here in Te Kauhanga, but up and down the country."

"Not good enough, Mayor, not good enough," Findlayson blustered and stepped away from the microphone which had been set up near the front of the chambers, between the gallery and the panel consisting of the mayor and councillors. He looked to the next speaker standing behind him, a woman with a red hat, hopeful she would have a better approach.

"My name is Kathleen MacLeod," she began. "I lived in Taumata while I was growing up. I've been away, but I have moved back up there. I want to believe the council has legitimate reasons for cutting this leg of Tāne Mahuta down, but even so, I want to express my sadness here to everyone.

"When I was growing up here, that tree saved my life. Some people in this room may remember. I was the little girl on the bicycle who would have been run over by the van that crashed into the tree. If you go up to Taumata, you can still see the marks in the trunk from the grill, though they are higher up the trunk now. Those aren't the only marks on that tree—there are scars from boys who have tried to climb the trunk with their rugby boots; there are initials from many young couples who have shared their first kiss and more under its canopy; there are pock marks higher up where we used to throw stones to knock down balls and frisbees and hula hoops we had errantly tossed into the lower branches."

"So it is very sad for us all," Sharon wrote of Kathleen MacLeod's words, "very sad indeed." The woman moved slowly back from the microphone, retreating to her seat in silence.

Stanley Kowalczyk, a surprising, and controversial attendee, considering recent rumours, had spoken favourably about the tree's longevity, claiming it as a role model for human conduct in its insistence on persevering, always reaching higher without diversion.

Blake Mānukau relieved the mayor in spells, reiterating key statements the council had prepared prior to the meeting.

Many others spoke and Sharon recorded all their voices. Some were sad but accepting like Kathleen's. Some were truculent and vitriolic, accusing the mayor and the council of wanting to keep firewood for themselves or blaming them for not looking after their town's greatest taonga properly. Others tried to present reasonable challenges to points that the mayor seemed determined to skirt.

"Is the tree sick, Mayor?"

"There is something wrong with the tree."

"But is it sick, Mayor? What exactly is wrong with it?"

"The arborists say it needs to come down."

"But why, Mayor? You're not telling us anything new here."

"There's nothing new to tell. We have been telling you everything you need to know."

"Is there a danger, Mayor? Should the homeowners in Taumata be worried?"

"There will be no danger once we have cut it down."

And so forth.

The room, while having started in an angry frame, remained agitated throughout the session. However, the mayor's stonewalling and persistent dousing of passions seemed, to Sharon, to be silencing the critics. The strange acceptance of people like Kathleen MacLeod began to dominate along with the sadness she espoused.

That is, until the final speaker approached the microphone. Sharon watched as, after the previous speaker had finished, a large Māori man stood at the back of the room and walked slowly towards the panel. She recognised him, only from reputation as he lived much further down the river, as Angus Tutemahurangi, an esteemed kaumātua with family and political connections that Sharon did not understand. The room was silent except for the sound of his footsteps and the intermittent tapping of his tokotoko, an impressively ornate carving which he wielded like a weapon. Sharon held her breath in anticipation of his words.

"Kia ora tātou," he said. His voice was awful in its tenor, as if his throat had been lashed by a razor tongue.

"Kia ora," came the rumbling response from many in the gallery.

"My name is Angus Tutemahurangi. Many of you know who my ancestors are, so I won't go through all that here and now." He raised his cane as he spoke. "I have come to warn you, Mayor, and this council, about the consequences of what you are planning to do.

"Kōwhi is our maunga," said Angus Tutemahurangi. "He is our ariki, our chief of all whose ancestors have lived in Te Kauhanga for a thousand years. He is the first leg of Tāne Mahuta. How can you cut down a pillar of the sky? Before we were here, he was here. Before the pākehā came, he was here, and after we have gone, he will be here. Never has a single branch broken from his canopy. His shade is all encompassing, and his roots uphold the very foundation of Taumata hill. Do you fear he will cause damage to our little, temporary houses? Don't you know that, without Kōwhi, there will be no foundation for those very houses you seek to protect?

"Who among us can chop down a mountain?" asked Angus Tutemahurangi. "Who can stand against our mighty Atlas and not bring down the wrath of the heavens on us all? Who could survive if Ranginui were brought back to Papatūānuku? The arborists? Who are they? What do they know? They measure and test and compare with other trees. They report back to men with ledgers and pathetic agendas.

"Who can say when it is time for a mountain to fall?"

"It is time," spoke a different voice from the back of the room. All heads in the room turned, all the heads that had been enthralled by Angus Tutemahurangi. All heads turned to see who would challenge this giant.

All heads turned to see the small figure of Koro Hohepa standing at the back, one hand on the shoulder of the young Māori man Montreal Perec has seen with him by the tree, the other hand held aloft like a saint from a medieval painting.

"It is time," he repeated, and that was all he said. For, at his words, Angus Tutemahurangi retracted from the microphone, walked back to where Koro Hohepa was standing, paused to look into his blind eyes, and continued out of the building.

Sharon had recorded the words of Angus and the old man, but in the silence of the moment, she was able to take a prolonged look at the kaumātua; and as she watched Angus walk to the back of the room, she saw the homeless man sitting along one aisle. He was looking at her.

"What do you know about Kupe?" asked BloodyLegend180.

It was a cool night, on the eve of February. The last few days had been stifling—the sun clear and strong during the lit hours, the clouds moving in through the evenings and settling over the area for the night, trapping the heat until more could be added in the morning. But this night, no clouds had arrived, and the heat had finally escaped. The coolness was refreshing outside and in Perec's lighthouse.

Over the previous weeks, Perec had continued his meditation, affirmed by Koro Hohepa's instruction that he was on the right track. He had experimented with new symbols for the dying tree but with limited satisfaction. Concurrently, he and BloodyLegend had continued their research.

"Kupe was a navigator," Perec typed in response, "allegedly the first Polynesian from Hawaiiki to arrive in New Zealand. He led, or at least inspired, the first waves of migration of Māori here—or of the people who would become the Māori. At least 200 years before Columbus, Magellan and Drake, he crossed 3000km of storm-tossed ocean to New Zealand."

There was no response for several minutes. Then BloodyLegend wrote, "I don't see any maps on here about him."

"No, it was too long ago, maybe a thousand years. There is only conjecture about the route Kupe piloted—nobody knows for certain where Hawaiiki is. Some say it was Tahiti, where Tupaia was from, some say Easter Island, others even say Taiwan."

"Don't Māori know where they come from, then?"

"Not really—it's lost to legend."

"I thought they were good at passing on genealogies, events, etc. Why not this?"

Perec wrote, "Hard to say—they didn't keep maps, and their carvings were pretty primitive until they developed better tools—stone adzes, that sort of thing. But I have another theory ...."

"What's that?" wrote the other.

"They found too good a home. After living in the ocean continent of Polynesia and needing to rely on long ocean voyages, the settlers here got comfortable. They didn't need to retain that knowledge because they and their descendants were here to stay. So, they lost their way back home. Māori say, '*Ka kotia te taitapu ki Hawaiiki*'—their sacred seaway to Hawaiiki was cut, their homeland was lost."

"OK," wrote BloodyLegend. "Whatever happened to Kupe?"

"Don't know. He made the trip back and, at some point, sent his grandson Nukutawhiti to lead another migratory wave. Another navigator, Turi, led the Aotea waka to the Taranaki Bight region under advisement from Kupe. Kupe had explored the rivers along the west coast—that's also where he planted his karaka tree seeds. The legends vary widely from iwi to iwi. Kupe either returned to Hawaiiki and stayed, or he's buried here, I suppose."

After several months of corresponding with BloodyLegend, Perec had decided that it was time he knew more about him—or her. More and more, perhaps because their progress had stalled, or perhaps because of one of his hunches, Perec began to feel that a better understanding of his colleague would lead to interpretation of the information they were sifting.

"Don't you think it's time you told me more about yourself?" he wrote, and held his hands above the keyboard, anticipating the initial response.

"Not important," was the reply.

To which Perec immediately typed, "I think it is."

Another long pause. *This is a good sign,* thought Perec. *Different from his usual repetitive refusals to elaborate.*

Several minutes passed, and Perec wondered if he was being ignored, not just delayed, when BloodyLegend wrote, "What do you want to know?"

"Are you male or female?" Perec wrote.

"Male."

"Where do you live?"

"In the islands."

"Which one?"

"Not important."

"Which one?" Perec insisted.

"Not important," the other persisted. "Next question."

Sighing, Perec wrote, "How did you get to Pureora forest?"

"Walked," BloodyLegend wrote. Then he added, "Just kidding."

"How then?" Perec asked, ignoring the joke.

The other paused, then wrote, "Boat—then car—then bicycle."

"How did you know the way? Had you been there before?"

"No—first time. Used a map, of course."

Perec sat back, unsettled. What was it that he really needed to know? He wasn't getting any answers that felt right, none that struck the chord he was sure he should be hearing. He wasn't asking the right questions, not touching the heart of the issue, the raison d'etre.

He thought about his own heart, his own motives for being here for almost three decades. Had he himself lost sight? Had he spent so much time circumnavigating life that he had neglected the interior? Like Tuki's map, he felt like he only knew the outskirts of himself, the exterior regions, easily mapped after so much observation. How could he identify his centre anymore? If he couldn't do that, how could he understand this man? How could he interpret with the soul, and not just with the conventional keys?

He wanted to know this about BloodyLegend. But, even if the other was willing, would Perec recognise the revelation when he saw it?

Finally, he sat forward over his keyboard. He typed, "Why are you helping me?"

Knowing his comrade by now, Perec expected a cheeky answer like, "I'm a bloody legend" or, "You hold the key," but instead, immediately, instantaneously, Perec read the response, "No treasure completes us like home and family."

TEN

It was on a Sunday that Stanley missed a run for the first time in two months. Kiri had rung him the afternoon before and asked to meet him at a café in town.

Stanley was nervous on the phone.

"Yes, Kiri, let's meet at Layola's. I'll come down after my run."

"No," she had said, "I want you to meet me instead of running tomorrow."

Stanley had wanted to protest. He was looking forward to his long run. He had been building up to it and had planned to run twenty kilometres for the first time—half-marathon distance. But it was Kiri.

So they met at Layola's café, located centrally on the main street.

She was stunning. She still nursed a limp as she approached Stanley but otherwise looked much the same as he remembered her. Instead of her formerly omnipresent running clothes, she wore a light summer dress with flowered print and elegant sandals. Stanley fell into her eyes which still radiated but did not welcome him to explore their new depths—and he remembered.

The morning was beautiful and sunny. Stanley wore sunglasses and a cap and was glad he did as Kiri wanted to eat outside on the footpath in the glaring sun.

"Hello, Stanley," Kiri said, but offered him no hug or touch. She put her handbag around one of the street-side chairs.

"Good morning, Kiri. It's really good to see you," said Stanley, and he wondered if he meant it considering the way he was feeling, the way he was missing his long run for this.

They ordered and ate and talked about daily matters. Physical therapy had been progressing well for Kiri, and she had started to run again, though only on a treadmill. She was looking forward to running outside, most likely in the autumn. They talked more of running—it was what bound them together as much as it had driven them apart. Despite the lingering shadow of the incident, the conversation flowed in and around their favourite topic.

"I was going to run twenty kilometres for the first time today," Stanley said.

"Well, I'm not sorry for making you miss one run, Stanley. I've missed a few, you know."

Stanley hated guilt trips. "It's been great out there for me—changed my life really. I owe it to you, I suppose."

"I could say the same for you."

Stanley could see what she was doing but was uncertain as to why. Dwelling on the past was unproductive in his mind. What point was she trying to make?

"We're both moving forward though, Kiri, both making progress."

"Stanley," Kiri's voice was tight, "it's not the same thing. I see you running every day. If I'm driving to physio, you're running. When I go to work, when I go shopping, when I visit my friends—I see you running. You even run by my house now—that's not on your circuit. How do you think that makes me feel, to see you running all around Te Kauhanga when I can't?"

Stanley tried to think of a way to excuse himself. "Is this why you wanted to meet me this morning—to punish me?"

Kiri saw the anger in him but wasn't afraid. "Yes, partly Stanley, but more to show you something. I want you to see the effect you had on my life."

"But I already see it," said Stanley. *What a waste of time*, he thought.

Kiri drummed her fingers on the table and resisted the urge to sigh, resisted any signs that would show her frustration with him. She had not intended to show weakness.

In the silence, the pair looked away from each other and at the cars passing in the street and the occasional pedestrian. Looking southward, outside the train station, Stanley saw the red cap. It seemed stationary, unwavering by the homeless man who was stretched out on his bench. But, as he watched, the red cap moved. The movement was practically imperceptible, like trying to watch a minute hand on a clock. The cap moved past the end of the station and into the empty car park and he could see the woman wearing it.

Stanley had first seen this woman's face at the council's open meeting, though briefly. He had been surprised to see her there and hear her story. He'd forgotten her name, but she lived somewhere in Taumata too. As she neared, he studied that face. It was very different from Kiri's—rounder, with mature skin, though not old. Her eyes were shaded as well, but, even so, her mouth was her prominent feature. She held it in a perfectly straight line. She looked supremely serene.

Kiri began watching her as well, though Stanley didn't notice, so lost was he in his thoughts about the woman.

"She walks so slowly," Kiri said.

"Have you seen her before?" asked Stanley.

"No," she said.

"She's incorrigibly frustrating," Stanley said. "Every time I run through town, she's walking through that same spot, between the parked buses and the station. She slows me down."

He felt Kiri's eyes turn on him. "You run through town?" she said.

Stanley, however, did not take his eyes from the woman in the red cap who was now just down the street from them. "Yes," he said. "I run several routes now."

"When did this happen?" she asked, but then said, "Never mind. I don't care. Stanley, why don't you run around her?"

Still watching the woman, Stanley bristled at the question. He didn't have to answer it, but he wanted to appease Kiri while he took a better look at the woman's approaching face. "You know why, Kiri," he said.

Kiri was agitated. At one point, she had wanted to help Stanley see things differently, live differently, live more freely, but it had cost her. Now she saw a pathetic man who refused to be helped, a man who wouldn't even look at her now.

In the meantime, the woman had continued her slow walk to the point directly across from them. She appeared not to notice Stanley staring at her. She appeared to be in her own world, slowly walking, barely minding the noise of the vehicles or the loud tones of Kiri who had stood from the table and hung her purse over her shoulder.

"Stanley, I've said what I came here to say and it's all been pointless. I don't even know what I was looking for from you, but, whatever it was, I didn't get it." She was flustered, not bothered by others in the café who had stopped their own conversations to listen to her.

"You're not an asshole—I don't know what you are. But you hurt me, and you're being a useless prick about it. Maybe I should have pressed charges—just to get you to fucking wake up—but what do I care? What do I care if you stay the way you are? Stay asleep, you wanker. Just—"

But Kiri had run out of words, run out of think, run out of care. She put both hands on the back of her chair and hung her head. She had not wanted to show weakness. But how could he have seen it anyway? He had not looked at her during her rant. She lifted her head and left without saying more.

Stanley heard Kiri speaking, and he heard her walk off. To say he was unfeeling would be too judgmental of Stanley, too inarticulate on the matter. Stanley didn't have a variety of nomenclature for his feelings and besides, emotions did not generally enter into his priorities for his sense of well-being or his decision-making. Yes, he heard her and he felt ... something ... but he was far more interested in the woman in the red cap who had not altered her pace this entire sequence. She moved past, northward on the footpath opposite him. She moved slowly and without any change in her trajectory.

She was magnificent.

February is the last official month of summer in New Zealand—and it is stinking hot. The sun burns skin readily through the ozone-thin sky. In fact, even on a cloudy day, skin will burn as if the country was rotating inside a microwave. Children return to school, summer holidays are wrapped up and the wealthier people who can afford beach baches return to the town's streets, unaware of how the poorer residents have continued without them.

Sharon had not taken holiday leave this summer. She was saving her time for June when she could attend her sister's wedding in the South Island. So she was very much in need of a statuary holiday on Waitangi Day. Waitangi Day meant little to Sharon, as it did to many citizens of the country. It was a day off—and although Sharon lived in a rural town steeped in Māori culture, she thought nothing of the messages of relationship and partnership the day espoused.

The Friday afternoon before the sixth of February, a Tuesday this year, crept by as she finalised accounts and ensured messages had been passed on to Blake, the mayor, and other councillors. It had been a busy day. The last weeks of summer had been quiet with many out of town. The phone calls about the tree had subsided. People were not about to let the issue interrupt late holidaying.

With only a few minutes of the work week remaining, Frances and Manu had left early, both to start preparing celebrations for local family the following day. The entire building was empty except for cleaners deeper in the interior. Sharon enjoyed these rare moments to sort everything in her own way, with no other voices or noises.

Just having ducked into the staffroom, Sharon heard the doors open and then close again. She returned to the reception area to see the homeless man who had already crossed the foyer and was waiting for her at the counter.

Sharon was shocked at his appearance. His hair was ragged, cut short with some implement—surely not scissors. His face was red and sore looking—she had never seen skin burnt as bad. He had discarded his usual swazi top she had seen him wearing in town, even during the hot summer months. He wore a ripped and sweating t-shirt with a faded picture of a palm tree. He was not wearing any pants, but had stripped down to a pair of boxers, also ripped. His feet were bare.

Sharon did not feel frightened. She had interacted with the man before and felt safe enough. She was more disconcerted by his appearance and his unknown purpose.

"Are you OK?" she asked.

The man nodded. "I am," he said, and stared at her.

Maintaining her receptionist's composure, Sharon said, "We're about to close for the day. Is there something I can do for you?"

The man nodded. "Yes, there is," he said. "Can I please have a drink of water?"

Sharon thought this through. She could see by his pallor that this was probably a genuine request, but to fulfill it would mean turning her back on him and perhaps leading him into the staffroom alone.

"Is that all you need?" she asked. "Nothing else ... you know ...

council-wise?"

The man smirked. "I'd like to pay my rates," he said and then, to Sharon's surprise, he laughed heartily before succumbing to a choking rasp. "I'm very thirsty," he managed to say. "A drink is all I need."

Sharon looked at the clock. It was past five.

"Come with me into town," she said, lifting her purse from under the table behind her. "I'll get you a drink there."

The man nodded without trying to speak again.

Sharon walked out beside him, keeping to his right, not allowing him to fall in step behind her. At the door, she let him out and locked it behind them. Together, they walked across and up to the main street, keeping under shelters. The heat sat on the day. The sun was still scorching.

Many shops were closed, and traffic was thinning after the 5pm traffic rush in Te Kauhanga. They walked in silence, Sharon immaculately dressed, the homeless man in his underwear, parched and dependent.

Minutes later, Sharon had bought a bottle of water for the man. He had refused her offers of a meal, but asked if she would sit with him while he drank.

The café was empty except for the owner and the young waitresses, who looked disparagingly at the man and, she noticed, at her. Sharon elected to sit in a corner nearest the front window, but out of range of the sun.

The man drank until the bottle was near empty. "Thank you," he said at last. His voice sounded fluid again, renewed and articulate.

"Are you all right then?" she asked.

"Yes, thanks. You're very kind."

"That's OK." Sharon decided to rectify a nagging curiosity. "I saw you at the council meeting—the one about the tree."

"Yes, I was there. I saw you too."

"I know," she said. "You were looking at me."

"Was I?" He chuckled, "Well, I suppose I might have been."

"Why were you there?"

"Would it be inappropriate to say I was there to see you?"

Sharon blushed and looked around the café as if worried someone had heard.

"Ha-ha—don't worry," he said. "I wasn't there for that." He

sipped his water. "I wanted to listen to the debate."

"Oh? Are you concerned about the tree?" Sharon didn't really want to hear any more about the tree, not during her days off.

"Not particularly. I've never gone up to Taumata. I can see it well enough from where I live. The tree and that bloody lighthouse."

"So, why did you want to listen to the debate?" she asked.

"I like a good argument," he said and sipped his water before leaning forward and over the table between them. "I also wanted to find out more about what the people in this town are like, what their values are. I wanted to see if there was any reason in this place, any intelligence beyond the name-calling and narrow scope I've encountered since I arrived."

Sharon asked, "Did you find any?"

The man laughed his hearty laugh again. "Sure," he said, "but there was probably more intelligence in the council recorder, simply taking notes, than in the rest of the room pontificating and over-dramatising and, worse still, obscuring reason with mythologies and cultural hierarchies."

"So, do you not agree with the council or with the kaumātua?"

"I don't agree with any of them!" he exclaimed. "Let things be, I say. Too much intervention in natural processes."

"But ... if the tree is sick, then branches will fall off ... the tree will eventually topple. We should cut it down so it's not a danger to houses in Taumata."

"Pffft," he scoffed. "If a community decided to build near a volcano, do you intervene to block the crater so it's not a danger? Or do you tell stupid people not to build near a volcano in future? I don't know if that tree is sick—doesn't look like it—but that doesn't mean it should be cut down."

Sharon frowned. "I disagree, of course. I live in Taumata."

"Well, that was a stupid idea, wasn't it?" he said.

Sharon shook her head, bewildered. "I think I should go. You are certainly an unusual man."

"Sharon," he said, stopping her as she stood.

How does he know my name? Sharon thought, but then remembered she was wearing a name tag.

"Sharon," he said again, "why do you think I live the way I do?"

She studied his red face and his shorn head. "I suppose," she said, "that you've fallen on some hard times, maybe from alcohol or

141

mental illness."

"Sharon," he said, and something in his voice changed—it was more consoling, not condescending, but pastoral and instructional. "Have you ever seen me drinking alcohol since I've arrived? Have I presented any signs of mental illness to you in our conversation today?"

"No ... no to both those questions," she said.

"Well, that's good—and I can say the same for you. So then ... think beyond the routine answers."

Sharon did think. "OK—you couldn't hold down a job. Maybe you have a criminal record, or you lost all your money and assets through gambling."

The man shook his head. "You're still thinking the same way. You're still thinking in terms of inflicted consequences—in other words, outside forces caused by poor choices. It's a way of blaming me and making me into a victim at the same time. Think differently. Why am I living like this?"

Sharon was finding it hard to think about what he was saying. His words no longer connected with his image. This sun-burnt, half-naked, parched vagrant was challenging her to think more deeply about his condition over a bottle of water in a mid-stream café.

"You don't get it, do you?" he said, and she focused on him again. "Sharon," he spoke to her as if she was an old friend, "I choose to live like this, just like you choose to live the way you do."

Montreal Perec paced around his house. It was another form of exercise and a way to exorcise some of his obsessive-compulsive demons. He walked from room to room, counting strides, translating them into millimetres for an, as yet, imagined map based on stride lengths rather than conventional measures. Starting downstairs, he made his way around, then up to execute the same process on the next level and then, finally, finishing in the lighthouse room at the top.

From there, suitably charged with his own circulation, Perec gazed out at the encroaching heat-induced haze of mid-day. *Waitangi Day tomorrow,* he thought, looking over the river which always made him think of the early Māori settlement in the area—made him think of the stories of Cook and Tupaia that brought him to Te Kauhanga.

Waitangi Day meant more to Perec than just a holiday. First of all, Perec didn't need a holiday. He was perfectly set-up with his online work and could take off any day he wanted. Secondly, the day marked the anniversary of his arrival in the country, this particular one his thirtieth celebration. And thirdly, Waitangi Day symbolised partnership between Māori and European—though it was the Cook-Tupaia partnership that intrigued him—and Perec loved symbolism.

Waitangi Day also meant taking his annual walk. The streets would, for the most part, be empty of shoppers and labourers, so each year, Perec walked, unmolested, down from Taumata hill into central Te Kauhanga and further north to the river.

"Why are you always online?" BloodyLegend had asked him earlier in the day.

"I'm not always online," Perec had responded.

"Every time I send a message, you reply immediately. Do you use a mobile device?"

"No," Perec wrote.

"So you're always online. Does that mean you're always at home?"

"Yes."

"Are you sick?" asked BloodyLegend.

"No."

"Are you under house arrest?"

"No."

"Why are you always at home then?"

"I'm going out tomorrow."

Perec did not need to explain himself to his island companion. It was enough to focus on their work together. But Perec would walk tomorrow. He would wake early, before any of the previous night's revellers stirred, and descend.

Each year, he noted that very little changed and he was certain it would not be any different this time. He had been watching, after all, noting and sketching and mapping. This was part of the appeal for him—to walk the streets and land features of his town map.

He would descend Taumata hill, sure to avoid any passing cars or curious pedestrians who might have seen him leave the lighthouse. He would cross through the underground, along the same route Stanley Kowalczyk took to work and, before going to the river, walk one way down the main street and reverse on the back street. As it had been the case each year, Perec anticipated he would see no-one but, if he did, once he was in town and no-one knew of his house of departure, he would be fine.

At the river, as he did each year, Perec would wade in his bare feet and legs. The water would be warm and remind him of the rivers of his Nova Scotian youth. This river would again help him recall the stories of the area, and he would feel the connection to the mouth, at the sea where his quarry had originated.

He would then turn and survey the area from the perspective of newly arrived treasure buriers and imagine where they went next. He would experiment in his mind with facts he had learned and wait for the next hunch to lead him onward, like a divining rod made from an alder bush.

Then he would return home the way he came and tuck himself away for another year. For, in three decades, Perec had yet to find that hunch at the river. After one year, he had been perplexed. After two years, he had developed some anxiety. After three years, he had settled with disillusionment. The answers, he had determined, would not come from dwelling on the past but from close inspection of the present. So, tomorrow, he would visit the river and again return unenlightened but satisfied that his ritual was complete, that he had once again shown the gods of time and space that he would not look to them, but that he would look closer. This is what had worked and what would always work.

======::::::

In small towns, as in the greater universe, there is, for every action, an opposite and equal reaction. As there is a Law of Multiple Encounters, there is also a *Law of Diminishing Contact*. This law is widely known, if not by name then by experience, and often confused with the infamous *Murphy's Law*. The Law of Diminishing Contact states that, after multiple and inconvenient encounters with another individual, once one desires encounters with that individual it becomes increasingly difficult to do so.

And so, this law also applied to Stanley Kowalczyk who, after discovering his latest passion for the red-capped walker, planned his next meeting with her. His first attempt failed when, despite maintaining his consistency of timing on his town route, he arrived at the train station too late. Upon his arrival, he saw the cap far off in the distance up the main street. Assured that, with her plodding pace and his swift speed, he would be able to catch up to her, he launched himself forward. However, she somehow eluded him, turning which direction he could not tell.

His next attempt failed in much the same way, only this time he did not see the cap at all. Instead, upon arriving at the station, he queried the homeless man about her, only to receive cryptic responses about poverty and free will before confirming that the red-capped woman had, indeed, passed by several minutes earlier.

After that, there was no indication that she ever passed that way again on the days Stanley ran the town route.

Determined, Stanley devised a new plan.

During his lunch hour—another sticky, hot lunch hour in Te Kauhanga—Stanley walked an extra block north to the council offices. Entering, he noted the spiral patterns created by the mosaic tiling on the floor leading to the receptionist's counter. His stomach swirled with the pattern, but he persevered, cutting directly across the arcing lines.

Frances met him there, shifting from her computer screen when she saw him.

"Hello," Stanley said.

She smiled broadly and greeted him in return. *This is a cute one*, she thought.

"I have an unusual request," said Stanley. "I wonder if I could speak to the council recorder who was at the meeting about the tree."

Frances said, "That would be Sharon. I'll just get her for you." She held his eyes as she turned, still smiling.

Sharon emerged from the staffroom. "Hello," Stanley said again. "You were at the tree meeting weren't you?"

"Yes, that's right, sir."

"I'm trying to find someone else who was at that meeting. She spoke at the microphone and gave her name, but I missed it. I'm wondering if you wrote her name down and if I could see the transcript or something."

"Yes, I can do that for you. The minutes from the proceedings are a public record. I'll get you the transcript now." Sharon turned and disappeared deeper into the offices.

What a lovely, professional woman, thought Stanley. He nodded at Frances who had reappeared part way though the conversation and was hovering in the area, pretending to continue with other tasks.

Sharon returned, brushing past Frances who flashed a curious look at her.

"Here you are," she said, opening a ring binder on the desk in front of him. She flipped some pages, slowing to scroll down the minutes with her finger. "Kathleen MacLeod," she said. "Does that sound right to you?"

"Kathleen MacLeod," Stanley repeated. "Scottish. Thank you very much."

He turned to leave when Frances' voice called out to him, "She's a real loon you know."

Stanley looked behind him to see Frances leaning on the counter, fluttering eyes at him. "Kathleen MacLeod—I went to school with her. She was strange then, and she's weirder now." Sharon stayed beside her, looking back at the name on the page. "Like, really weird," Frances said.

Uncertain, yet wanting to learn more about his new fixation, Stanley asked, "How so?"

"Haven't you seen her walking around town? It must take her a bloody hour to get from one end of the street to the other. At school, she was the total opposite—she was manic, a real crazy person. You didn't know what she was going to be like from one encounter to the next. You know how she said she was nearly killed by that van—the one that rammed the tree?

Stanley nodded.

"Well," said Frances, casting a look sideways at Sharon, "Most of us in town don't believe it happened that way. We think—no, we know—she made that story up. You know that guy up in Taumata who lives in the lighthouse?" Stanley nodded. "He's a weird one too—have you ever seen him Sharon?—big hairy fella. Well, when that van crashed into the tree, Kathleen was about seven or eight I think, and she used to try and see him. She'd hide outside his fence for hours trying to catch a glimpse. Her parents had told her to cut it out. They told her it was because he was a strange man, but I reckon it was because they knew they had a strange daughter.

"So when that van crashed, she wasn't supposed to be around that area. She made up the story about nearly being hit by the van as a distraction—to get her parents to forget about what she was doing there in the first place."

Frances stopped and reached out to touch Stanley's arm over the counter. "So you don't really want to bother with her, sweetie," she said. "How about you and I grab a coffee, though? I can take a break right now if you'd like."

Stanley recoiled. What strange information this was and what a strange proposition from a strange woman. "No, thank you," he said. He didn't elaborate but turned and walked back over the spiral-painted tiles and out the door. He didn't see the smiles on the faces of the two women or hear their laughter.

"You don't have to live this way!" A voice, crying in the wilderness—or at least near the town square. Standing on his bench, the homeless man had finally gathered his audience.

"It is not a crime to be alive!" he called out to, and over, the heads of three Asian tourists. Their bus had stopped in Te Kauhanga for a thirty minute reprieve. It was the attentive crowd that had caused Sharon to stop across the street where she watched from behind an awning post.

"What does the law say about lifestyle? In what ways do you acquiesce when no law dictates? Yet, it is not the law that compels you is it? It is fear that drives you. You have more freedom than you know!"

The man's voice was rich, filled with tone, resplendent in tenor. Sharon shifted imperceptibly to sneak a better view. She was captivated. The man wore the same clothes she had first seen him in. The Friday lunchtime crowd seemed less interested. It was high noon—hot.

"Apparently he's been performing like this all week."

It was Blake, and he was beside her. Sharon stole a look at him but then resumed watching the orator. She said to Blake, "I hadn't heard. Anything being done by the police?"

"Oh, they've spoken to him," Blake said, "but his rants only last ten minutes or so—and none of the townsfolk have been complaining. It's like the roosters in the park—you'd think he'd be considered a public nuisance, but instead he's become part of the woodwork around here, another part of Te Kauhanga's special character, our very own homeless preacher."

"I was once like you!" the homeless man continued. "Trudging through life, trapped in my choices—choices I wasn't making on my own. Did you know the choices you are making are designed for others' benefit? You are sheep!"

"I've met him, you know," Sharon said. "He's been into the council offices a few times." She continued to watch him. "He's quite intelligent."

Blake examined the side of her face then looked back at the man. He sipped his cappuccino. "How are you anyway, Sharon? You all right?"

Sharon bristled at the condescension in his voice. "I'm fine." She checked the time on her cellphone.

The homeless man had lost his Asian trio and collected an old woman on a mobile scooter and the young runner with the limp. "How do you know when you have broken free? How do you know when you have gained true autonomy and self-sufficiency?" he called.

This caught Blake's attention. "What does he know about self-sufficiency?" he scoffed. "The poor schmuck is a victim of our world's vices. He's got no power, no assets, no options. Self-sufficiency's about standing on your own two feet, about taking control of the space and the resources around you and bending them to your needs, not caving to consumerism ... not letting things control you." Blake stepped closer to Sharon, filling space in front of her, partially obscuring her view of the preacher, compelling her to look at him instead.

"Sharon," he said, "have you ... have you taken control of your situation yet?"

She shoved him then, out into the street, knocking him a glancing blow off the post. "Don't crowd me!" she yelled, and it was loud enough to stop the preacher mid-sentence. His audience turned towards the sound, but Sharon didn't notice. She only saw Blake's face and realised he had not meant harm.

"Just ... don't crowd me, Blake ... please," she said, then tuned into the silence in the street—no ringing voice, no bustle of footsteps behind her, not even the intermittent rumble of lunch-time traffic. In the silence, she flushed, overly aware of the moment. How did she get here? How did she get to this place, at this time ... far away from her Wellington, amongst these small-town, small-minded people? How did she end up losing control of her *situation*? The moment held her—Blake standing between two parked cars, uncertain of what to do in front of the onlookers, and the preacher, brushing through his small crowd and crossing the street, his eyes fixed on her. She noted that his hair had grown out, emphasising the unevenness of its strands. He had ripped the sleeves from his swazi top so that it looked like a tattered tunic.

He arrived behind Blake's shoulder, and the moment released Sharon with his words. "Is this man bothering you, Sharon?"

Blake was released too. "No," he said, moving away from the man and back onto the sidewalk, but no closer to Sharon. "I mean ... if I did, Sharon, I'm sorry."

"It's OK," she said to Blake. Then, to the preacher she said, "It's OK." Her voice was stronger.

Blake never looked at the man, only nodded at Sharon and walked away, turning down the side street which led to the council offices.

Sharon focused on the homeless man. The small group of stalled passers-by had moved on with Blake. The audience across the road must have determined that the man's ten minutes were expended for the day. The man said nothing. He seemed to be waiting.

Sharon gave him what he wanted. "I need help," she said.

The sound woke Perec as it did everyone in Taumata that night. In fact, people all over Te Kauhanga reached for their laptops and mobile devices, certain the sound was the result of an earthquake, and searched online for a report of its magnitude.

Perec knew it wasn't an earthquake. He knew it was a cracking. The sound resembled one he'd heard at Stanford Lake one winter. He was ten years old and staying with his uncle and aunt while his father nursed his mother through one of her bouts of inertia. Temperatures on the lake reached minus thirty that winter, and the lake responded with terrific displays of shifting ice. The first night he'd heard the lake was terrifying. He sat up in bed at the sound—a rumble that shook the foundation of the house as it passed from one end of the lake to the other. He heard the excited, yet exhausted tones of his surrogates and was relieved when they turned lights on throughout the house. They called for him to come out from his room, which he did, joining them on the front balcony, bundled in his blankets. His aunt put a hat on his head, and they listened.

For as long as they could stand the cold, the trio had listened to the ice cracking, shivering and shifting its way across and around the lake. The entire stretch of air above the ice was filled with the sound, a splintering rumble which never reached a crescendo, never conformed to a pattern, but which elicited awe in its onlisteners. It was a spectacle of sound.

So Perec recognised the auditory spectacle on that warm February evening in Taumata. He recognised the cracking, the splintering and the awe, and he knew of only one possible source.

From his three-story house, Perec peered into the darkness and saw the great branch, illuminated by the street lamps and the newly lit houses nearby. It looked rooted on its own, but fallen over, as if it was itself a tree that had surrendered to its own lean. The trunk of the branch rested stolidly against the base of the tree proper, as if it had slid neatly along the bark rather than tumbling haphazardly down through its fellow members, banging and crashing as it most certainly had done. The length of the branch lay across and inside the church, whose roof was now divided in two, each half perfectly symmetrical with the other. Surely, the altar had broken the branch's fall as nothing short of divine intervention could have kept it from penetrating the very crust of the earth and wedging itself deep within its core.

The stillness of the moment counterbalanced the alarming activity which preceded it. However, houses were alight, and Perec could hear voices starting to cry out as fathers called to their families to stay inside, that the tree had broken. The town fire alarm sang, a pathetic echo of the branch's dramatic collapse, and soon trucks climbed their way up the incline. No-one dared venture towards the tree itself except for the mirrored figures of Koro Hohepa and Father Sennheiser, each on either side of Centre Street. Perec watched them from his perch, both men standing in shadow, the first reciting karakia in Māori in front of his broken maunga, the second, kneeling beside his broken temple.

ELEVEN

The overnight events, and the subsequent deluge of people, vehicles, and chaos in Taumata, did not deter Stanley from visiting Kathleen MacLeod at her house the next morning. And why would they? If there was one thing Stanley Kowalczyk knew, it was how to stick to a goal, how to maintain focus, how to finish the line of action he had started.

Only, this line took him off his beaten path. Despite his repeated encounters with Kathleen MacLeod on the main street and the subsequent revelation that she too lived in Taumata, Stanley could not deduce why he had never seen her between these two locations—until he set out to find her house.

It was easy enough to find, of course, as Taumata is a small, self-contained neighbourhood. But Kathleen lived on Hauāuru Street. Since moving to Taumata five years earlier, Stanley had never been on Hauāuru Street, unless it was to drive his car for an out-of-town trip. It is not an out-of-the-way street, by any means. In fact, it was the main street between Taumata and Te Kauhanga, but you will remember that Stanley bypassed the routes of ordinary citizens, cutting through neighbours' yards in order to reach town. Thus, he consistently negated any necessity of walking down Hauāuru Street.

Nor did Stanley ever run on Hauāuru Street, as he either left his house to run behind Taumata or through his neighbours' properties into town. For Stanley, Hauāuru Street was a void, a limbo, an empty place on his mental map of his residence—until he was given Kathleen MacLeod's address.

So, on Waitangi Day, on the morning after the first ever branch fell from the Taumata tree, Stanley first set foot on Hauāuru Street.

And what a busy street it was. Fire trucks which had ascended that morning passed by him as they returned to town. Voyeurs drove past him slowly, either turning into the neighbourhood, or coasting by in hopes of a view of the branch or demolished church without embroiling themselves in the activities. Other walkers meandered by him, speaking in excited tones about where they had been when they heard the noise and affirming the council's proposal to cut the menace down.

Stanley ignored the vehicles and the voices and made a beeline for Kathleen's house, having cut across Tonga Street—his street—on an angle that established him precisely on the corner, before deviating slightly to the right and straight down Hauāuru.

Kathleen's house was situated exactly half way down to the next corner. It was a tidy place, with a central front porch jutting out from a squarish mainframe whose roof angled in such a way that it gave an illusion of roundness so that, Stanley thought, the entire structure looked like an igloo or a tortoise. Behind the house, across the unseen yards of the Heke and Findlayson families, loomed the tree. Standing on the footpath, Stanley considered two things: the tree now had a gaping hole in its canopy, already being filled by branches from above who were eager to hide the space left by their brother, but still showing, for the first time at that elevation in a thousand years, brown-white skin rather than green fronds. The other thing Stanley considered was that, in his efficient path-making to work, he had been walking around the red capped woman's house this entire time.

This was his more prevalent thought as Stanley entered the small front gate, a gate not unlike his own, and ascended the short, hydrangea-flanked steps to the porch. He rang the bell without hesitation and with his rehearsed opening lines on the tip of his tongue.

In mere moments, the red capped woman was opening the door in front of him. She said nothing, but waited for Stanley to initiate the salutations.

"Hello," he said. "My name is Stanley." So far, the words flowed exactly as he had planned—right pace, right tenor. Kathleen MacLeod said nothing.

"I live around the block," Stanley continued. "I was given your address at the council. I saw you at the town meeting—the one about the tree." He waited.

"OK," was all she said, but she looked lovely.

"Well, I heard your story that night ... you know ... the one about the van running into the tree."

"Yes?" she said, turning her head and furrowing her brow in hopes of prompting purpose out of him.

This was harder than Stanley had thought. In his conjectured conversations, he had started with this connection, and the red capped lady had reciprocated, offering some recollection of having seen him there or volunteering questions he might answer about the meeting. This felt like a dead end. Stanley was losing his line of reasoning and felt his opportunity collapsing into her beautiful eyes. He had never felt this tongue-tied by a woman.

A chainsaw roared to life in the centre of Taumata.

"Well ... I guess ... I found your story interesting, that's all—oh, and I've seen you downtown sometimes. You like to walk."

"Yes," she said, holding her quizzical expression, but then adding, "I've seen you too."

Alleluia, thought Stanley.

"You have?" he said.

"Yes, you run."

"Yes, that's right. I've run by you a few times. You always wear a red cap."

This brought a smile to Kathleen's face. "Stanley, is there something I can do for you this morning?"

"Um ... well ...," Stanley said, holding out his hands in a pleading fashion, "I'm glad you asked. I guess I'm here to ask you to go on a walking date with me."

"A walking date?"

"Yes. Would you like to walk together sometime?"

"I thought you ran," she said.

"Well, I do, but I thought it might be nice ... you know ... to go for a walk with someone. I used to ... I used to run with a friend, but we don't run together anymore."

"Is that the friend who was yelling at you at the café last week?

The one with the limp?" Kathleen asked. She didn't sound accusatory, but Stanley was taken aback.

"No, no ... it was a guy friend," he said. "He moved out of town."

Kathleen shifted her weight so that she brought the door closer to her body, blocking the view inside her home.

"I walk pretty slowly. I don't think you'd enjoy it."

Stanley felt his chance collapsing again but not into her eyes— there was hope in her eyes, hope for a good response.

"I can honestly say," and he said it in his most honest, most level voice, the chainsaw desisting for added effect, "I would sincerely like to go for a walk with you, and I know I will enjoy it. Besides," he lied, "I think it's time I slowed down."

✠

Sharon had cleaned all morning. Never had she felt so self-conscious—not before a date, a job interview, not before Blake's first visit to her house. She felt propelled by the contrast between her home and her impending visitor.

She had not slept well. She, like all her neighbours, had heard the branch, but she had been awake when it fell, unable to sleep for the thoughts of her appointment in the morning. She and her cats had investigated the sound in the middle of the night, walking out to her back yard, chatting and querying with David Humboldt, her nearest neighbour. He had maintained calm, reassuring his wife and daughter that all was well, and this brought Sharon some comfort. Still, as the news shivered down the block of the tree's decline and the damage to her church, she couldn't shake the more devastating feeling that she had made a mistake.

She wasn't ready and yet, hadn't Father Sennheiser often preached that Jesus takes us as we are and cleans us up, rather than waiting for us to clean ourselves enough to meet with him? The cleaning metaphor wasn't lost on Sharon, but she took it more literally than most. She felt dirty all the time.

So, even after learning about her place of worship, Sharon returned to her mess inside to hide from it all. And, perhaps because of what happened to her church, she heard a voice say to her simply, "It's time."

She cleaned from the time she went back inside until the knock on her door at the prescribed hour. What were the results? Many dishes were found and washed, clothes were collected and hidden in bedrooms, opened magazines were closed and bookshelves were dusted. Nothing had been discarded beyond food-related scraps and packaging. The waste bins were fuller now than when she'd started though difficult for a stranger to locate in this landscape.

At his knock, Sharon opened her door to the homeless man.

He looked out of place, even for a vagrant. In fact, he looked much as he had when she asked for his help downtown. He wore the same sleeveless swazi. His hair was matted but partially hidden by a tan fedora hat. His body language suggested discomfort even with the porch beneath his feet.

"Hello, Sharon," he said. "I found you."

"You found me," she said. "I'm glad you could make it."

"This is my first time up to Taumata," he said. "The air is different up here."

Sharon furrowed her brow. "Just up here? It's not very far from town."

He nodded. "Not in distance if you measure it in metres or in stride-lengths, but it is a big step for me. I've imagined what it would be like up here, with the tree and the lighthouse."

Sharon had not yet stepped back to invite him inside. "I suppose that's all you've seen from downtown? There's a little less tree to see now. Why haven't you come up before?"

"It wasn't time," he said.

Sharon breathed deep. What was she doing?

"Aren't you going to invite me in?" he asked, and Sharon remembered herself and her manners.

"Of course," she said. "Come in. Don't worry about your shoes."

She opened the door wide and held it long enough for him to support it while he walked in behind her. "Watch your step," she said, but led him forward without further hesitation. She had done this with few others, but once she made the decision to invite someone in, she proceeded as normal, prepared to ignore reactions her guests might display. She heard nothing of the sort from behind her, as she navigated her way through the piles of books in the hallway then climbed over the boxes and loose stacks blocking the entrance to the kitchen. She heard no gasps, protests, comments, queries, or stammers. At one point, she cast a glance over her shoulder in the pretence of checking his status, and observed he formed no facial expression of judgment or concern. He simply followed her, trodding in her wake until they arrived safely in the kitchen.

"Tea?" she asked, and motioned for him to sit in the same chair she had offered Blake months earlier.

"Absolutely, Sharon, thank you," he said, and sat.

He doesn't even look around, thought Sharon. It was true. The man didn't do the newcomer lolly-gag—that open-mouthed turning of the head of a person examining the quality of the walls, accounting for the significant features of a person's home. No comments of, "Nice place you have here," or, "This place looks like it's good value." No, the man simply sat and waited for his tea. He did observe Sharon, however, as she moved within her cooking space.

As the host, Sharon felt compelled to create conversation. "What is your name?" she asked. "You haven't told me it yet."

"My name is Rico," he said, "just Rico."

"*Just* Rico? No last name?"

"Rico is my last name," he said, "and my first."

Sharon poured the newly-boiled water into two cups and tossed a teabag in each. She smiled. She was growing used to his crypticism. "Did you hear the tree last night, Rico?" she asked.

"I did," he said. "The whole town heard it, I can assure you. I watched all their lights come on and listened to their voices."

"What did it sound like where you were?"

"It sounded exactly like ... a giant tree branch falling." He smiled, and accepted the cup Sharon offered as she sat across from him. She didn't need to move anything out of the way. *Thank goodness I cleaned in here*, she thought.

"I heard it too. I was awake late last night," she said. "I guess the council has been right all along. The tree needs to be cut down."

He nodded. "Perhaps. But sometimes solutions bring their own problems." He sounded magnanimous.

"What really upset me," Sharon continued, "was that it landed on my church. Did you see it on your way up?"

Rico sipped his tea. He hadn't had a cup of tea for several days. It was good. "I did. I walked by the lighthouse. I didn't go any closer. The fire trucks were there, and they've cordoned the road. The branch did a pretty good job."

Sharon squinted at him. *A good job?* She wanted to ask him what he meant but felt too intimidated to challenge him on even a small thing. She watched him take another sip of his tea and look around the room. He was finally starting to pay attention to her surroundings. She waited for it, but it didn't come.

"You called it *your* church, Sharon. Are you Catholic?" he asked.

"I am."

"Have you always been Catholic?"

"I have—born and bred. I went to a Catholic primary school in Island Bay, then a Catholic boarding school. My parents were good Catholics, as was my grandmother whom I lived with when I first moved here—faithful people."

"And you, Sharon—are you a faithful person?" he asked.

"Of course," she said. "I go to church every Sunday ... well, I did. I guess I might miss this weekend. Father Sennheiser will have Mass somewhere though."

Rico raised an eyebrow. "I thought Catholics had to have church in an actual church, with a tabernacle and an altar."

Sharon nodded. "That's right. But in circumstances like this, Father Sennheiser will sort out an alternative—for now. It won't be the same though."

"How do you mean?"

"Well, as you say, Mass should really be in a church."

"I didn't say that, Sharon," Rico said, "but why does it matter to you?"

Such questions, Sharon thought, feeling her personal space invaded. She hadn't articulated her faith to a non-Catholic since university. "Well, all our rituals are tied up in a church and with what's inside it."

Rico pressed further. "So, what happens exactly? When you go to church and go through all those rituals there?"

"Lots of things. We bless ourselves with holy water, ask for forgiveness, listen to the readings, sing songs, take Holy Communion."

Rico leaned forward and said, "You haven't mentioned God at all, Sharon. Does God have anything to do with these things?"

Sharon laughed. "Of course He does!" she said. "It's all about God." Then she remembered some of her teaching. "Jesus meets us in a special way during Holy Communion."

Rico smiled again and sat back. "And so, God is part of all the rituals Sharon?"

"That's right," she said.

"And the rituals are embedded in the church building and the various parts of it—the tabernacle, the altar, the holy water?"

"That's right. It's God's house."

"And so God meets with his people through the rituals in His house?"

"Yes," she said.

"Sharon," Rico said, his voice close to a whisper, "do you really believe that God can be contained in a house?"

Sharon thought for a moment, retracing her steps through his statements. She was no fool. She started with his premise and examined his logic. Finally, she said, "It's not about containment, Rico, it's about ... a meeting place. It's about a special place we build for him so he can meet us there."

"That's fine, Sharon, I have no problem with that, but I'm asking you to think about the limitations you are putting on yourself—and on God—when you say that your meeting with Him won't be the same without the building. Can't you meet Him elsewhere? Can't you meet Him by the river? Can't you meet Him at work? Can't you meet Him ... downtown?"

This creeped Sharon out a little to be sure, but, after studying Rico's face carefully, she determined she was not dealing with a case of Messiah complex.

"What you're saying makes sense," she said, "but I'm still upset about our church."

"Of course," Rico said. He paused and let the moment sit between them. He finished his tea which had cooled as they spoke. Outside, a chainsaw growled through its work.

Sharon released them from the silence. "I suppose what you're saying is that God is too big for a building?"

"I don't need to say that. That's a truism—totally obvious. Look," Rico said. "Look at me. Am I alive or not?"

Sharon laughed. "Of course you're alive."

"How do you know?" he asked.

"You're talking, you're breathing, you're moving."

"That's right," he said. "Now, you've met with me in several places, haven't you? At your workplace, downtown, and now in your home." He waved his arm around as if to emphasise the place was hers.

"Yes," said Sharon.

"And did I seem more alive in any of those places?"

"More alive?" Sharon asked. "What do you mean?" But she was sensing the connection.

"More alive—more talkative, more breathful, more mobile. Those were your criteria for being alive."

"Well, no, that seems silly. You can't be more alive—you're alive or you're not, I suppose ... unless you're mostly dead." Sharon laughed. She was enjoying him.

"That's the one, Sharon," said Rico, "I am as alive in your home— this building—as I am at your workplace or downtown."

"And it's the same with God?" she asked.

Rico nodded and pointed around the room with an index finger, indicating the mass of material surrounding them. "It's the same with you, Sharon ... it's the same with you."

Montreal Perec was agitated. All the activity and attention around the tree during the morning had prevented him from taking his Waitangi Day walk. He had paced his house like a horse who had stood too long in its stable. *One walk*, he thought, *one walk each year is all I want. Can't they hurry up and go?*

But, of course, if they had left, Perec would not have exited his house immediately. He had missed his chance to wander through the quiet streets of Te Kauhanga before others awoke.

So, he paced. In three decades, he had never missed this morning walk. It was as much a part of his calendar as his annual sketching of the township and his plumbing. He was in no mood to correspond with BloodyLegend, either, or with anyone at all. His computer was shut down, his modem was switched off.

As he paced, he listened to the chainsaw and the voices of the council engineers arguing with the works foremen. He passed by his front door and looked from his upstairs windows, noting their progress, before continuing his circuit of the house. With each passing, the giant branch shrunk in chunks, and trucks filled with firewood. They had worked from the trunk of the great branch, leaving the crushed church for last. By the end of the morning, the engineers had gone. By the end of the afternoon, the foremen had followed. By twilight, the chainsaws had stopped, and the crews had left, leaving a pile of sawdust and firewood, a condemned church, and a closed road to deal with in the coming days and weeks.

Perec did not lament for the tree—the loss of its branch and its subsequent confirmation that the tree was indeed dying. Nor did he lament for the church. He was not a religious man or sentimental about such things, not even to the point of feeling sympathy for his fellow residents of Taumata who had lost their place of prayer. In fact, he resented that part of the community who gathered at dusk to hold a candlelight ceremony, further delaying his exit.

Perec decided he would still walk on Waitangi Day. He would not delay until morning.

Stanley and Kathleen, Stanley and Kathleen, Stanley and Kathleen. Stanley liked the sound of the phrase and imagined his family and her friends saying it for years to come. *Kathleen and Stanley, Kathleen and Stanley, Kathleen and Stanley.* He repeated the phrases to himself as he finished drying and putting away his dishes prior to preparing for his walking date with the red-capped woman. He hoped she would wear the red cap.

They had agreed to meet after tea, though later than usual as Kathleen had scheduled a video chat with family overseas. By the time she arrived at his front door, the clouds had moved over the valley, and the day had turned to a dusky grey. Some heavy rain drops fell, though intermittently.

"Are you still keen to go?" she asked Stanley, who was dressed for the occasion, wearing his new running shorts and his less colourful shoes—not his favourite but, he thought, more impressive for a walking date with Kathleen.

"Absolutely," he said. I don't mind running in the rain or in the dark."

"What about walking?" Kathleen asked. She wore plain shoes, with no evidence of any extra features, a simple pull-over and track pants—and she wore the red cap.

"Of course," Stanley smiled. "I walk in the rain too."

He locked his door and the pair walked through his front gate.

Stanley felt some tension knot inside him, but he had prepared for this. "How about we walk the loop?" he asked Kathleen.

"I'll walk anywhere you like. It's all good to me," she said.

As they started down Tonga Street, Stanley started the stopwatch on his wrist.

"Why are you doing that?" Kathleen asked.

"I always time my runs," Stanley said.

Kathleen stopped, causing Stanley to do the same. He stopped his watch as well.

"Look, Stanley, are you sure you want to do this? I did warn you that I walk slowly."

"Of course I do," Stanley answered. "Like I said, I need to slow down anyway. I always time myself so I can log it, even if it's a walk. It's fine."

Kathleen looked dubious but began walking again. Stanley restarted his watch and stepped alongside her.

"How often do you walk?" Stanley asked.

"As often as I like," she said, not glancing at him.

As they reached the corner of Tonga and Hauāuru, Kathleen diverged to her right, towards her house.

"Oh ... um ... I thought we were walking the loop," Stanley said. He stopped his watch.

Kathleen stopped in the middle of the road and said, "I thought you meant our regular loop ... you know ... the one where I see you downtown."

"No, I meant the 5K loop around Tautaungara." As he said this, Kathleen shrugged her shoulders and started to return to the verge where Stanley was standing. But Stanley overcame himself and said, "You know what? It's all good. Let's go your way."

Kathleen shrugged again. Stanley restarted his watch and the pair walked down Hauāuru Street.

Her pace was incredibly slow. Stanley had to make a conscious effort to stay in stride with her, each step of his lunging ahead with a life of its own. His legs were longer, and the trained muscles pulsated deep in their tissues, yearning to stretch and exert themselves. By the time they passed Kathleen's house, Stanley had checked his watch three times, trying to do so as he deliberately fell behind her—as difficult as that was—in an attempt to avoid her notice. According to his watch, Stanley would normally have been at the bottom of the incline. Calculations automatically ran through his head. To complete the loop, it may take them as long as five hours. His chest tightened. He needed something to focus on, something lovely. Alongside his companion, he stole glances at Kathy's euphoric eyes. Falling away from her, he pinched perusals of her jogger-clad bottom. He thought, *I might survive this after all.*

As Stanley struggled, Kathleen walked and said nothing—no idle chit-chat, no space-filling banter, no commentary about the weather, the tree or their life histories. The rain was falling harder now—unpleasant, but not so heavy to elicit complaint from either trekker. Reaching the top of the incline, they saw a brilliant pink horizon slowly relinquishing its hold to the thick bank of clouds. They made their way down by streetlight. Even walking downhill, Kathleen set a slow pace for the two.

Finally, they reached the bottom of the incline and the back road running between Taumata and Te Kauhanga. It was a quiet night. During their walk, they did not see a single vehicle, nor did they hear one from town.

Stanley commented on this. "Another Waitangi Day in Te Kauhanga. Do you and your family do anything special for it each year—or did you, when you were growing up?" he asked.

Kathleen stopped as if there was oncoming traffic. Stanley paused his watch.

"Not too much," she said, looking directly into his eyes, "but I do ring them—or chat with them each year. They live in Australia now."

Stanley, perplexed by the stoppage, said, "How long have they lived there?"

"Long enough," Kathleen said, then released his gaze and walked onto the road. Stanley restarted his watch and followed her, enjoying the view, and beginning to appreciate her odd conversation style.

They walked together, under the railway tracks, through the underground, and onto the main street. It was deserted as far as they could see. Shop lights dimly illuminated footpaths across the road. They turned towards the train station and their usual encounter point. As they reached the homeless man's bench—even that was unoccupied—Kathleen stopped again and said, "I want to check something in that window across the road. Coming?"

Stanley stopped his watch. "No, that's all right, I'll wait here for you."

Squinting and tilting her head, Kathleen smiled and walked across the road. Stanley watched her stand in front of the jeweller's window for several minutes before she turned and walked further, along her side of the road. He started his watch and walked parallel to her. Two shops along she stopped again, this time peering into the bakery. Stanley stopped himself and his watch.

After half a minute, Kathleen carried on, and so did Stanley, each repeating the process as they made their way along the main street—she stopping to look in a window, he stopping his watch and waiting. Each time, Kathleen reduced the amount of time she looked, until Stanley picked the game she was playing. He could see her reflection in the windows as she must be have been able to see his.

"I know what you're doing," he tried to laugh. "But this is supposed to be a walking date isn't it? Why don't you come back over here?"

"Why don't you come over here?" she answered still looking at his mirror image.

Stanley felt the tension's shadow again. "I prefer to run on this side," he said.

"But, Stanley ... we're not running," she said. "We're walking."

"It's ... it's the same thing to me really, but I prefer to be over here. I want to finish my loop."

"*Your* loop?" Kathleen turned to face him across the still-empty street. "I thought your loop was on the other side of Taumata. This is my loop." She didn't laugh, but Stanley could hear the mirth in her voice. He didn't like it. But God, she was beautiful.

Stanley thought about that. He thought about her beauty—her eyes, her cap, her bottom. Wasn't it worth it?

"Come back over, Kathleen. I'd really like to walk with you over here."

"If you'd really like to walk with me, come over here. There's another place I want to check out." With that, she turned and walked, ever so slowly, past the final shop on the block and disappeared around the corner towards Stanley's offices.

Stanley looked at the space she had occupied and missed her already. He considered his loop, his line from home and back to home again. He considered her allure, her whimsical, strange humour and light.

Stanley left the path and followed. It wasn't as if it was a complete deviation—he knew the streets well. It was, he realised, the handing of control over to her. Who knew where she might lead him next?

As he left the path with this in mind, he felt free. So free, in fact, that he ran to catch up to her. Not only did he run after her, but he ran into the freedom, zigzagging across the road, stopping and tap-dancing in the middle of the street before chasing her down outside his offices.

"You came," she said.

"I came," he said.

She reached out a hand to touch his arm and said, "Is this where you work?"

"Yes," he said.

"Is it good work?"

"It is for me."

Kathleen slid her hand down Stanley's arm, until she twined her fingers with his. "Let's walk back like this," she said.

Tingling, Stanley nodded, and the pair returned to the main street and carried on with their loop.

It didn't take five hours, but Stanley wouldn't have minded if it had. Despite the increasing rain, Kathleen led him on several more detours, each one less distressing and more filled with the excitement of the night. His legs no longer strained and complained. The tension still prodded him, but a squeeze of the red-capped woman's hand dealt it mortal blows until its shadow all but disappeared.

Still, the downpour forced them back. Walking out of town and towards Taumata, they approached the zigzag track. Kathleen spotted him first. She whispered, "There's a man ahead of us, just starting up the track."

Stanley could see him too—a large man, bearded, wearing a short-brimmed sun-hat and raincoat. He looked as one who carries the weight of the world on his shoulders. Even so, even in gumboots, his pace was crisper than the pair, and it surprised Stanley when Kathleen said, "Let's get closer to him and see where he's going."

In the spirit of the evening, how could Stanley refuse? Still holding hands, he set the pace, checking her expressions to ensure she was all right. She was. The track was sodden with the rainfall, allowing for quiet footfalls behind their quarry.

Emerging at the top of Taumata, they could not see him. The smell of damp sawdust filled the neighbourhood. With his new-found spirit of adventure, Stanley made the quick decision to turn left, away from his path home. It was the only way they would have seen the man, for, as soon as they navigated onto the footpath, they saw the figure enter through the front gate of the lighthouse. They could see him by streetlight, just as Stanley could see Kathleen's expression in the light above them.

She removed her red cap. Her mouth hung open and her eyes— her lovely eyes—turned lusty. From her lips, Stanley could hear the name, barely breathed.

"Perec."

⁜

"Fear," said Rico, petting a cat which had walked within his reach. "Fear is at the heart of all our problems, Sharon."

It was a new day in February, on the weekend after Valentine's Day, for those who recognised it. To Sharon, it was simply Sunday. Rico was back in the chair with another cup of tea. It was his third visit since Sharon first requested his help.

Sharon had attempted, once again, to clean up the space around his chair. She had gone so far as to shift several stacks of magazines and two boxes of books onto various other surfaces in the house. This created a space with only a bare coffee table between her and Rico.

"Fear is what drives us, even when we think we are motivated by something else," Rico continued. "Remember when I told you I choose to live the way I do?"

Sharon nodded. She had become a willing acolyte to Rico's talks.

"Our ability to choose is the only power we have over fear. Everything else we do is dictated by the fear inside us. Why did you clean this room?"

Sharon blushed. She was glad he noticed but embarrassed to have it pointed out. "I wanted to make a space for you ... so you would feel more comfortable."

"Thank you, Sharon, that's very kind," Rico said. "Do you think I feel more comfortable with space around me?"

"Well, it's just that you live outside, and it's a bit crowded in here."

Rico surveyed the room. "I'm not claustrophobic, Sharon. I was as comfortable during my first visit here as I am on my bench. I think it's more important to determine if *you* think it's crowded in here."

Sharon shook her head. "No ... well, not most times. Maybe when I'm in a hurry. I love my collection. I think I'm the opposite of claustrophobic. I love to come in here and be surrounded by my things. It's comforting."

Rico nodded. "That's interesting, Sharon. Most people don't see much difference between comforting and comfortable. Why do you need comfort? Is your job stressful?"

Sharon thought of Frances first, then the phone calls and the accounts, then jobs she had in the past—the library, Tom. "No," she said, "I've had worse."

"Tell me about the worse," Rico said.

Sharon crossed her legs on the chair under her and sighed. She had never spoken to anyone in Te Kauhanga about her previous job. "The worst was the best," she said. "It was a relationship that made it awful."

"What happened?"

"I worked at the Alexander Turnbull Library as an archivist—my dream job. I spent my days cataloguing and procuring and assisting university professors and lawyers in locating historical documents. I was in contact with some of the most significant artefacts in this country's history and with the people who created them: Marsden, Pompallier, Busby, Hobson—our founding fathers, really."

"So, you were in charge of storing old stuff?" Rico said.

"Not just old stuff—important treasures that help us understand where we come from and who we are as a nation."

"Of course," said Rico, seeing her defensiveness. "What happened then?"

Sharon eyed him, pausing her narrative. What could it hurt? "I had a relationship with our curator—my boss."

Rico nodded. "That complicated things?"

"It was wonderful at first. Tom was wonderful—so learned, so connected, such an amazing man. We would have dinners in the library itself. We both loved being there. It wasn't just a job for us. But," Sharon said, "I suppose it ended like it does for many golden couples—"

"Another woman?" Rico asked.

Sharon nodded, and her first tears in weeks crept down her cheeks. She stood and extracted a towel from behind a pile of newspapers. When she sat back down, she continued. "I was heart-broken. I knew I couldn't stay with him, but I loved that job so much. He was the bonus—he made everything richer and alive ... but I realised I didn't need him. I wish I'd never dated him. I could still be there ...."

"You're grieving, Sharon," Rico said, and her tears flowed faster. He leaned towards her and spoke softly. "You're grieving, but it's not for Tom is it?"

Sharon shook her head, wiping her eyes.

"You're grieving for the job," Rico said.

She wiped another tear and composed herself. "It wasn't a job—it was a calling." Her voice was shaking, angry. "Now look at me—answering phones in this shit-hole. I'm a bloody receptionist—taking messages for morons, entertaining mindless chatter and gossip for loose women who can't see life over the fucking hills, dating some local-yokel who thinks he's God's warrior against consumerism when all he does is limit his shopping to top-of-the-line products. I lived in the capital. I lived amongst the best of our country—past and present. Now I'm stuck in this town with a house no-one will buy because a tree's going to fall on it."

There was an awkward silence, broken suddenly by Sharon's laugh. "A tree's going to fall on my house! Just like the church!" She laughed again, hysterically at first, then she calmed down until she was sighing deeply in her chair. "So ... yes," she said to Rico, "yes, I find my house comforting. It's the closest thing I have to the archives."

Rico nodded. "Thank you, Sharon. I think I understand. You feel more alive here."

Sharon stopped wiping her face and thought about that. "I do," she said, "but ...."

"But we know that's not possible," Rico said, smiling.

"I don't know," Sharon said, shaking her head. "I don't know."

"Sharon, you said you need my help. What is it you want from me?"

Sharon sniffed. "I saw how free you were on the street that day. I saw what an ass Blake was. I guess I want to know how ... I want to know how to feel better."

"Feelings are ephemeral and deceiving things, Sharon. You feel more alive here, but that's not possible. You feel trapped, but I've told you that you have the power to set yourself free. It's fear that binds you Sharon, not feelings or circumstances." Rico laughed, "I can't do much about the tree—that's too big for the two of us—but I can show you how to break free from the fear of things bigger than us, things too wild for us, things too conventional for us. But I can't promise this will look like what you're hoping it will look like. Are you willing?"

Sharon said, "I'm willing."

"Good," Rico said. "Then let's start with all this stuff."

Cartography has advanced into many fields since the days of Ptolemy, Eratosthenes, and Mercator. No longer is it acceptable to fill in gaps with dragons or Biblical illustrations, and arguments still reign over the political motivations of map-makers who, with a choice of scale or symbol, emphasise the importance of one country, continent, race, or economic system and shape our perceptions of the world even from primary school days.

No, map-making, in its origins, was never solely about navigation—finding one place after leaving another and returning again. Which ocean should feature in the centre of the map? Why do we place the northern hemisphere at the top? Have you seen the size of Greenland lately? No, it is important to be scientific, with no other agenda than to present an image of the world as it really is.

And not only the world. Cartography is now responsible for mapping the human genome—whatever that is—and mammalian circulatory systems, even the workings of our minds, our very thoughts.

Montreal Perec did not consider himself a scientist. He was old school and believed interpretation and intuition were valid elements in map-making. But he did think about the mapping of his own mind. Far from a narcissistic exercise, Perec simply viewed this as another cartographical challenge. To map the internal workings of his mind was an extension of mapping the internal workings of his house. It was another result of looking closer.

And what did he see? Symbols, of course. Symbols for synapses, firing and lying dormant—awaiting their next missions, their next message to transport across the brain waves of his mind from one point to another. Symbols for categories of thought and feelings, colours and shapes to indicate ideas or memories, sadness or frustration. He saw frustration as a synaptic symbol, alight and ready to fire, but held back either by a force from behind or an obstruction in front. He saw this symbol appear in his mind more and more following Waitangi Day.

Some thoughts launched across the surface of his mind. Some were lost to the deeper recesses—sunken vessels never to be heard from again, unless raised by a team of thoughts who recognised their merit and re-joined them to the fleet. Some thoughts circumnavigated his mind, docking at other ports before reappearing at their origin, usually in the frontal lobes, to re-present themselves to Perec's consciousness with new findings, new treasures, like explorers returning to their king.

And when Perec mapped his mind in this way, he reaffirmed his stance that intuition and interpretation were as much a part of cartography as in the Arts, for that was how he saw his craft—a glorious enterprise bridging the worlds of art and science. And in this world, as in his mind, Perec saw the leaps, the conjectures, the gap-filling that were necessary, that were inherent in the activity. In his mind, he saw his symbols disappear and reappear from their paths, with no explanation for where they had strayed in the meantime. Like appearing and disappearing electrons, they existed and did not exist at the same time. Like light, they behaved as waves and particles as the need demanded, as the measurement prescribed. The landscape of the mind did not always follow the rules of reason, so why would we expect the landscape of our world, our neighbourhoods, our domiciles to behave any differently? As soon as a map maker completes his work, the landscape changes, and the map is inaccurate. Could it ever have been accurate in the first place?

And so, Perec was used to frustration. In fact, after so many years of patient map making, of drawing and re-drawing maps of places that fluctuate in their nature and impression, Perec hardly knew what frustration was—he was that patient, that understanding of these matters.

But in mid-February, he was frustrated. He could feel it, and he could see it.

His trip to the river, once he had made his break from the house, had gone as expected. He had descended into town undetected and walked his streets, enjoying the proximity to the sources of his symbols. He had waded in the river, in the water that would travel to the mouth, the origin of Tupaia's and Cook's journey inland. He had exited the river, pausing to allow the moment to speak to him, to allow his intuition to reveal the next step for him. And, as expected, as he was used to, he had received nothing. He had ascended the hill to Taumata as normal, albeit in the rain. He had gone to bed, satisfied he had completed his ritual, satisfied he had played his part, but unsatisfied ... and frustrated.

The next morning the frustration began its full-scale assault. Slowly at first, Perec sensed it forming on the horizon of his mind. Over the day, the fleet grew to an armada, and Perec realised he must attend to it. He remained offline and endeavoured to complete an extensive mind-map, marshalling his resources to root out the source of the threat. He worked in silence. To see him sitting in the upper room of his lighthouse day after day, hour after hour, you would believe he was in a state of deep spiritual mediation.

Thirty years. On his sixth day, Perec uncovered the phrase, buried, not like a treasure in a hole, but like a layer of magma underlying the surface of his mind. The phrase moved like the mantle of the earth, at times like a stable layer, at times like a molten boil, striving for the surface where pressure would be relieved.

Thirty years. This was the source of the frustration. For in that boiling mass, Perec saw other symbols, like flotsam and jetsam, buoyed by the molten waves but with no direction, no purpose. He saw symbols for family—for his parents and cousins he had long-neglected; he saw symbols for pleasures he had denied in his life—the love of a woman, friendships, and horse riding; he saw symbols bottlenecked from years of obsession—oak trees, coconut fibres, the money pit; he saw symbols of his homeland—lobster traps, bagpipes, beaches, docks and lighthouses.

He watched these symbols, these buried treasures, toss and turn in the thirty years. He felt them there in his mind—bound and buried, disconnected—and he felt the frustration. On the surface, the armada swarmed him, overwhelmed him in the thousands. There could be no resistance and no acquiescence. As the fleet fell on him, the surface burst and thirty years of symbols flooded Perec's mind.

The silence was broken in Perec's house. The frustration turned to anger as magma turns to lava upon the breach, and Perec had no defence. He raged in his upper room, smashing his chair over his desk, scattering large sheets of parchment on the floor. He tore curtains and sheers from the windows. He flung open a filing cabinet and tossed files upon files around the place, ripping at some, cursing them for unknown sins.

He stormed down his stairs, knocking framed maps from his walls, leaving a trail of broken glass in his wake. He kicked at the walls as he descended, broadening holes where he had pried back the scrim for views of pipes and wires.

His rage had no focus, no direction. He wandered from room to room, indiscriminately tossing, kicking, pushing or smashing, until the thirty years abated, until the armada relented and returned whence it came.

Thirty years, he thought, once he could form thoughts again. *Thirty years* was his only thought for some time as he settled onto his sofa, still unaware of the carnage surrounding him from his rampage. Perhaps out of habit, perhaps because he thought he was still mind-mapping, Perec returned to his examination and barely recognised what he saw. Thirty years covered his mindscape like a flood, blocking the pathways and ports common to his mental survey. The symbols floated as debris, mixed with his usual thoughts and feelings, past and present, this life and the life he might have had all jumbled in one mess of symbols.

But the flood was receding. Perec was aware of the thirty years seeping below the surface, taking symbols back with it, from both the past and the present. He watched, curious, as an objective observer. What would remain? What would he find left after the devastation?

Perec watched as thirty years swirled back down at various points. Symbols for lobster and love of a woman vanished alongside some neighbours in Taumata and maps of Te Kauhanga. Gone were the hills surrounding him and memories of his voyage to New Zealand. As the thirty years receded, Perec began to see symbols that had survived the onslaught like trees or buildings that had survived a tsunami. He saw other neighbours, the tree, his laptop, and many symbols from the legends he had created over the years. He saw the river, and his office, and symbols for his pipes and wiring. He saw the symbol for the treasure of his ancestors. Relieved, Perec began to think more clearly. He was OK. It was not all for naught.

Still, he watched as the last of the loose symbols swirled around their vents, until his attention was drawn to the sound of an obstruction. Stuck over its vent, refusing to be swept away by the thirty years, was the symbol for the lighthouse.

PART 4D

AUTUMN

TWELVE

Autumn has less to do with falling leaves in the North Island of New Zealand than it does in Nova Scotia. That's why it is rarely referred to as *Fall*. Instead, temperatures moderate rather than fluctuate—varied but not extreme.

And so, the poets here are more restricted in their use of cyclical metaphors than their Northern Hemisphere cousins. Death seems less dramatic and, while as prevalent as anywhere else, more surreptitious and stealthy.

Leaves do turn and leaves do fall, and the bush and farms quiet for a time of waiting and yearning, but, like bark concealing its rings, the surface plane shows little of its inner dimension.

"Where have you been?"

The question was the first thing Perec saw when he signed into his WiCharts account. BloodyLegend180 must have seen his name appear when he logged on.

"I've been here," Perec wrote back. "Offline."

"Everything all right?"

"Never better," Perec wrote, and he meant it. "I know what I need

175

now—very close."

"Tell me more."

Perec typed. He told BloodyLegend about his trip to the river. He told him about his frustration and his mind-mapping. He told him about the symbols and the lighthouse. He left nothing out.

"What sort of lighthouse was it?" BloodyLegend asked when he'd finished.

"A Nova Scotian lighthouse."

"What could that have to do with anything?"

"I live in a lighthouse—though a different kind."

"I'm not following you."

Perec typed, "It's a sign. I'm in the right spot after all. Somehow, my living in this house has something to do with finding what I came for."

There was a long pause and Perec waited. Finally, he received his response. "Seems far-fetched."

He typed back, "Yes, but it's the most significant sign I've had since you went to Pureora. Somehow, you're part of it. The spirals are part of it. This house is part of it." He paused, then added, "Lots of parts."

"Speaking of Pureora, I still say it makes more sense for you to go there."

Perec sighed. *Sense*, he thought. *What does that mean? Reason? Intuition? Sight? Insight?* "I'm close," he wrote, "I just need a key."

"What sort of key? A map key or a door key?"

"I don't know—anything that will unlock it all. Do you have anything for me?"

Another long pause, then, "Just Pureora, but never mind. No, nothing new. Nothing to do with lighthouses." Perec didn't respond right away. The next message came as an addition. "You sound as if you're being guided."

Perec had thought of this. How could he be guided? He didn't believe in any kind of god or universal force that might help him. But he couldn't help but feel a destiny of some sort, as if he was intended to find something. He'd always felt this way—as if he'd been put on earth to fill in the blank spaces of some map, to find some answer, to uncover some treasure. It had been a driving force rather than a calling, a force so strong it moved him to leave his family and homeland for this part of the world, this house. How could he explain this to his companion on this leg of the expedition?

"Something like that, maybe," he wrote. "Don't worry—nothing spooky."

With no new revelations to share and with an agreement to stay in contact should anything present itself, the two cartographers logged off, and Perec went about his new business between searches: restoring his damaged home.

He pushed in his chair and walked up his flights of stairs to the lighthouse room. He had re-filed his papers first, in the hopes that a key might reveal itself there—some old document that he would recognise in a new light. He found nothing, but his time in the room had been well spent. He would soon be ready to map this room as he had his study. At the same time, with the lighthouse symbol in mind, Perec had taken to long bouts of surveying his surroundings via the windows which offered him a panoramic, 360 degree view. Perhaps, he surmised, the key was to be found from his vista, the highest point in the area.

And so, he looked closer—closer than he had done when mapping from this room. In between ponderings, he cleaned his mess and worked on restoring the damaged walls, still bruised and in want of stitching after his kicking and throwing.

This day, he worked on the wall to the left of his desk. A wayward stapler had punched a hole in the scrim. Unlike his map-making, when it came to home repairs, he was much better at opening holes than closing them. He picked up the bits of scrim from the floor, determining their uselessness before discarding them. He would need to find someone with some spare material—builders didn't supply scrim anymore, everyone preferring gib. Perec adjusted the blade on his utility knife and drew fine lines in the scrim around the hole. At least he could tidy and prepare it for future repair. Once he had cut deeply enough, creating a uniform square grid around the hole, he gently pried the perimeter scraps off.

It was the smell that caused him to look closer—an earthy, organic smell emitting from the square hole. Perec leaned into the wall, putting his nose inside. The smell was definitely stronger, and nothing like scrim—though that smell was mixed with it—and nothing like paint or any other building material you would expect. He looked down the hole but could see only so far for the size of it and the amount of light it allowed. He would need a torch and a bigger opening.

It seemed a minor thing to Perec, but his curiosity had always been a rewarding master. He retrieved a torch from downstairs and returned with his larger utility knife.

The smell had filled the room in his absence. It seemed more recognisable now—no longer a dank, trapped smell, but a fragrance that had been set free to send its signals into the world like sonar pulses. It seemed less threatening, more inviting.

Perec tried to see more with the torch alone, but the hole's size was awkward. With his new knife, he enlarged it by cutting down almost to the floor, leaving enough room to maintain the scrim's integrity and allow for a patch to be applied later. He pulled the excess away and poured his torch light in.

At the end of the light's reach, below the floor and out of arm's length, Perec conjectured, was an object of some sort. It seemed to centre the space between the internal wall and the scrim of the room below him. If need be, Perec thought, he could cut a hole in that room as well, but far better if he could reach it from the entry point he had created.

He reached in with his arm, elongating himself on the floor under his desk, his feet scraping the wall opposite. He couldn't reach it, but the smell grew stronger in his nostrils. Curiosity led him to cut the hole that much further, all the way to the floor board, giving him another few centimetres. He tried the torch again. Was the object moving in the light? Like a black hole, Perec could not see the object as much as he could see there was something different in the centre of all that blackness.

He lay prone again and stretched his arm to its fullest extreme. He could feel it. It felt like the end of something—something longer and attached to something larger. It felt rough to the touch except for a soft cluster at the end which Perec could just wrap his hand around. It broke off in his palm.

Perec, not wanting to lose his capture, released the rougher extension and withdrew his hand. In the light of the windows, he sat against the wall and opened his fingers.

He held a leaf.

"Why do you walk so slowly?" Stanley asked. He and Kathleen were embarking on their fourth walking date since their hand-holding night. In between, Stanley had continued with his running routine. He had worked out a plan whereby his walks with Kathleen would replace some of the easier long runs in his schedule. He still stopped and started his watch with their feet.

"Is it bothering you?" asked Kathleen as they meandered left around the corner of Tonga and Hauāuru, this time taking Stanley's loop behind Taumata Hill.

Stanley smiled, and he meant it. "No, it doesn't," he said. "I pretend we're holding hands and it helps me slow down beside you. It's nice. I told you I needed to slow down." As he spoke, he took her hand in his and held it as they walked. She accepted it.

"I just wonder why you do it. Don't you ever run or power walk? You know, to get fit or to train for something?"

"No," she said.

He had grown used to her curtness as well.

"I mean ... don't you think you are limiting yourself? Wouldn't you like to push yourself?"

Kathleen stopped. So did Stanley's watch. "I find it funny to hear you talking about me limiting myself, Stanley."

"What do you mean?"

"Don't you think you have your own inhibitions?" she asked, nodding towards the watch.

Stanley started to defend himself but paused long enough for the better thought to present itself. "Fair enough," he said. He removed his watch and put it in his jacket pocket.

"Happy?" he said, and the pair walked on.

It was a cool evening with a fresh southerly breeze. After several minutes they reached the bottom of the hill and their entrance to the 5K loop. They walked in silence, listening to the early autumn whistles of birds. Thirty minutes passed at their pace. Stanley absorbed the grey-blue sky beneath the clouds. He paused the two himself, stopping to pet a horse who greeted them by the bridge and stream. He noticed the cracks in the footpath and the scars on telephone poles from errant cyclists or long-removed garage sale posters. When they reached the edge of the golf course, he said to Kathleen, "You still haven't answered my question."

"Haven't I?" she said, cryptically.

"No, you haven't," said Stanley.

"Why do I walk so slowly?" Kathleen enunciated. "I walk slowly because I don't want to miss anything. Look."

They stopped to watch a flock of starlings swarming above a large pine tree. Stanley had seen this flock on previous runs, hovering over this area. Tonight, just as the birds converged on the tree, they diverted their course and flew several hundred metres away, over the small valley, only to return again en masse, swaying and swinging until they hovered above the tree again. They repeated this pattern several times as Stanley and Kathleen watched until, finally, the entire group descended on the tree and remained hidden in its branches, presumably resorting for the night.

"I've never seen that before," Stanley breathed.

"Exactly," said Kathleen. "Let's walk some more, and you can tell me what else you see."

Around the golf course they trekked, hand-in-hand except when they pointed out sights or sounds to one another as if playing a slow-paced game of *I Spy*. Stanley would nominate objects or sounds and Kathleen would encourage him and elucidate: "I don't like to miss things, Stanley. There's so much around us all the time. Some people are only focused on getting from Point A to Point B, or climbing to the next level. But we live in a wide-open space, Stanley—three dimensions. All around us is a circle—everywhere you go. You are the centre and everything else is on the circumference or in the area in between. What about Point C? What about Point Z? What about Point Infinity? When you get to a new plateau, do you stop and enjoy everything that is there? Or do you climb on?"

She spoke slowly, of course, interrupting herself whenever he or she paused to admire a new view, until they came to the house of Kiri's friend. Stanley stopped and looked long over the golf course.

"What do you see, Stanley?" Kathleen asked.

"I see a tree," he said. It was the tree Kiri had hidden behind.

"Do you want to take a closer look?" Kathleen asked.

"I do."

He took her by the hand and led her to the fence separating the road from the golf course, and the pair climbed over. They walked as they had done, but without speaking. While Kathleen absorbed her surroundings, Stanley fixed his position on the tree. There were no golfers playing. The tree was next to a putting green. Stanley let go of

Kathleen's hand and reached out to touch the bark. It didn't matter to him what sort of tree it was, or how the bark felt, although he did feel it on his palm in a way he had never felt tree bark before. He stepped around the other side of it to where Kiri had been hiding, where he had been afraid to go—or too truculent to go.

Kathleen, unsure of what he was feeling, placed her hand on his shoulder and felt him shudder. He did not cry or explain himself. Instead, after a few moments, he turned to Kathleen with a broad smile and said, "Let's dance."

He took her by the hand and placed his other hand at her waist, and the pair danced around the putting green of the sixteenth hole of Te Kauhanga's Tautaungara golf course, creating circles and triangles and even spirals—sometimes making no pattern at all.

Sharon and Rico were progressing. For the second time during the year, Sharon set aside a weekend to clean her house, to normalise her life—only this time she had a new philosophy and a new coach in Rico.

"Attachment is an enemy as well. It breeds fear—the fear of losing things, whether it's losing books, magazines, collections, or whether it's people, buildings, churches, pot plants." It was a repeated message, a broken record. Rico had warned her he would do this, and she had given him permission to revisit the precepts upon which they agreed: they were going to remove objects which formed unhealthy attachments in Sharon's life.

Rico held up another magazine for Sharon's decision. "Toss it," she said without hesitation.

"Excellent," Rico said. This had been their routine, established in the morning and carried through after lunch. Bags were filling with torn, soiled magazines and newspapers. Boxes surrounded Rico as he sat on the floor, awaiting Sharon's verdicts, sentencing some books to rubbish, others to charity, others to be kept.

"Let's move onto some more books," he said, standing and shovelling boxes closer to a shelf near the doorway of, what was again becoming, Sharon's bedroom. "What about this one?" He withdrew a large copy of *The Riverside Shakespeare* from the top of the unit.

"Keep," Sharon said. "It was my grandmother's." Rico replaced it without argument.

"Next?" He showed her a collection of New Zealand short stories.

Sharon thought for a moment. "Charity—I have most of those in other volumes."

"Very good," Rico said, placing it in a box. "You're making choices like a normal person." Sharon laughed. "And this?" He held up a copy of *Ancient Celtic New Zealand*.

"Keep," she said quickly.

"Really?" Rico said. "Tell me about this book." This was another part of their pattern and his method. He watched for signs of attachment, particularly to unusual things, and to her demeanour when presented with them.

"On the inside, you'll see it was a gift from a friend."

Rico opened the book and read aloud, "*For my dearest Sharon, an invigorating and controversial read. Love, Tom.*" Rico studied Sharon's response to the words. "So," he said," this is *the* Tom?"

"Yes," Sharon said. "It's not a very good book really, too informal in its research method and filled with conjecture. But I don't dispose of books that were given to me as gifts."

"Why not?" Rico challenged. This wasn't the first time Sharon had thrown down a non-negotiable.

"Because it's like throwing out a part of them—a memory of their part in my life."

"The same can be said for practically every object we own Sharon. Remember, it's the healthy attachments we want to maintain, not the ones we're afraid to lose."

"I'm not afraid to lose Tom anymore, but I want to keep that memory," she said.

"So you're afraid to lose the memory?"

Sharon hesitated, looking for a better answer, one that would validate her position. "Yes," she conceded.

"Sharon," Rico's voice changed, dropping in register in a way Sharon now recognised as consoling yet compelling. "Sharon, you've shared with me that you have an unhealthy connection to this man. You can free yourself from that right now with this simple step. You will not lose your memory any more than one loses contact with God without a church. I've seen very little attachment to Tom in this time I've spent with you—you can do this."

Sharon nodded. She could do this. "Bag it," she said, and laughed. "It really is rubbish anyway." Rico smiled and complied, tossing it in a bag.

"How do you feel?" he asked.

She breathed and motioned to the bookshelf. "Let's keep going."

Several more volumes were quickly processed, including more from the infamous Tom, until Rico emptied the shelf to reveal a mound of disgusting rubbish hitherto hidden behind the unit. Shovelling the putrid mound into the bag, he uncovered one further large volume. It was *The Book of Hours*.

"This is a curious one," he said. "It looks like it should be in a museum."

Sharon bristled. "Keep that one."

"Tell me about this book," Rico prodded.

She frowned. "Keep it."

"Tell me about it first, Sharon," Rico said. He began leafing through the vellum pages. Sharon remained silent, watching him until he found the picture. "Here we go," he said. "Is this Tom?"

"Yes," she said. "Put it back and we'll carry on, eh?"

"Is this actually your book, Sharon? How did you get ahold of this?"

"It's mine. It was a gift."

"Another gift from Tom?"

She nodded.

"Sharon, I realise this one is probably pretty special to people in the book collecting world, but remember what we are trying to do here. Look, let's try this. What happens when I separate the picture from the book? Here, you can have the picture." He handed it to her.

"Now, think about the picture and the book as two different things. What shall we do with this book, now that it has nothing to do with Tom?"

Sharon looked at the picture in her hands and kept her head down. "Keep it," she said. Her voice was tense—unrelenting.

Rico considered moving on. He had done so at other sticky moments, but he sensed something deeper going on, an attachment they hadn't identified yet.

"OK, how about this? Let's get rid of the picture of Tom instead?"

Sharon continued looking at the photograph which shook in her hand. She nodded. "OK," she said, and handed it back to Rico.

Rico looked at Sharon's posture, her shaking hand and her quivering lip, exposed just below her tilted hairline. He took the photo and held it ceremoniously above the rubbish bag, waiting for a last minute reprieve, a protest to arrest his fingers and save Tom. There was none and he dropped it in the bag.

Sharon's shoulders eased and, with them, the atmosphere in the room eased.

"Good, Sharon," Rico said. "Now, about this book—"

Sharon's head whipped up. "You said I could choose between the picture and the book!" Her voice was child-like.

"I don't think this book belongs here, Sharon. It should probably be in a museum or maybe back at the archives you used to work at."

"It's mine!" she cried. This was a new voice from her. "It's mine! It belongs with me!"

"Sharon," Rico said, keeping his voice calm and level, "you have to let things of Tom go."

"It's got nothing to do with Tom." Sharon stood. Her voice was quieter now, but more threatening. "I just showed you that. Give it to me. Give it to me or get out."

"If I give it to you, can we still talk about it?" Rico asked.

"Give it to me!" she yelled. Her face contorted and she held her hand out. It was no longer shaking.

Rico placed the book in her hand and she sat in the chair with it on her lap, covering it with both arms. Rico would not let the issue go—there was no point in him continuing after losing a battle like that. He stood, prepared to leave, when Sharon spoke.

"This is from my job," she said. She looked at him and then at the book. Her voice was monotone. "My wonderful job. I was surrounded by books like this, books that few had access to, and those who did accessed them through me. I was their guardian and their gatekeeper—and I was good at it. I can look after this book."

Rico returned to his position on the floor next to the bookshelf. "I'm sure you can, Sharon. Tell me more about the book."

"It was one that Tom first shared with me, but it has nothing to do with Tom anymore. I understand what you are trying to show me. I'm not afraid of losing Tom anymore or memories of him. But I loved that job."

Rico nodded. "Grief, Sharon."

Sharon wiped her eyes with her sleeve, keeping her other arm planted on the book in her lap. "Thank you, Rico. Yes, that's what it feels like."

Rico was close now, both physically and to the matter. "It makes sense, Sharon. You didn't just lose an income, you lost status and position."

Sharon nodded. "I did."

"Those are attachments, Sharon." She tensed again at the words, pinning the book to her legs and glaring at him with one eye through her fallen hair.

"I need to say it, Sharon. It's why I'm here—to set you free from fear. You're afraid of losing the status and all the benefits inherent in your former job. That's why your clean-up with Blake didn't work. He wanted you to clean up to improve your status, but that's backwards. Letting go of attachments to such things is the only way to overcome fear and then live the life you want. I don't care if you live in a mess, if that's want you want. But the stuff is controlling you. This book is representative of your attachment to something you no longer have but are afraid to release."

As he spoke, Sharon's shoulders eased, her breathing slowed, but her grip on the book held fast. She raised her head to look into her mentor's eyes only a couple of metres away, kneeling in front of her, and said, "I'm not ready yet."

Rico leaned back with his elbows on the floor supporting him and sighed. "OK, Sharon. What do you want to do then? Are you willing to keep going?"

Sharon nodded and smiled. "Yes, I am Rico—and thank you"

Rico stood and surveyed the assortment around him. "We have almost enough for a skip here. Are you OK with that?"

Sharon laughed. "I am," she said," I actually am."

"Well, sometimes you have to look at the battles you've won, not the ones you've lost." Rico pulled a box from behind his chair. He reached in and extracted a *New Zealand Listener* magazine from 1974. 'What about this one?" he asked.

"Toss it!" Sharon squealed and rocked in her seat, clutching *The Book of Hours* like a doll.

They continued in this way for the rest of the day and for all of Sunday. In fact, Sunday seemed more like a party than work. They played music throughout the day, and the atmosphere was rife with delight and freedom.

Rico played along as best he could. There were very few challenges and no more scenes made over documents or artefacts like *The Book of Hours*. He had seen to that. For, whenever he spotted a dubious object, one that looked as if it belonged in a museum, he would set it aside and wait for Sharon to make a cup of tea or use the toilet. Into the rubbish bag was tossed a compendium of treasures—letters signed by famous New Zealand military figures, original novel manuscripts by Shadbolt, poems by Baxter, church documents bearing the seal of Bishop Pompallier, and one very old, soiled map of the North Island which looked, by today's standards, as if a child had drawn it or as if it had been copied from the deck of an early explorer's ship.

By the end of the weekend, the skip they had arranged was full to the top and a phone call had been made for a truck to swing by the next night to collect the small mountain of boxes to be taken to the town library and to the local St. John book sale.

Exhausted, Sharon and Rico toasted their work with a glass of wine and, for the first time since he arrived in Te Kauhanga, Rico slept with a roof over his head.

It was about time he replaced all that old scrim with gib anyway, Perec reasoned. He stood, surrounded by masses of the stuff he had torn from his study wall, below his lighthouse room. The smell of the tree now filled the room and Perec was able to see what he felt in the darkness from above.

A tree branch was growing inside his wall, and at the tips it bore leaves—faded green leaves with tinges of brown, but leaves that were certainly alive, soft to the touch and moist despite their lack of sunshine. The branch stood tall in front of him between the wall struts, wider at its base which Perec had yet to uncover as it disappeared into the black space behind the wall of the room below. He would need to delve deeper.

—————::::::

"I'm thinking of adding an extension to my house," announced

Stanley as he and Kathleen walked past Robinson Builders on Stuart Street, two blocks behind Te Kauhanga's main drag. The couple had finished a lovely walk through the town's central domain. It was a Saturday morning in late March and the rugby and netball season had kicked off. Neither Kathleen or Stanley were fans of sport, but they circled the area to engage in a smattering of community spirit. They had decided to call their jaunt a day and return via the incline.

"Won't that upset some symmetry in your place?" Kathleen asked. She had visited his home several times.

"I think I'm ready for it." He eyed Kathleen sideways. "I really do!" He laughed, noting her raised eyebrows.

"All right," she said. "Way you go."

It was a beautiful day, a calm day, a day for sunglasses and long pants, shaded caps and covered shoes.

"What do you see?" Kathleen asked as they turned off the main street to cut across the green, gardened area in front of the entrance to the underground. They had enhanced their game, adding an element of playful competition.

"I see red leaves," Stanley replied, "green only two days ago, on the magnolia by the memorial. What do you see, Kathleen?"

"I see an empty park bench, empty again for the third sighting this week."

Stanley murmured his approval. "I see what you did there—seeing something that's not there when normally there is."

"This isn't my first rodeo, son."

They continued on in relative silence with an estimated time of arrival at Kathleen's house of twenty minutes. They enjoyed the feel of the soft grass beneath their feet, compensating their footfalls for the more arduous demands of the asphalt on the neighbouring footpaths and streets. A slight breeze was blowing, cooling skin that was still sometimes scorched by the autumn sun in the ozone-depleted sky. The two did not hold hands as often, but they regularly rubbed shoulders or brushed arms against the other's shifting hips. Stanley was enjoying the growing intimacy—no pragmatic rush for contact and explorations. Instead, each new part of her was experienced surprisingly and inadvertently, without plan, without intention, but with welcome reception.

They walked. To describe the details of such sauntering would be to extend a patient narrative and take advantage of a reader's good faith. So it is with stories, as it is with any journey, that the highlights of such a chase must be cut to.

It was Stanley who saw the map. He didn't know it was a map, of course. He saw the corner of a larger body of paper barely visible between leaves and long grass. Later, he would tease Kathleen for not noticing it: "It's no longer my first rodeo either ... it might be time to hang up your spurs."

Her only defence was to claim that it was too close to her house, that, just as a prophet is not received in his hometown, just as most vehicular accidents occur closer to home, she did not notice because she was overly used to the views around and in front of her home, even in in her own yard. In her own space, she glanced over the ordinary.

He would scoff at this rationalisation and claim that she had simply grown complacent and that his vigilance was the key, but he would admit that she had taught him everything he knew about smelling out fine roses such as this map.

And they both knew it was a find all right. After Stanley extracted it from the branches of the hydrangea bush, they took it inside. Laying it out on her table, they examined it.

"This is no ordinary paper, Kathleen. It's thick—and look at the corners—they're frayed, not ripped, as if it's been through a few wars."

"It is a map though, isn't it?" she asked. "It looks like the North Island, at least near the top. The bottom is flat, like it's been chopped off."

"And there's no sign of Lake Taupo," Stanley added. "See there? That's Taranaki Bight, so Taupo should be about here." He drew a line with his finger from the western coast to the bottom centre of the island.

"Be careful," Kathleen said. "We don't want to wreck it by touching it too much. It looks fragile."

"Well, it survived a trip into your hydrangea. How do you think it got there?"

"Who knows?" she said. "It must have blown in there somehow— no-one would have placed it there, surely. Maybe it flew out of someone's window when they were driving by? Although I couldn't imagine someone being so careless with this."

They persevered, commenting on every detail they could spy,

continuing their sport of trying to notice something the other hadn't. Kathleen logged onto her laptop to compare with digital maps of New Zealand online. They matched significant shapes and the limited amount of water features included on the parchment.

"Maybe this is a copy of a famous map or something. Run a search on it, Kathleen."

Kathleen typed in the keywords, *old New Zealand map,* and the couple scrolled through the image results, finding no matches. She narrowed the search by adding, *north island.* The two gasped together as soon as the next batch of results were revealed.

"Is it the same?" Stanley asked, leaning over, and sometimes on, her shoulder.

"I think so. If it's not, it's uncannily similar. Maybe one is a hand-drawn copy of the other."

The two stared back and forth between the screen and the map laid out on the table beside the laptop. They mentally scanned around the perimeter looking for any variations, any deviations, sharing their thoughts in hushed but excited tones.

"I don't think they're exactly the same. What is the map on the screen, Kathleen?" Stanley was squatting beside her, his head leaning against her shoulder. He could feel her breath on his cheek.

Kathleen clicked from the image to the accompanying web-page. "Tuki's map," she read. The two read further in silence. They read about Tuki and his companion, Huru; they read about Lieutenant Philip Gidley King and Norfolk Island and Lieutenant Hanson, the commander of the *Daedalus*—and they read about the map Tuki had drawn for King.

"Stanley," Kathleen said when they'd finished reading, "if this is Tuki's map, or a copy of it, then it should be in a museum or in the national archives or something. How did it get here?"

Stanley stood and brushed one corner of the map. It was fragile, he thought. He carefully folded it back on itself. Kathleen inhaled as he did so. "I'm just checking the back," he said, "for any markings, maybe an indication of where it came from."

He laid the map out again, this time face-down. The two studied it in their ponderous way, but found nothing.

"OK," Stanley said, "we'll have to take it to someone—but who? The town library? The police? The council?"

Kathleen's eyes widened as he listed possibilities. "No, none of those," she said. "I know exactly who to take it to."

Sharon felt lighter.

She had felt lighter since she and Rico farewelled the skip from her property, watching the less valuable items in her collection shimmy and shake away, out of Taumata and out of her life. They had delivered boxes of saleable items to St John's, and she had gifted others to the town library. In exchange for his loving-kindness and guidance, she had invited Rico to move in.

It was temporary, of course. She had insisted, incapable of imagining sending him back to his bench after all he had done for her. He had relented with little protest, happy enough to recover himself in a dry environment and welcomed her hot shower and the daily meals she prepared when she returned from work.

In her dreaming, in her fantasies, she had always pictured herself dramatically changed at the council if she could only clean up her situation. She had imagined higher self-esteem, a firmer handle on Frances, a bold outpouring of fortitude in which she would give her co-worker a right telling off if she tried bullying her or embarrassing her again.

But these things did not eventuate. Frances knew something was amiss, Sharon was certain. However, the best way Sharon could describe it to herself, and to Rico, was to say that Frances' manoeuvers seemed much smaller and insignificant than they had only a week prior.

On the Monday, during morning tea and after Sharon had arrived, late, having launched the skip and delivered her other goods, Frances made not-so-subtle innuendos about Sharon's weekend and its possible effects on her tardiness, force-fitting it into other conversation topics.

"You know, I don't think it's right that we have such boring weekends and Sharon has all the fun." They had been talking about Manu's children and their results at a swimming carnival on the Saturday. Sharon pretended not to have noticed the comment as she was rummaging in the staffroom cupboard for sweeter biscuits.

Manu ignored it too, or didn't realise the topic had shifted from her children. "Elizabeth's coach said she has never seen a pupil improve so much in such a short amount of time. I'm not saying she's bound for the Olympics, but I am just so proud of her."

Sharon re-joined her co-workers at the table, pushing the newly opened biscuits to the centre. "How did Hori go?" she asked. Normally, she would ask this type of question to keep the conversation going and away from Frances' agendas, but this day she felt a genuine interest in Manu's life, more open to listening, as if her head was also uncluttered.

After Manu provided an update on her son, Frances took the opportunity to blatantly switch topics. "What did you get up to this weekend, Sharon? Your neighbour—what's her name again? The one who works at the supermarket? She told me you had a visitor—a man."

Again, a week before, Sharon would have felt all sorts of anxieties about Frances' questioning. She had pre-meditated about this, however, and decided ahead of time that she would not answer. She had deliberated with herself about it. She felt no fear, but pondered if it would it be better to show this fearlessness to Frances by proudly, or at least directly, proclaiming the identity of her guest and his role; or by retaining the information, and not feeding Frances' need to own that part of her.

So ... Sharon simply smiled and said nothing.

It was an extraordinarily awkward moment for all three present, lasting far longer than Sharon intended, but, then again, how long had she intended? She really didn't know what would happen. But she felt no fear at all in that moment and quite happily waited until Frances caved first.

"Okaaay Sharon ... well, that was a strange way to respond, wasn't it?" Her tone was condescending, mocking. "I guess we can take silence as affirmation, can't we?" She winked at Manu in an attempt to paint herself as the victor.

As the week waned, Frances grew more uncomfortable with the changes in Sharon. There were moments of tension in which she would slip in snide remarks about keeping secrets or diminishing staff morale. There were moments of ignorance in which Frances would pretend Sharon didn't exist, sometimes only addressing Manu or Candice in conversation or proceeding with a topic as if Sharon had not added anything at all. There were moments of sheer rage in which Frances snapped at Sharon, only to follow it up with a joke, veiling the intensity of her comments. At no point was Sharon afraid and she revelled in this during her debriefs with Rico in the evenings.

Of course, this newfound courage was to be challenged to breaking point, as is often the case.

It was on the Friday of that same week. The council had been meeting in their chambers for the afternoon. With councillors occupied and Frances in attendance at the meeting as minute secretary, Sharon had the opportunity to tidy loose ends while Manu handled any stray citizens who visited the front desk. Tonight would mark one week with Rico in the house, a week she had continued to enjoy and learn from and one she would try to extend that evening with her famous corn chowder—an attempt to persuade him to stay with her longer.

When the doors from the corridor leading from the chambers swung open, and she saw Frances walking out with Blake, Sharon knew she would need to endure one more push from her nemesis before going home. Frances' face was positively alight. Sharon knew the look well. It was the look Frances wore when she had garnered some inside knowledge, the type that solidifies a relationship and a network and one that excludes others alien to these.

As they walked closer to the desk womanned by Manu, Frances spoke to Blake in secretive tones deliberately broadcast loud enough for Sharon to hear. "I loved the way you stood your ground in there," she said, touching his arm. "That's why I really respect you as the mayor's aide. The people of Te Kauhanga don't know how lucky they are to have you working for them." Sharon resisted the urge to make eyes at Manu. She wouldn't get it anyway, and Sharon was no longer feeling threatened by Frances' tactics. Still, she listened, aware they were leading to something.

Blake, bowing his head to the flattery, simply thanked her, then allowed her space to carry on in the same vein.

"You know," Frances continued, "What's really a shame is that more people don't come along to council meetings to find out what you guys really do for them. They are public forums after all. Hey, you guys," she addressed Sharon and Manu, "you should have seen Mayoral Aide Blake in there. He was amazing." She still hadn't looked at Sharon yet. Her eyes were for Blake.

"What happened?" Manu asked. Sharon wanted to roll her eyes, but it wasn't simple Manu's fault. Frances would find a way to reveal it anyway.

Blake cut in. "It was nothing really, just a debate. We had to decide a course of action, and some of the older councillors needed persuading to make a move that needs doing sooner than later."

"Gosh, you're so humble too," Frances said to Blake, stroking his arm again. To her co-workers, and finally looking directly at Sharon, she said, "I've never seen him so passionate, so concerned for the welfare of people, so determined to push past silly concerns."

Blake raised his hand as if to slow her down, but Frances continued unabated, "They finally voted to cut that old tree down, and Blake was the one to show them the way."

Sharon stood. She was surprised by the rush inside her, as if all the fear she had swept away over the past week had returned in one condensed wave.

Blake turned to address the other two women. "Yes, but we really think it would be best if no-one knew about this decision just yet. We don't want any fall-out in the community."

Sharon tried to gather herself, tried to recall words from Rico to help her focus, to help her feel free from the fear which now gripped her at the throat. She managed to say, "But it was decided in a public forum. Anyone could have attended, so anyone could have heard." Frances glared at her.

"Well, yes that's true," Blake said, "but we really were in committee at the end when we all agreed that it would be best for the community not to know yet. There was a lot of flak from the first announcement and, as you well know, we've been dealing with a lot of upset since the branch fell. As employees here, I'm sure you'll be keen to co-operate with us in this." He looked at Frances in reprimand but also for assurance.

"Of course we will be," she said. "We just want what's best for everyone. We understand." She surveyed Manu but settled her eyes on Sharon. She wanted something from her and, against her will, Sharon gave it to her.

"This is terrible," Sharon said, her voice and lips trembling. "I live up there. What's going to happen to us?"

"Look, I don't want to have to explain it all again out here," Blake said, "but it needs to be done *for* you, Sharon. What if a branch lands on your house? Or your neighbour's? Wasn't it your church that was crushed up there?" Frances echoed each of his statements with a pitying nod.

Sharon was hearing the response, and was conscious of its logic, but felt adrift in a sea of fear. How could the tree not be there? How could they cut it down without it falling on someone else's house? Questions cascaded through her mind, not one of which she could articulate. Instead, she snapped, "You bitch, Frances. You're loving this. You don't care about the people of this town. You just want Blake's hands down your pants. Trust me, he won't take you as high as you want to go."

Sharon walked out as she spoke, fleeing as she was fighting. She tried slamming the front door to the foyer, but it only swung slowly on its hydraulics, allowing her to hear Frances' laughter as she walked down the footpath.

THIRTEEN

Perec made short work of the scrim in the pantry below the study. Inside the wall, the branch grew thicker. It had no smaller branches emanating from it, no leaves in addition to the few at its tip. Inside the wall, Perec pried floorboards free. Standing back from his demolition, he absorbed his torch-lit view below the foundation where his house met the ground.

The branch was growing straight out of the earth.

There was no trunk. There were no accompanying branches with their own leaves—no offshoots of any sort—just one long branch growing straight out of the ground and into the walls of his house.

Perec abandoned his hammer and fetched his crow-bar and a shovel from his back porch. He would need to dig.

There is a warning in the Bible that once a person is cleansed of a demon, it may return with several others to fill the empty space, and the poor host would be worse off than before. The warning suggests the person must ensure the space is filled with something else—God's Spirit, good works, a righteous heart—something that will prevent future occupation.

Sharon had been tempted to go shopping. She told Rico about the day's events when she returned home, armed only with bags of groceries for the night's dinner. Rico listened, as he helped Sharon empty the bags onto the bench in her near-immaculate kitchen.

"I almost went straight to the bookstore because I knew they'd still be open, but I remembered what you said about fear being the cause of my hoarding. It didn't make sense to me that buying some books would solve my problem with Frances or the tree or whatever! There was no connection, so I had to be acting out of fear."

She handed him a bottle of spaghetti sauce which he set beside the cheese on the bench. "So I did what you said and slowed down. I didn't stop altogether—I just slowed down long enough to let the fear subside and my mind settle. By the time I reached the main street, I was able to walk right by the shop and bypass it to the supermarket."

Rico observed her carefully between the cans and bottles. She was brandishing celery stalks as she spoke, waving them around like a teacher's ruler or a baton. She spoke rapidly, in a higher register than he had heard all week. "That's terrific, Sharon. So, why aren't you smiling?"

Sharon stopped and let the celery hand drop to her side. Rico watched tears well over their casements as she shook her head. "I know, right?" she said. "I should be smiling."

"Let's talk about it, Sharon, but not here—in the lounge."

She didn't move. She felt more comfortable surrounded by the unpacked grocery bags and the mounting ingredients of their meal. There was hope in this room, hope she had planned and plotted all day before things fell apart.

"It's that bloody tree," she said, looking out the window above the sink. She could see it in the distance and hear the omnipresent saws playing.

"Tell me about the tree, Sharon," Rico said.

Sharon recognised the tactic and welcomed it. "For the past five months it's been all about that bloody tree. I must have spoken to every resident in Te Kauhanga about it over the phone. So many demands, so many memories, so many lives affected. Some people, like old Mrs Boyle, made it their business to ring the council each week for an update from me. Ha—then the Council tells *me* to keep my mouth shut when there's actually an update worth passing on."

Rico nodded, searching for indications of where this was

emanating from. "Who told you not to tell anyone?" he asked. "Was it Blake?"

"And Frances."

"Mhmm," said Rico. "So it really was quite a test for you today—two people you used to fear, pressuring you as a team. It's funny how we are tested."

"Funny?" Sharon repeated.

Rico nodded. "You don't think it was coincidence, do you?"

Sharon waved this away with her hand. "Whatever—but it was a test, and I'm OK with how I handled it. What I don't understand is why I was so upset."

"You mean why you were upset about the tree?"

"Exactly—I mean, I've hated that tree since I arrived here. It blocks out the sun twenty-three hours of the day, it destroyed my church, and it's a threat to every property in Taumata. If they don't cut it down, whose place will be next? Our property values have surely plummeted." Her eyes filled again. "No-one is ever going to buy this place when I want to leave."

"Why leave?" asked Rico.

"Because I never intended to stay. Because I only meant to get my feet under me again, financially and emotionally. I never wanted to be stuck here."

"You're not stuck, Sharon. You are free."

Sharon dropped her head to study her hands resting on the bench. "Simply saying I'm free doesn't pay the mortgage. Am I going to end up like you—destitute and homeless?"

Rico paused, biting his tongue. "I'm not destitute, Sharon."

"Well, that's fine for you then!" she said, raising her head with her voice. "You choose to live your way. I didn't choose to live under a dying monstrosity!"

"It sounds like you should be happy the council is cutting it down. You'll be all right. They'll cut it down, free up some sun for you. The church will rebuild, property values might even go up."

"No, they won't. You have no idea how many tourist dollars that bloody thing brings into this town. It's on all our postcards, our t-shirts, our website. How will people identify this place after it's gone? By the river? There are thousands of towns on rivers in New Zealand. By the railway lines? That's a dying industry. There's talk of cancelling the one stop-over we have as it is. This place is doomed and I'm going down with it."

Rico had heard these sorts of surface arguments before but knew he needed to tread carefully. To abruptly challenge each point or to minimise them would risk minimising Sharon as a person and alienate his influence.

"Sharon, do you like the tree?" he asked.

Sharon looked hard at him. "What do you mean, 'Do I like the tree?' Haven't you been listening?"

"It's just that, sometimes we form attachments unknowingly—often with things around us that we never intended to value, but whose lustre shines brighter as separation approaches. It happens when an acquaintance is dying—someone whose loss makes us feel guilty for not having paid them more attention or included them inside the periphery of our lives."

"There's nothing peripheral about that tree," Sharon muttered. Still, she listened to Rico.

"Do you think that might be the case, though? Do you think that, despite all the arguments for and against cutting it down, you might just miss it? You might just want to save it because it warrants saving?"

Sharon tried to hold onto her perspective, tried to return in her mind to the day she arrived in Te Kauhanga and swore she would get in and get out faster than a bank robbery. But eight years of toil and turmoil overwhelmed her thoughts. Five months of community voices echoed in her mind, drowning out her own. She said to Rico, "It doesn't make any sense."

"That's because it's an emotional thing, Sharon, it's irrational. But I need you to dig deeper inside yourself and find me the answer. Don't think about arguments. Don't think about mortgages or property values. Don't think about others' opinions, even mine. Think about it like you did with Tom's book. I need to know if you are attached to that tree."

Rico's voice helped clear her mind. How far had she come in this past week? How much could she trust this man? She held onto his words and held onto the thousands of choices she had made with him. *Tom's book and the tree, Tom's book and the tree.*

"I'm attached to it," she said, finally.

"Tell me about it," Rico prompted.

"I love it. It's what this town is: strong, resilient, steeped with history. How many lives has it traced? How many children have played around it and, maybe in its earlier days, in it? It shades us, it cools us and, if the legends are true, it holds this whole hill of Taumata together."

"Would you pay money to see it stay standing?"

"Absolutely."

"Would you continue living here, despite the risks?"

"I would."

"Would you fight against the council, protest even, to see it protected?"

Sharon considered the face of the enemy, the tactics, the path Rico was paving for her to see.

"Yes, I would," she said.

Rico smiled. The pair had not left the kitchen during their conversation. "Let me help you finish putting these away Sharon," he said.

Sharon, feeling as if she had just renewed her baptismal promises, shook her head, adjusting her senses to the shift in the moment. "OK, but what are you thinking, Rico? Tell me what you think."

Rico handed her the frozen mince. "Do you feel better?"

Sharon surveyed her feelings. "Yes ... yes I do." What had he done?

"Well, that's good." He extracted a punnet of cherry tomatoes from one of the bags.

Sharon smiled. She did feel better. "I thought we'd have spaghetti bolognaise tonight. I bought a bottle of wine too."

Rico did not hesitate in responding, though he did not speak unkindly. "I won't stay tonight, Sharon. I'm going back down. You should know that I'll be leaving town by the end of next week."

This revelation left Sharon reeling. "Leaving?" she said. "Where? Why?"

"It's my time, Sharon, just like it was your time to break free from your collection. It's my time again."

Sharon was about to protest, but Rico held up his hand. His face was stern. "I *am* going Sharon. But, before I leave, I will have another gift for you."

—————::::::

Despite her protests, Stanley had made Kathleen promise to wait for his return from a conference out of town before taking the map to Perec. "We're in this together," he had pleaded. "We need to make the right decision. Take your time, just like you've taught me."

And she had waited, though it tested all her well-worn patience. When Stanley presented himself on her front step, he was shamelessly pleased to see the agitation in her—the same agitation he once felt walking with her. He was still a passively vindictive creature, comforted when he saw his shoe on another's foot.

On the way to Perec's house, Stanley held the map close to his chest, as Kathleen articulated and gesticulated frantically.

"He's a brilliant man, I just know he is," she said. "He knows all about maps. He's got hundreds. I've seen them." Her pace was quicker than usual.

"How do you know?" Stanley asked. "I hear he's nutty."

He expected a sarcastic comment from Kathleen, something alluding to his own nuttiness, but she stared straight ahead and said, "I used to visit him as a kid."

"Visit him? Did your parents know him?"

"My parents were fools," she said, coldly. "They thought he was strange, like everyone else does in this sinkhole. He's from Canada, you know."

As they neared the lighthouse, Stanley noted the activity on Centre Street. Since the falling of the branch, the council had closed the street entirely, barricading the area with high, wired fences. Inside the enclosure was a compendium of vehicles, men with orange vests, an arborist's truck, and the sounds of voices, hammers and saws. This had been going on for weeks as repairs were made to the church, the branch was further decimated and the situation was monitored and re-evaluated.

"He's got quite the view these days," he said.

As they stepped onto the verge of 22 Tūāraki Street, Stanley asked, "Again, are you sure it's all right to do this? Shouldn't we speak with someone more official? What if he's some sort of hoarder and he just keeps it for his own collection?"

Kathleen opened the gate leading into Perec's yard and held out an upraised palm to Stanley. "Give it to me, and I'll do it. It was on my property after all. I can do what I like with it."

Stanley was taken aback by her abruptness. He hadn't seen this level of curtness in her before. She seemed manic, threatening in her demeanour, her eyes wild and glazed.

He held onto the map. "No, that's fine Kathleen. We'll do it together."

She turned quickly and ascended the steps to Perec's front door. "Don't worry, Stanley. He's not some Boo Radley. I used to watch him open up for visitors—mailmen, plumbers, and the like." She rang the bell.

At first, there was no answer, of course. Montreal Perec was far too engaged to be answering doorbells. After some time, she rang again.

"Maybe he's not home," Stanley said.

"He's *always* home."

Still no response. They listened for any noise from inside, but it was pointless with the resurgence of the chainsaws behind them.

Kathleen rang again, this time adding three solid raps to the door itself. Then—footsteps.

She sucked in a breath and stepped back, watching the door handle turn.

The door opened only enough for a hand and a face to appear. Stanley retreated as well, off the bottom step and onto the walkway. Perec's face was wild and filthy. His hair was curled round his cheeks and matted from oil and dirt. His eyes, suspicious and accusatory, leapt out at them from the caked earth on his visage. His hand was equally soiled, smearing dirt on the door frame. He said nothing, curious about the two visitors, but his mind was too preoccupied to present any expected words of social convention. The woman, with one hand covering her mouth and the other tucked under her arm, seemed familiar.

Kathleen, too, was dumb-struck. Here was Perec—her fascination, her youthful obsession, the man about whom she had generated so much mythology.

He was disgusting.

Stanley, noting Kathleen's muteness, stepped forward. "Hello ... Mr Perec ... we wondered if you might be able to help us with something?"

Extended lack of use and a dust-encrusted throat created a voice that even Perec didn't recognise. "Busy," was all he could muster. He closed the door.

Kathleen, as if Stanley had slapped her on the back of the head, was stunned out of her trance. Like an uncoiling snake, this slow walking vision launched herself upon the door. She wasn't about to lose contact again.

"Perec!" she yelled. "We have a map!"

Just as quickly, the door flung open, revealing the hermit in his entirety. The muddy mess was not limited to his face and hand. It covered his body. It was impossible to discern what he was wearing. He was clothed in the earth itself. Beyond him, like a giant tail, the dirt extended down the corridor and into a room within the interior. At the doorframe, a great pile of dirt leaned against the wall. Perec had a shovel in his other hand.

The bearded man cleared his throat and said, "What sort of map? I have many maps."

"I know," spoke Kathleen, causing Perec to re-assess her familiarity. "This one is quite old." She motioned to Stanley to show it to him.

Stanley held the map out to Perec, wary of the dirty hands and shovel. Perec, however, kept his hands to himself and merely stepped forward, brushing past Kathleen, to look closer.

To describe the map through Perec's eyes would be like trying to put on glasses to simulate the multi-lensed vision of a housefly. As Stanley unrolled the map in front of him, the landmass appeared to him, at first, as a key—wide at the bottom where one would expect to see Wellington now, and long and narrow at the top along Ninety-Mile Beach and leading to Cape Reinga. That was how he first saw it, and it arrested his attention. As he looked closer, the key seemed to move in upon itself, spiralling like a spinning wheel until, finally, the motion ceased and Perec saw the North Island as Stanley and Kathleen saw it and, as he did so, one word deserted his lips: "Tuki."

Kathleen and Stanley exchanged glances, then Perec said, "No ... not Tuki."

"It's not?" Stanley asked. "Is it different somehow?"

But Perec was not speaking to them. He was looking closer, comparing the lines, imagining the ancient cartographer's hand sketching this beauty out, feeling the shape as much as seeing its form, feeling the nuances that differentiated this map.

He zoomed in, ignoring the smell of cat urine on the artefact, starting at the centre, imagining himself present in the map, present at its geographic centre, its Pureora Forest. He found nothing. No symbol marked the centre as found on Tuki's map, enhanced by BloodyLegend180. But, as he zoomed out, like a hot air balloon drifting vertically, other features came into focus. He did find the marking—the same paperclip marking as on Tuki's map—but in a different location and alongside a feature not marked by Tuki: a river.

"Where ... where did you get this?" Perec stammered, looking at Stanley.

"We found it ... last week ... in Kathleen's front yard."

Perec turned on Kathleen. "Where do you live?"

Kathleen blushed. She had so longed for his attention. "I live just down the street ... around the corner ... on Hauāuru."

Perec stared at the map again. "Right here in Taumata ... all this time?"

"Well," said Stanley, "we don't know how long it was there. We reckon it blew out of someone's vehicle. I suppose it could have belonged to someone in Taumata."

Perec seemed to ignore him. "I ...," he coughed some dirt into his hand, "I would very much like to study this more closely." He gathered his wits, conscious that there were protocols he needed to follow in order to cooperate with his visitors. "What were you wanting to do with it?"

Kathleen and Stanley looked at each other. They hadn't discussed this far. Kathleen took charge. "We really only wanted to find out if it was important or not. That's why we took it to you. We don't have other plans."

Perec nodded. "Would you ... would you mind if I held onto it? I can do some more research. I can tell you, it is not Tuki's map—I'm not sure whose it is—but it is very old." He looked at Stanley who now appeared the more uncomfortable of the two. "I will return it to you. I don't buy and sell maps. It will be well-looked after."

Again, Kathleen took the initiative saying, "We trust you completely, but ... we'd like to find out more as well. Can we come back once you figure it out?"

Perec studied the woman's face. As distasteful as the thought of a return visit was, Perec nodded out of expediency. He looked at his hands and said, indicating a point just inside his door, "Would one of you mind setting it on my table there?"

Kathleen plucked the map from Stanley's hands and walked in

beside Perec to do as he requested, but before she could survey the interior any further, Perec was ushering her back outside. It would have to do.

As she returned to the front step, considering her farewell remarks, Kathleen was stopped short by Perec's raspy voice.

"You're the girl that caused that van to hit the tree, aren't you?"

"Well ... I didn't cause it," Kathleen said, "but, yes, that was me."

Perec nodded towards the tree and all the activity surrounding it and said, "Look what you've done, eh?" before closing the door.

As in war, an explorer must endure horrendous periods of anticipation—extended empty spaces in which no new ground is won, no new patches of a map are completed. In that time, between the excitement of initiating the enterprise and the flurry of activity at its completion, the intrepid must resign himself to the notions of patience and steady fortitude.

Thirty years had passed since Montreal Perec launched his treasure hunt; thirty years since he crossed the great lands of North America and the even greater waters of the Pacific; thirty years of dogged diligence, at times interrupted by moments of revelation, but mostly filled with lack of moments and lack of movement.

And, as in a war which ends with a furious battle, or as in exploration, a flurry of discoveries was unleashed once Perec found the key he had been seeking.

After farewelling Kathleen and Stanley, Perec studied the map, still standing in his entrance-way, covered in the earthy foundation of his property. He dared not soil it with his touch, so he showered before re-attending to it without distraction.

Having done so, he spread the map across his kitchen table, his study now so filled with scrim as to make it unsuitable. He noted the new rain falling outside and settled in. He removed a framed print of Tuki's map from his wall. He knew they were not the same but studied them, already theorising that one map may have been copied from the other. Cartography has always been about altering and adding on to the prior knowledge of others. Much like the Gospels, one map would be created as an improved copy of the original, perhaps adapted for a different audience. The question for Perec was: which one was the original?

So many similarities—he could understand why his benefactors had believed it was Tuki's map. The general outline of the North Island was almost identical. The South Island was drawn as a similar, non-descript blob. Even the proportions were incorrect in the same ways when compared to accurate modern charts.

Back and forth, Perec shifted his eyes. He peered closer at the centre of the island, again noting the paper-clip spiral near the river to the south east of the same symbol on Tuki's map at its geographic centre. What was he missing? Was this to be the only difference? And if so, what was the significance of the difference? This latest map may only be a copy of Tuki's, perhaps with an error in the placement of the symbol. Or perhaps it was another paper version of Tuki's, sketched from the same dizzying heights.

Once again, however, Perec *felt* there should be more. He left his maps momentarily to fetch his magnifying glass—square with a broad handle—from his mangled study. Again, he started from the centre, but, finding nothing more, he ventured out towards the coastlines, down the river from the paperclip to the west coast and Taranaki Bight, and tracing northward up past Auckland and Hokianga, all the way to Cape Reinga, before descending southward past Tuki's territory around Doubtless Bay; past Auckland and its harbours on the eastern side, round the firth of Thames and back up and around the Coromandel peninsula, stretching down the elongated eastern coastline to Gisborne, as far east as the North Island extended.

Perec, ever so closely, studied the coast—the same coast so often visited by explorers from the north and east, so heavily populated by Māori in those great days.

Failing, Perec retreated and paused before retracing the coastline back north. It was at Whitianga and Mercury Bay that Perec saw the aberration and, at first, that was all it appeared to be. The new map was such a close match to Tuki's—as if two individuals had sat down beside each other, hand-drawing copies from the same original. You would expect a degree of variation, but this shore appeared as if its craftsman had suffered a stroke mid-sketch. The lines were interrupted by loops and swirls, certainly not representative of any geographical feature—unless via symbolism.

Perec was looking so closely that the symbols loomed in his mind, casting shadows over his reason, and he paused waiting for his intuition to solve the riddle for him. However, there was no revelation, no sudden flash of insight. Reluctantly, he withdrew, leaning back from the map to rub his eyes and scratch his head. It was as he did so, in the motion of zooming out, that he saw the names.

Woven into the coastlines, amidst the loops and whirls, were written two names, and Perec could see them as clearly as if he had written them there himself: *Banks* and *Tupaia.*

Rico was gone. Sharon had released him after their meal, which had been pleasant, but without any further cryptic comments from her guru and without any sense their separation was permanent.

She hadn't seen him again all week. She had replaced her lunch-time shopping excursions with a simple coffee and sandwich in town, across from the train station. Each day, she visited the same café in hopes of seeing him. As the week dragged on, Sharon began visiting the bookstore on her return to work. She only bought one book and a half dozen magazines for her weekend reading.

She had deliberated with herself all week about the tree and the council. She was confused after her conversation with Rico. He appeared to be prompting her to take action, but something didn't feel right. Nothing felt right, and she spent her evenings in her backyard, sitting in her lawn chair wrapped in a blanket, and studying the tree from afar.

It was on one of these nights that she rang Blake at home.

"Sharon? Hi ... I missed you at work today. The mayor has really had me hopping lately."

"Blake, I'm ringing you about the tree," said Sharon.

Blake remained quiet on the other end of the phone, but not from lack of confidence. His tone was sure and dismissive as he said, "OK, Sharon, but isn't that a work thing?"

"Not for me it's not," she said. "Look, I'm not ringing to argue about it. I just want to say something, and I want you and the council to hear it."

She heard Blake sigh faintly. He didn't say anything. Sharon took this as a cue to continue.

"The council announced their proposal in the summer, when half the town was at the beach ..."

Blake protested, "Now, hang on, Sharon ...."

"Never mind that," she said. "We both know it's true, but that's not my main point. The council reported it in the summer, then held a brief, stone-walling forum. Then, last week you told us about their decision—a decision that is still being kept secret."

"Yes ... well, as I said, we were in committee, and we don't want to upset anyone needlessly, Sharon—"

"What I'm trying to say," she continued, "is that the council seems to be setting itself up to seek forgiveness after the fact, rather than permission from the community before." She wasn't sure if she was saying things clearly or forcefully enough, but Sharon felt the sustaining wave of self-righteousness. She would not back down. She would be heard.

"That's simply not true, Sharon—," Blake tried to interject.

"Never mind, Blake. My point is that the community needs to be allowed to say goodbye to the tree properly. Plans need to be in place to involve the community, to involve the local kaumātua, to invite national dignitaries here. People need their rituals. They need their closure."

Blake sighed, more audibly this time. "There can't be much more time, Sharon. It's dangerous. We think the tree was infected with fungi. The interior is rotten, perhaps down through the roots. People can't see what we know, Sharon ... and they won't accept it if we tell them."

"I told you, Blake, I'm not ringing to argue with you, but I want you to promise me the council will do things properly. No secrets—transparency. The community deserves that much."

After a pause, Blake said, "All right, Sharon, I promise." But there was loathing in his voice.

Too exhausted to dig, and too excited to sleep, Perec contacted BloodyLegend180, who responded immediately.

"I've found the key," Perec wrote.

"Tell me about it!" came the reply in the chat window.

"It's in a map—an old map, older than Tuki's. It was made by the chiefs at Whitianga. The ones Charles Heaphy wrote about."

"From Cook's deck? The one witnessed by Te Horeta te Taniwha?"

"Yes."

"How do you know?"

Perec told his companion about the names in the coastline. "We've all been wrong," he typed excitedly, his fingers scratching several typos. "It wasn't Cook who was the goblin that came inland with Tupaia. It was Joseph Banks, the botanist. That makes even more sense. Banks was far more interested in exploring the interiors of countries and continents like Australia and Africa. He was further entrenched in the Royal Society who wanted the treasure buried in the heart of Terra Australis Incognita."

"How did you find it?"

"It just showed up at my door," he wrote. "I really don't know where it came from."

There was a long pause. Then BloodyLegend wrote, "What makes it the key?"

Perec's fingers shook over his keyboard. It had been an exhausting, exhilarating day. He was not used to strenuous physical labour, and his mind was overwhelmed with the significance of the events.

"In the centre of the map—*near* the centre of the map—is the same symbol as on Tuki's: the paperclip spiral. It's at the end of a river connected to the ocean in the Taranaki Bight."

Perec waited for his words to sink in.

BloodyLegend responded, "You'll have to connect the dots for me."

Perec smiled and typed, "Cook had a map when he circumnavigated New Zealand—*this map*—a map we thought had only been drawn by the chiefs in charcoal on the deck of the *Endeavour*. That's the story told by Te Horeta te Taniwha who was 12 years old when Cook visited his region. Someone must have transcribed it onto parchment.

"This is why it looks so much like Tuki's map. Tuki was about a year old when Cook first visited, but Cook met his grandfather who must have shared this knowledge we're seeing embedded in the maps and in the symbology. Somewhere along the way the location of the spiral changed or was marked in error or perhaps corrected. Maybe it was meant to mark the geographic centre or maybe it was meant to mark a great taonga—a great treasure! When he and Banks had Tupaia with them, they had *this* map showing the river and marking a spot at its end. If my theory is correct about Terra Australis Incognita, this is where Banks and Tupaia went to hide the Oak Island treasure. They wanted to bury it in the geographic centre, but the chiefs or this map's maker marked it incorrectly."

"In Te Kauhanga?"

"Yes. This explains why I shouldn't be looking in Pureora!"

"But—"

BloodyLegend paused, longer than usual, and Perec felt uncomfortable. He was about to ask him what he was thinking when a new message appeared.

"But, Te Kauhanga is not at the end of the river. The end of the river is in the mountains. And why would the chiefs tell them to bury something there?"

"I don't know," Perec wrote, "but it has to be here. This is where the stories of Tupaia and his European companion led."

Another pause. "Of course," was all the other typed.

Perec stopped for a few minutes. He listened to the rain outside, a distant, though prevalent, sound in his house with the roof higher than others, but a sound he knew intimately after so many years inside. He felt his isolation more than ever. His correspondent's questions had planted seeds of doubt where there had been only grounds for certainty moments earlier. It made him feel alone again, trapped in his house, tantalisingly close to his treasure.

Leaning forward, he typed, "There's something else," and waited for a reply.

Receiving none, he continued, "I have a tree growing inside my house."

His companion wrote, "What?"

"I have a tree growing inside my house—inside the walls."

"That's weird. What does it have to do with anything?"

"I don't know yet, but I have to keep digging."

FOURTEEN

In his digging, Perec had uncovered interesting yet insignificant items: sections of plumbing below the top layers of pumice leading to his curbside toby, beer bottles, a workman's cap, a metal gasoline can—all presumably left behind by the house's former occupants and perhaps its builders. He had discarded these with the dirt, shovelling all of it into a heap inside his kitchen and intermittently shifting the pile further into the house to create space as he extracted more. He employed the same techniques he and his childhood friends had mastered digging snow tunnels in the largest of their roadside ditches.

After signing off from WiCharts, Perec had returned to his dig. The adrenaline rush of sharing his findings with BloodLegend180 had spurred him to continue. It was dark outside and the rain was falling heavily, but none of this affected Perec in the dry, dark pit in the centre of his house.

He toiled with a spade and a torch, following the course of the tree branch growing inside his walls. He dug around it as one does when removing an entrenched tree from the garden, looking for base roots, hoping to cut the plant free at its core.

But, as he dug, in a haze of sweat and soil, Perec suspected this branch had no such origin. The longer he dug and the deeper he travelled under his house, the branch stretched on and on, no longer widening as a branch does, but stretching onward like a giant tentacle.

As he dug deeper, Perec found new objects and, much as a

scientist measures time via the strata of rock formations, Perec discovered older artefacts. His first such find was easily recognisable in this land—an adze head. Unlike many basalt versions in the North Island, this adze head was made of greenstone. Perec studied this in the light of his torch. It felt more significant. An adze was used for carving—carving canoes, carving wharenui, carving pou whenua, carving any number of wooden implements used by Māori. As valuable as it was, Perec discarded it amongst the shovelfuls.

Still deeper, he discovered another adze head of similar composition and quality, then another—this one a tanged quadrilateral-sectioned variety—then another. This was unusual—so many in one place, but nothing to do with his search. Similarly, he discarded otherwise fascinating items—small, tooth-shaped necklace units and a whale ivory pendant.

Still deeper, following the branch which, if he had maintained his bearings, was moving southward beneath his house, Perec discovered rope. Examining it in the heat and congestion of his underground tunnel, his heart nearly exploded from excitement. The rope was fibrous, which was not such a surprise, as rope was once made from flax in these parts, but Perec was certain he had seen rope like this before. He was certain it was made of coconut fibres, similar to that discovered in the shafts below Oak Island. In ocean-voyaging eras, coconuts provided, not only food and drink, but material for cordage, basketry, rigging, even shelter.

Still deeper, and with renewed vigour, he dug. The strain was immense, but he renewed strength with every discovery. In and out of his tunnel, Perec dug and emptied his loads of soil, re-hydrating before returning to the task. Time had stopped for him. Whenever he returned to the surface, he listened to the rain outside and, in his heated state, longed to indulge himself in the exterior shower—but he pressed on.

And pressing on as he did, as he had always done, led Perec to the pottery. Lying deep under the earth and further south again from his house, Perec found large shards made, as he only recognised from his study, of shellfish—lapida pottery. As with the adzes, Perec may have discarded these, as curious as it was to find lapida pottery this far inland, but turning over his largest piece in the torch-light, Perec cried out, "It's here!" For on that shard was the clear impression of a paperclip-shaped spiral.

In his tunnel, Perec leaned against the branch he had thus-far uncovered. Wheezing from his exertion in the dank, warm air, he contemplated what this meant for him. If he had indeed connected the dots between Cook's treasure, the map, and this place, how could he go about finding where it was buried? It could be anywhere in Te Kauhanga. And what on earth was he doing digging up this tree?

The tree, he thought. He turned and looked at the branch by his torch-light. Deep in his pit, it was difficult to maintain a sense of up or down, north or south. He had attempted to calculate his bearings with each exit and entry into the tunnel, but could not be one hundred percent sure. Looking at the branch now and considering the distance he had travelled, Perec arrived at the notion that the base of this branch was above him, no longer below. He arrived at the notion that this was no branch at all. It was a root.

What Perec did not see—above him, where the root arced towards its source—was the skeleton, buried in a crouched position, its severed head replaced above the shoulders. Would it have mattered if he did discover this inestimable treasure? How could it have possibly fit with his hunt? How much more importance would he have given it than the adze heads or the beer bottles?

He also did not see, nor did anyone else in Te Kauhanga, the dark figure starting a journey from the river's edge, moving through town in the rain, towards Taumata.

Dawn would arrive soon enough. Perec had abandoned his tunnel, resurfaced, and stood in his lighthouse room, staring at the tree. The rain was relentless, and the accompanying thunder and lightning reminded anyone awake in Taumata that it would be a prolonged torrent. He stared at the tree, imagining his route hidden below Centre Street, mapping out its undulations in his mind in the hopes that he would understand.

The area was illuminated still by streetlamps, those steadfast stalwarts against the storm. From his vantage point, Perec could see portions of every street in Taumata. He erased them in his mind as he would errant markings on his hand-drawn charts. He removed them entirely, along with the footpaths and driveways, the houses and the demolished church—all erased from this plane atop a hill, all replaced in his projection by the original inhabitants: ferns and flax, tōtara and macrocarpa, native bush and trees, kith and kin to the giant Kōwhi in their centre—their last testimony to a flourishing time, a legacy to their one-time dominance.

He imagined men arriving below the hill, from the river—Banks and Tupaia and perhaps Turi Nukutawhiti, or the great Kupe himself. How they must have encountered this minor peak. How would Kōwhi have appeared to them? One of many?

And where, in all this space, would they have positioned their taonga? This gave Perec pause. He couldn't dig up all of Taumata.

A noise—a voice. Amidst the shattering sound of the pummelling rain and after a lightning strike, but before its subsequent thunder, Perec heard it. At first, he thought it was a signal from his computer—another inquiry from BloodyLegend180—but then he heard it ring out again, a sound carried by the wind and followed by its own echoes: a voice.

Perec strained to hear, strained to see through the haze which obscured any details below. The apparition manifested between sheets of rain like an image behind the static on an old television set. It was a man, sure enough, and he was walking between the trucks and the woodpiles, circling the tree. Perec was captivated, watching this scene replay itself as the man circled, and he could hear the voice rise and fall with the wind—until he fell.

The man folded as much as he fell, collapsing in his tracks, and he lay prone on his back, his face seemingly at the mercy of the elements.

Perec looked around the five streets but, of course, there was no-one to help, no-one to see. There was no-one awake.

He descended his two flights of stairs, extracted his raincoat from a hall closet and drew it over his dirt-encrusted frame. He no longer owned gumboots, so Montreal Perec walked outside in his sandshoes. The rain barely touched him as he dashed his way forward, towards the man sheltered by the tree.

In seconds, he was squatting beside the figure whose voice was now stilled, though his lips were still moving.

It was Koro Hohepa.

At first, the old man did not acknowledge Perec's presence, but continued to stare straight ahead into the cloaked night sky. Perec lifted him under his shoulders, supporting him enough to help him breath, for the old man was struggling.

"Koro Hohepa," Perec said, his own voice still sounding untried and gritty with the wages of his subterranean labour.

Koro's blind eyes released their hold of the firmament and moved to Perec's face, which was now caked where the deluge had but briefly met the soil. He moved his lips again and, at the same time, raised one arm and one finger, pointing to the sky.

"Koro," Perec rasped above the howl around the pair, "I can't hear you."

Koro raised his arm again, setting his blind eyes along its trajectory. Seeing the cue, Perec leaned in to hear the words.

"Hawaiiki," said Koro, "Hawaiiki," and he closed his eyes.

Perec lifted his head. The old man had died, but his arm remained fixed. Perec looked to where it pointed. He hadn't pointed to the sky—he had pointed up the tree.

. ııllllıı.
'ıllıllıl'

The dark figure moved slowly, as if the wind and rain impeded, but just as certainly as if they inspired. Along Drew Street, past the insurance company's office, past the council building, but unprotected by the awninged shop-fronts, the figure progressed directly, unwaveringly, until diverting diagonally across Donaldson and through the underground.

The sun was beginning to rise, though its benefits were far from realised through the dark clouds which retained the blackness of night. Perec knew that, if it was to be done, it was to be started quickly.

He had shifted Koro Hohepa to his house, hefting the tiny man over his slick shoulder. He returned to the tree with his shovel and, from its base, assessed its scale.

He had watched the arborists for several weeks, harnessing their gear and digging in with crampon shoes, like ice mountain climbers, to ascend the tree on behalf of the council. None had climbed higher than Perec's house. There was no need to risk life and limb or offending the tangata whenua.

Perec easily procured the equipment, smashing truck windows with his spade. He did not take any harnesses. He knew he would only have used them when he was high enough to reach the lowest branches. After that, they would only serve as an unnecessary encumbrance. He donned the arborists' spiked boots and began his ascent.

Perec struggled, several times needing to detach his foot from the trunk. At one point, he managed to reach the lower lover's oaths, but the strain on his exhausted shoulders was too much, and he could not master the spikes which resisted penetration when driven, and stuck stubbornly when needing withdrawal.

Though the rain was held at bay by the enormous branches, the wind threatened to shake him like an autumn leaf. He pressed on, almost to the mark left by the van that avoided that Kathleen girl. *Strange girl*, Perec thought, and his legs gave way.

Were it not for a slippery fit, Perec's feet may have stayed inside the embedded shoes and ended his ambition. Falling away, Perec landed on his back and, winded, he lay still on the dry ground.

Above him the winds blew strong—strong enough to bend and shake Kōwhi's branches with a force Perec had not seen in his thirty years. The branches creaked and moaned, the shudders starting at the tips and resonating inward and down the trunk. The ground shook beneath Perec, and he traced its vibrations back up into the giant canopy. Amidst the rumbles, a higher-pitched scraping reached his ears. Perec, breathing again, sat up and identified the source. It was the branch he knew intimately, silhouetted by the dimly rising sun. It had finally reached the roof of his lighthouse.

He rose again, hobbled north on Centre Street, up his front steps, inside and past Koro Hohepa lying in his corridor between mounds of Taumata Hill soil, and up his two flights of stairs. In his lighthouse room, still very dark, Perec opened the window facing the tree.

It would mean jumping, but nothing he couldn't overcome. He

took the tip of the branch, bare of leaves as if its last growth could ill afford the luxury of green, and steadied himself. Climbing onto his roof, he discovered the true source of its nudity—his guttering had collected the falling leaves of the tree. These leaves had not been replaced by a new generation. Holding tighter to the branch against the terrific wind, Perec ignored the pelting drops he had avoided under the tree. With extraordinary focus, Perec jumped.

After days and nights of digging, Perec's arms and legs were racked to breaking point—but they held, wrapped around the thicker circumference of the branch. Already, he was protected by the branches above and around him, and he was even more so, as he shimmied along its radius into the tree.

At the tree's centre, Perec rested, still prone on his stomach. In the dim light, he could make out the markings below him—markings that, until then, had only been sighted from below. And he could see markings directly in front of him—more initials, though these were more difficult to identify. But Perec was there to climb. He stood on his branch, setting one foot on its higher neighbour.

And from that branch, he reached another, and then another, and his confidence grew. He avoided looking down and, in doing so, convinced himself that climbing this behemoth was no different than climbing the oaks and maples of his childhood. Joy filled him—the exhilaration of childhood exuberance and endeavour mixed with the adult comprehension that, at least for the time being, there was nowhere to search but up.

As he climbed, the foliage grew thicker and the rain seemed to desist, though this was a credit to the tree, not to any subsidence by the storm. At the last point of clarity, where he could see out beyond the leaves, he saw he had finally risen higher than his lighthouse and could see hills beyond the hills of Te Kauhanga, lit by the sparse sunlight in the east. But with one more step up, the view was lost and he was subsumed by the tree.

Atop Taumata Hill, arriving at the base of the tree and as aware of the dawn as Perec was, the figure discovered, from the broken glass and gaping window, that the first part of his mission had been completed by another. Climbing back out of the arborist's truck, he wielded the 50" bar chainsaw.

Under the shelter of its canopy, unmolested by the rain, the figure set to work, firing up the saw.

Encompassed as he was by that same canopy which, while buffering him from the wind and rain, also soundproofed him, Perec heard nothing below. Euphoric and sensually overwhelmed after so many years inside, he allowed the tree to absorb him and to lead him.

Perec climbed—branch upon branch with no sign of thinning. As he climbed, fatigued and slowing, he wondered what it was he was meant to see—and how he could possibly see it. His view of the outside world was completely shielded. His view of the inside world was completely condensed.

But he climbed. And as he climbed and the exhilaration and joy subsided, he began to slip into a pattern. The air thinned. Branches looked the same. Leaves felt the same. The smell of the tree consumed his senses until he couldn't remember a scent before the tree's. And the wall of bark, ever in front of him, rose like a highway, stretching towards a horizon and an apex he could not see.

But the bark did change. It grew smoother, more pleasant to the touch, like a baby's skin—only the bark at this juncture seemed older. Being the only changing element, Perec looked closer, noting not only its texture, but its change in pattern for, as he climbed, it became more and more like a blank slate, more like a map.

It is, of course, only when there is empty space that you can see objects within. Who could see the stars if it weren't for the ether? Who could hear a child's laugh in a sports stadium? Who could follow an argument in a sea of inane chatter? Who could know themselves in a crowd of imitators?

In that space, as he looked closer, Perec saw the symbols. At first, it was an island—an easy thing to plot on a cartographical canvas of ocean. And there were more like and unlike it as he climbed higher. In between them were symbols for ocean currents and wind currents. There was space on the bark all around these symbols, but they were contained all the same, elongated over time, warped in their dimensions but appearing to retain some measure of their proportions.

Below Perec, the saw roared and cut deep. The man knew what he was doing, establishing an undercut in the pre-dawn. He knew what he was doing, and he knew where it was going.

The rain and wind hesitated. The residents of Taumata roused.

Even so, Perec never heard the saw. Instead, he felt the shaking and, this day, Kōwhi, the tree of Taumata Hill, truly lived up to its status as a maunga—a mountain for iwi Māori. The shaking felt as Perec imagined it would feel standing on the lip of a volcano.

The tree shook, and he shook with it, clinging to the branches under his feet and under his arm. Despite the alarm, he did not take his eyes off the bark, enraptured as he was by the carved symbols.

As the tree shook, aged branches broke free above the cartographer. He was in no position to dodge them as they crashed above, around and below him. As they cleared away, he could hear the rain and wind again, tremendous forces to encounter at such a height—and a dizzying height it was as, only for a moment, Perec took his eyes from the bark and set them on the newly revealed horizon.

To the east, beyond the hills of Te Kauhanga and beyond the hills that shadowed them, the sun had carved a path through the clouds. It was wide enough for Perec to capture a view never before seen from the peak of Taumata. Perec's gaze reached to the coast and the ocean and maybe, he thought for a flash, maybe to other lands beyond that.

Then the tree broke.

Like no iceberg cracking, like no mountain rock splitting, like no lightning bolt striking, the sound of Tuamata's tree's demise thundered down that solar highway.

Perec fell with the tree and, as he did so, branches broke away with him, littering the space around him and revealing the map carved into the bark. Perec's mouth fell open. Like Tupaia's chart, there were the stars and the islands and the ocean and wind currents, spread out across the great Polynesian continent, connected, as only Perec could see, by a giant paperclip spiral, pointing to a landmass clearly represented by a symbol that could represent but one thing.

"Home," Perec rasped and then was gone under the debris and the very trunk of the tree.

EPILOGUE

You can no longer see it from space. Descending into this world, in the largest area of blue, near the centre of the North Island of Aotearoa, the grey mountains, the lake, the farmland and the dense bush dominate the scene in the same way a family congregates around a lost member.

The township of Te Kauhanga, still resembling a patch sewn into the land, now bears a scar as straight as an arrow, pointing from the top of the Taumata hillside to the river, pointing due north as if from the centre of a compass. Ranginui's sun dial had fallen.

The scar was only one of the remnants of the tree left since it had fallen on the last day of Autumn—one day before it would have completed its final ring.

The sky did not fall with the felling of this leg of Tāne Mahuta, but much damage had been done. Tomo—sinkholes—had appeared over several months in Taumata, some beneath houses where owners discovered strange roots left behind. Works engineers predicted that, in the coming year, the hillside of Taumata may in fact collapse in on itself. It appeared the legends were true.

Sharon, bereft at the felling of the tree, and realising her financial fears, sold up before many others, absorbed her losses, detached from Te Kauhanga altogether and returned to Wellington to live with her daughter. She never heard from Rico again and still speculates about his promised gift.

In her wake, many others vacated the hill, and the neighbourhood declined. Stanley and Kathleen, in their fortunate circumstance, liquidised their properties, pooling resources to purchase a house together in town. It was an odd-shaped place notable for its aversion to symmetry.

The lighthouse at 22 Tūāraki Street was demolished by the tree, for that was the line it had taken as it fell, first landing on the house of Montreal Perec, leaving a gap only above the road below Taumata, then crashing across the railway line, above the underground, and along Drew Street. Fantastically, no buildings in town were badly damaged except for Stanley's office and the council building whose facades were scraped off. Stanley's insurance company ensured both were repaired. Otherwise, the town's reflective roofs were temporarily dulled by the unwanted blanket of branches and leathery leaves.

The upper reaches of the tree splayed out across the park areas alongside the river—that ancient landing point frequented annually by Perec. Of course, the tree was finally measured, and it was confirmed for the residents of Te Kauhanga that they did, indeed, once host the largest tree in the country and in the world. The symbols, though free from their branched covering, were unrecognised by the works crews who dismembered the tree, and even by the kaumātua who chose this section to be made into a carving, plinth-like, which now marks the space formerly occupied by the great trunk—bypassed by the two lanes of Centre Street, surrounded by empty houses, the abandoned church property, and tomo.

Two other notable elements of this tale went equally unrecognised. Perec's tunnel was never discovered, such was the force of the tree's falling and the depth of its impression along its line from the trunk to the lighthouse. Similarly, the body of Koro Hohepa, secured by Perec, was never recovered when the atomised debris of the lighthouse was cleared away. This led to speculation about his disappearance, many believing he had been mystically transported to the home of his fathers with the demise of his maunga.

Perec's body was found. His climb would not be recorded in legend. No witness could attest to it. None could say why he, after so many years inside, would be outside on the night the tree was felled. Some, of course, proposed that he had been the lumberjack despite the fact he had been found near the river, while others claimed they had seen another figure present in Taumata. So it was with some controversy that his grave was shifted, following a period of clearance and preparation, to the site of the lighthouse ruins. It was thought, by Kathleen and others, that he should be buried as he lived—rooted to that spot.

After those long winter months, the gravesite stood lonely, threatening to be overwhelmed by the spring growth of grass and weed. Perec had no visits from family nor, not since the first days after his memorial had been established, by any curious parties.

And so it was small wonder that Kiri, who no longer lived in Taumata but frequently included the hill in her runs, should notice the stranger there paying his respects.

Running east along Tūāraki, Kiri noted his posture—head bowed, hands folded at his waist. From side on, he looked good to her. He wore sunglasses, a leather jacket (which she thought to be too warm for only a breezy spring day), blue jeans and, as she witnessed once she had closed the gap on him, jandals containing his bare feet.

As she approached, he raised his head, and she slowed to a walk, conscious she might be disturbing him. *Not bad*, she thought. From a distance, she had thought he was also Māori, but now determined that he was Polynesian though she could not pick his origin more specifically.

Seeing her, he removed his sunglasses, clearly intending to initiate conversation, so she stopped. His eyes were stunning, though weary and somewhat closed to the burgeoning sunlight which was now breaking through above them. It was close to high noon.

The man nodded. "Hello," he said.

"Kia ora," replied Kiri, adjusting her respiration, but ensuring it retained an attractive level of breathlessness.

He indicated the grave. "Did you know this man?"

She looked at the headstone and shook her head, "No—no-one did, really. He never talked to anyone."

The man smiled. "What about this place? What was this?"

"We all called it the lighthouse," she said, returning her attention to his face. "He lived in it."

"Lighthouse," repeated the man. "Interesting." He looked out over the ruins beyond the town, scanning the hills of the valley opposite. He turned and looked back down Centre Street, at the plinth in the distance.

"Where are you from?" Kiri asked.

He looked back at her. "I'm from the north," he said.

Kiri laughed at his answer, then pointed towards the hills, along the stretch between the plinth and the river, along the scar of Te Kauhanga. "Well," she said, "you won't have any trouble finding your way home from here then."

He followed her direction and smiled again. "I suppose I won't," he said. "Thank you." He said it in such a way to make Kiri think it was his way of ending a conversation since she wasn't sure what he could be thanking her for.

"No worries, mate," she said. "Might see you around then."

As she jogged away down Centre Street, Kiri hoped that, if she looked back, she might catch him watching her move. Reaching the plinth, she stole a glance over her shoulder. If he had been looking she had missed it, for the stranger had turned so that she could only see the large patch on the back of his leather jacket.

Maybe another time, she told herself, then thought, *I wonder why he wears the number 180?*

ACKNOWLEDGMENTS

I don't have many ideas. I am not a prolific writer, filling journal volumes, mass-producing manuscripts of short-stories and poetry, or blogging 24-7. I work a job, raise a family and live a life hopefully worthy of a muse's time. After writing my first novel, *Redeeming Brother Murrihy*, which consumed any creative brain space for many years, I wondered if and when the next idea would come.

Te Kauhanga began as an idea—a different sort of space exploration. Unlike *Murrihy*, I wanted to write a story in which the characters don't travel, but play out their lives in a small space, intersecting and influencing each other in unexpected and unknown ways. I had in mind Stephen Leacock's *Sunshine Sketches of a Little Town* and DL Smith's *The Miracles of Santo Fico*.

From there, I imagined characters—characters who would need to exhibit some unusual traits in relation to space and to their setting. From characters, I developed symbols, plot, etc.

With an idea, it helps to bounce it around with others. Many thanks to my colleague and friend, Dale Thomas, who listened patiently and offered further reading including Georges Perec's *Species of Spaces*. He, along with Megan Dickens, provided sincere and valuable feedback as the first readers of my manuscript. Leanne Reynolds generously designed a brilliant cover for the second edition.

Once again, it is my immediate family who need utmost recognition: my wife, Mary, and my children, Sam and Katie, who put up with a tired and distracted husband and father who chose his word processor over time with them. Again, I hope you are proud of the work I've done.

I invite readers to provide feedback via my website: antonymillen.com. Who knows where that next new idea might come from?

Kia ora,

Antony Millen
January 2017

FURTHER READING

While my preparation involved more than listed, I recommend these texts and links for any who are interested in finding out more about the topics in the book.

Atherton, Jo. *Oak Island Treasure: Home of the Oak Island Money Pit Mystery.* n.d. 2013. oakislandtreasure.wordpress.com.

Chavasse, CPG and JH Johns. *The Forest World Of New Zealand: Realm Of Tane Mahuta.* A. H. & A. W. Reed, 1975.

Coleman, John. *Mysteries in Nova Scotia.* n.d. 2013. www.vortexmaps.com/novascotia.

Doutre, Martin. *Ancient Celtic New Zealand.* de Danann Publishers, 1999.

Druett, Joan. *Tupaia: The Remarkable Story of Captain Cook's Polynesian Navigator.* Random House NZ, 2011.

Garfield, Simon. *On the Map: Why the World Looks the Way it Does.* Profile Books, 2013.

Jefferson, Christina. "The Dendroglyphs of the Chatham Islands." *The Journal of the Polynesian Society* (1955): 367-441. www.jps.auckland.ac.nz.

Perec, Georges and John Sturrock (trans). *Species of Spaces and Other Pieces.* Penguin Classics, 1998.

The Navigators: Pathfinders of the Pacific. Dir. Sam Low. 1983.

ABOUT THE AUTHOR

Antony Millen is a Canadian living and writing in New Zealand.

Originally from Pictou County, Nova Scotia, Canada, he moved to New Zealand with his wife and two children in 1997. In 2013, he launched his first novel, *Redeeming Brother Murrihy*. He followed this with *Te Kauhanga* in 2014 and *The Chain*, his first novel for young adults, in 2015.

Antony is the winner of the 2014 Heartland short story competition (*Fishing the Pungapunga*). He also won third prize in the 2015 NZSA Central Districts short story competition (*Aukati*), a competition in which he was awarded Highly Commended in 2014 (*The Boy at Ohinetonga*).

His short story, *The Homeless Men of Mahuika*, was published in Issue #4 of *Headland* in 2015. His short story, *Aukati*, was published in *Landfall 231*.

FOR MORE INFORMATION:

antonymillen.com

ALSO BY ANTONY MILLEN

Available now in paperback and e-book editions:

Amazon & Amazon Kindle

Fish Pond   Mighty Ape

Chapters Indigo   Book Depository

antonymillen.com